trouble in twi-town

travis & trouble
book one

Henry Vogel

Published in the United States of America by Moranderin Media, an imprint of VL Publishing.

Cover art by Miblart.com.

First publication: November 2022

ISBN: 978-1-959859-00-0 (ebook)

ISBN: 978-1-959859-01-7 (hardback)

ISBN: 978-1-959859-22-2 (paperback)

Originally published in serial form online.

In memory of Dave Hayslett. I miss you more than words can convey.

a whiff of trouble

THE TUBE TRAIN hissed to a stop in the industrial district that earned Carnegie Station its name. Boisterous steelworkers got in a few last jokes and jibes with their buddies before clocking in at work. I walked among them, silent and out of place, as always. The crowd shrank with each foundry we passed, slowly reducing the odor of close-packed humanity. That's why it took me so long to notice a subtle scent, as out of place in this industrial setting as I am.

The fragrance teased of exotic locales, tropical nights, and all-consuming passion. It promised dimmed lighting, cold liquor, and warm curves. It tempted. It lured. And I followed.

It led me down a wide corridor, past industrial sites on the left, past their associated offices on the right, to a lone door beyond them all. Neat lettering on the door read TRAVIS BARRETT. Smaller type below the name added INVESTIGA-TIONS & RETRIEVALS.

As I opened the door, a Robosec looked my way, and her face screen assumed a pleasant, smiling visage. The smile faded when she saw me.

"Oh, it's only you, Boss," she said. "I hoped it might be someone important."

"I love you, too, Rita," I said. "Say, you have an olfactory module, right?"

"Sure, Boss, though my module is so far out of date, it ought to be called an *old*factory module." She fed a sniff through her vocorder, just to make sure I understood her dissatisfaction with the module. In a coy tone at odds with her metallic body, she asked, "Why?"

"There's a fragrance in the air, Rita, one I smelled over the hot odors of sweat and molten metal. It's stronger in here."

"Yeah, so?"

I glanced askance at Rita. "I'm told the latest model Robosecs have polite respect built into their core personalities."

"You can't afford one of them. I know. I do your book-keeping."

"Maybe someday..." Rita ignored that comment, as she always does. I returned to my original question. "Can your olfactory module identify the fragrance?"

"It sure can, Boss."

I waited five seconds before asking, "And?"

Rita's voice lost its bantering tone. "Trouble, that's what it is, Boss. Trouble with a capital T. It stands for Tina, it stands for Tate. And it all means trouble with—"

"A capital T. Yeah, I got that, Rita." I scratched my head. "Tina Tate. Why does that name sound familiar?"

The eyes on Rita's face screen looked past me and out the window in the office door. I turned and followed her gaze to a huge, blazing sign fifty yards away.

TATE STEELWORKS.

"Oh. So, this Tina is one of *those* Tates."

"You're kidding, right, Boss?"

"About what?"

"You haven't heard of Tina Tate?"

"Should I have?"

"I see you reading the news webs all the time. You mean to tell me you never read about Carnegie Station's very own glamour girl?"

"Most of what I read is news from the inner planets, plus the sports report. I never read gossip sites unless work requires it."

"Your loss, Boss." Rita waved a mechanical arm towards the door to my office. "You better get in there. Trouble is waiting for you, and she asked for you by name."

Rita turned her attention back to her comp screen. That's her way of telling me she'd said all she was going to say. With a mental shrug, I opened my office door and strode through it. Only to be brought up short by a lithe, female form blocking the way to my desk.

Tall and slender, she wore a one-piece outfit that clung to her body like a second skin. She faced away from me, so I had time to appreciate red hair cascading to her shoulder, beautifully rounded hips canted to the left, with long, shapely legs supporting it all.

Without turning around, she asked, "You know what would really make this office pop?"

"Twenty pounds of dynamite?" I growled, as I sought a way to slide past her.

"Cute. Wrong, but cute."

Her head shook.

Red hair bounced.

Impure thought cavorted through my mind.

"No," she said, "a big, oak desk. With a matching chair, naturally."

Despite my best efforts, I snorted. "Gee, why didn't I think of that?"

I lifted her by both elbows, moved her two feet to the left, and finally had a clear path to my desk.

"What's wrong with oak?" she asked, as I slid behind my government surplus metal desk.

"It only grows on Earth, we're in the Belt, and my last name isn't Tate."

I leaned back in my chair and got my first good look at Tina

Tate's front side. Bright blue eyes regarded me from a heart-shaped face. A well-manicured finger tapped luscious, kissable lips as she considered my words. A long neck gave way to shapely shoulders over the gentle swell of—

I wrenched my mind away from Tina Tate's considerable physical attractions and suddenly understood Rita's warning. "But you didn't come here to discuss interior decorating, Miss Tate."

"Call me Tina," she said. "Everyone does."

"I am not everyone, Miss Tate. Now, what may I do for you?"

She bit her lip in a fetching manner, then said, "I want you to find Nick."

"And Nick is...?"

"My little brother."

"Just how little is Nick?"

"Twenty-two. Three years younger than me."

"That makes Nick an adult in the eyes of the law, Miss Tate."

"Which is why I came to *you*, Mr. Private Investigator."

Touché.

"A fair point, Miss Tate. When was the last time you saw your brother?"

"In person, three weeks ago. He commed me every other day while he was gone. But his last comm was six days ago."

"I gather your brother is not on Carnegie Station?"

"No."

I sighed, "Miss Tate, this would go a lot faster if I didn't have to drag the information from you."

"Nick disappeared on Mercury."

I stared at her for a second, then asked, "You know I earn a daily rate plus expenses, right?"

Miss Tate cocked her head to the left. "And?"

"Do you have any idea how much round trip passage to Mercury costs?"

She gave a nonchalant wave of her hand. "Not a clue." Her

mouth curved up in the first devilish smile I'd seen since I was a boy. "But, unlike you, my last name *is* Tate."

Score another point for the heiress.

I leaned forward, rested my folded arms on the desk, and caught her gaze. "May I ask a different, perhaps sensitive question?"

She mirrored my posture without breaking eye contact. "Shoot."

"Why are you here?"

"I've already told you. I want you to find Nick."

"Let me rephrase my question. Norman Tate is the richest man in the Belt. With his only son missing, why hasn't he hired one of the Inner System's big name investigative firms to find him?"

"I begged Father to do just that. He refused." Miss Tate dropped her forehead onto her folded arms, and whispered, "Mr. Barrett, I don't think Father *wants* an investigation."

A single tear splashed onto my desk, and Miss Tate's body shuddered silently. I kept my arms folded on the desk and maintained a cool, professional expression. But this display of vulnerability gave the beautiful glamour girl just the right touch of girl-next-door familiarity that it took all my self-control to maintain my aloof pose.

As usual, Rita was right about this one. Trouble, indeed.

She drew a long breath, swiped at her eyes with the back of her hand, and sat back in her chair. "Please excuse me, Mr. Barrett. I just..."

Her hands fluttered in her lap as she sought an explanation for her emotional display.

I held up a hand to forestall any explanations. "There's no need to explain, Miss Trouble. I—"

Her eyes widened. "What did you just call me?"

"I called you Miss Tate. Now—"

"No, you called me Miss Trouble."

I replayed our conversation in my mind. I *had* called her Trouble instead of Tate.

"I apologize, Miss Tate, and will completely understand if you wish to take your business elsewhere."

"Nick always called me Trouble when it was just the two of us."

I couldn't think of a useful response, so I just said, "Oh."

Miss Tate's dazzling smile—the one that could get a guy like me into a lot of trouble—lit her face. "I *knew* you were the right man for the job!"

I had the feeling I'd lost the thread of the conversation. "You did?"

She gave an emphatic nod. "Before I even walked through your door."

"Not because I called you Trouble?"

"No, but knowing you and Nick are on the same wavelength cinched the deal."

I gave what I hoped was a sage nod, and said, "I see."

Miss Tate leaned forward again, propped one elbow on the desk, and rested her chin on her cupped palm. "No, you don't."

"You're quite correct, Miss Tate."

"Call me Trouble. At least when it's just you and me."

"It wouldn't be proper."

She flashed that devilish smile and said, "Call me Trouble, and I'll tell you when I knew you were the investigator I needed."

I realized Miss Tate would not budge on her demand. With a sigh, I asked, "You win, Trouble. Are you satisfied?"

In a throaty voice far more appropriate for the bedroom than for my dingy office, she said, "Very."

I caught myself leaning closer to the mercurial woman with the apt nickname and made myself lean back in my chair. "What about your promised explanation?"

"Oh, that." She sat back, grinned at me, and said, "I knew you were the man I wanted as soon as I read about your dishonorable discharge from the Space Patrol."

I hardened my gaze, and my tone of voice dropped to absolute zero. "You're gravely mistaken if you believe I will bend or ignore the law on your whim. I can say with certainty that I am *not* the man for your job." I gestured towards the door. "Good day, Miss Tate."

"Oh dear, I'm afraid I didn't explain myself well at all."

I turned my attention to my web screen. It wasn't even turned on, but it faced away from the woman, so she wouldn't know that. "Why are you still here, Miss Tate?"

"Will you stop playing the offended man and let me explain?" she asked. Without waiting for a response, she continued, "I don't want you because you'll do *wrong* for the right price. I want you because you'll do *right* regardless of the cost."

Against my will, I found my gaze sliding back to Miss Tate. My tone of voice even warmed to merely frosty when I said, "I disobeyed an order from my superior officer. Because of my decision, twenty-four members of my ship's crew died and my ship was destroyed."

"But your decision saved the four hundred and seven civilians onboard the starliner *Euphoria* from the most notorious space pirate in the solar system."

"That fact was irrelevant to my case." Once again, I pointed towards the door. "As I said before, Miss Tate, good day."

Despair washed over her face, but she remained seated. "I need you on Nick's case, Mr. Barrett. You're the only man I can count on to stand up to Father when he offers you a valise full of money to relinquish the case."

Despite my previous words, her comment piqued my curiosity. "What makes you think your father will do that?"

"He's already done it twice, Mr. Barrett."

"Ah, so I wasn't your first choice?"

She shrugged. "Originally, I simply contracted the biggest names in the business. After Father bought off my first two choices, I did my homework."

"And my tarnished reputation caught your eye?"

"The only difference between tarnish and sterling is polish and effort, Mr. Barrett."

The intercom on my desk crackled, and Rita said, "Oh, that's a good one, Boss."

Miss Tate's eyebrows rose as I turned a glare on the intercom. "How many times have I told you not to eavesdrop, Rita?"

"Eight hundred and thirty-six times, Boss."

"Then why do you keep doing it, Rita?"

"Because I never know when you're going to need my advice."

"I never need your advice, Rita."

"Uh huh," Rita said. "So, are you taking Miss Tate's case?"

"Not that it's any of your business, Rita, but I haven't decided yet."

"You should definitely take it, Boss."

"What happened to the Robosec who warned me that Tina Tate was trouble?"

"Oh, she's trouble all right, Boss," Rita replied. "But she's *your* kind of trouble."

I thought, but did not say, *Oh, Rita, you are right in more ways than your circuits can imagine.*

"Does that mean you'll take the case?" Miss Tate asked.

"Yes," Rita said.

"Rita does not speak for me," I snapped.

A static-filled laugh came from the intercom. "But you'll take the case, right, Boss?"

I looked across at Miss Tate, "I have a feeling you're going to cause me a lot of trouble, Trouble."

"Probably. Nick says I'm quite good at it."

"Okay, Trouble. I'll take your case."

Trouble's dazzling smile lit her face. "Thank you, Mr. Barrett!"

From the intercom, Rita said, "You should call him Travis."

"*Rita!*" I snapped.

"What? I'm just greasing the gears of your relationship with our new client." She paused for a second, then added, "Mentioning grease and gears, I'm overdue for my yearly maintenance appointment."

"You're the one who makes those appointments, Rita. Why drop it in my lap?"

"Because you're the one who earns the money to pay for them, Boss."

"Is that your subtle way of reminding me to discuss my retainer with Trouble?" Without waiting for an answer, I turned to Trouble. "I usually charge three days in advance, but that will barely cover my travel time to Mercury."

"Don't you mean *our* travel time to Mercury?" Trouble asked.

I pulled out my Space Patrol commander's voice and said, "Absolutely not."

Trouble smiled sweetly. "I'm Belter born and bred, Travis. How are you going to stop me?"

"I could refuse your case. Since no money has changed hands, we have no binding contract."

"You *could*," Trouble agreed, "but you won't."

"Because...?"

"If I read you right, your sense of honor won't let you go back on your word once you've given it to a lady in need."

"She's got you there, Boss!" Rita said.

I turned my sternest glare on Trouble and watched it slide right off of her. "The last thing I need with me on Mercury is a damsel in distress."

Trouble's hand dipped into a purse I never noticed because it was below her cleavage line, and pulled out a gleaming blaster pistol. "I'm a lady, Travis, *not* a damsel."

She showed excellent trigger discipline, kept the business end pointed at the ceiling, and treated the gun with respect. Even so, I asked, "Do you even know how to use that thing?"

The blaster disappeared into her purse. "What part of *Belter born and bred* did you not understand, Travis?"

"Let me guess, you learned all about guns as a little girl while sitting in your daddy's lap?"

I expected confirmation, accompanied by a nostalgic smile. I didn't get it.

Something flashed behind her eyes, but it was gone before I could figure out what it was. "Father's business consumed too much of his time. He had a member of his staff teach me."

I squelched my rising curiosity about Trouble's relationship with her father. She wasn't hiring me to meddle in her paternal affairs.

"Fine, it's possible you can take care of yourself in a pinch," I said. "But that still doesn't explain why I should take you with me to Mercury."

"Since I'm buying the tickets, isn't it more accurate to say *I'm* taking *you* to Mercury?"

"Could you please just answer the question and stop being so—"

"Troublesome?" She grinned. "I'm coming with you because I know Nick better than anyone. I may not know how to track down clues or follow up leads, but I can help you interpret them."

"I can always send a message back to Carnegie Station if I need that kind of help."

Trouble shook her head. "And let the trail go cold while you wait hours for the message to reach me, and more hours for my reply to reach you? I don't think so."

I released a long sigh, which brought a wide smile to Trouble's kissable lips.

She's your client, Travis. Stop thinking about her like that!

"That's a yes, then?" she asked.

As I drew breath to answer, Rita said, "That's a yes."

I gave a nod and said, "It's a yes. Though I don't know why I even bothered taking part in this conversation."

"You won't regret it, Travis!"

"So you say," I muttered.

"What now?"

"Pack for the trip to Mercury. Practical clothes, no designer outfits. And especially pack practical shoes."

Rita made a throat clearing sound over the intercom.

"Thanks for the reminder, Rita." To Trouble, I added, "Give Rita my retainer on your way out. Oh, and pick up a lot of hard currency. That always comes in handy on a case."

Trouble rose gracefully to her feet and turned towards the door. Over her shoulder, she asked, "Do you think fifty-thousand dollars will be enough?"

I'd been thinking a couple of grand, but she *was* a Tate. "Sure, Trouble, that should be plenty."

I followed her into the outer office, waited while Rita transferred my retainer fee from Trouble's account to mine, and then held the door while she sashayed through it. I stood there staring at the door long after it swung shut.

"What's got you thinking so hard, Boss?" Rita asked.

"I'm trying to get a handle on Trouble. Especially her relationship with her father."

"What about it?"

"There's something off about it. I mean, consider how she calls him *Father*. Most girls like her call their father *Daddy*. It helps them wrap the man who controls their bank balance more tightly around their little finger. But not Trouble."

"I'm just a Robosec, Boss, and my programming doesn't go deep into father-daughter dynamics. But I'm sure you'll figure it out."

I headed back to my office. "You're just saying that to make me feel better."

"Correct."

I barked a short laugh. "Don't forget to make that maintenance appointment, Rita."

"Will do, Boss."

I closed the door to my office and immersed myself in preparation for our trip to Mercury. An hour later, raised voices in the outer office drew me back to reality.

I pressed the talk button on the intercom. "What's going on out there, Rita?"

A gruff man's voice said, "Tell 'im Hammerhand Houlihan is here."

In a prim tone, Rita said, "A Mr. Ham-handed and associate to see you, Boss."

I expected someone to visit about now, but I'd hoped it would be someone civilized. Instead, I got the muscle.

"Send them in, Rita."

The door opened, and the massive form of Hammerhand—onetime heavyweight boxer—squeezed into my office. Apparently unsure the office would hold him, Hammerhand's associate, a skinny, ferret-faced man with slicked back hair, lounged in the doorway and grinned at me.

"I'm sorry, gentlemen," I said, "but I'm not taking new cases at the moment. May I recommend you take your business to one of the other investigative firms on the station?"

"Hey, Slick, we got us a comedian," Hammerhand said. "Ain't he funny?"

"Hi-larious," Slick agreed.

Hammerhand leaned on my desk, and I swear the metal groaned under his weight. "We ain't here to hire you, Barrett. We got a invitation for you. One you ain't gonna refuse."

"I hope you're not asking me to the station ball, Hammerhand," I said.

"Ha ha. Funny, again. Right, Slick?"

"I can't stop laughing," Slick agreed.

Listening to the goons, I felt like I'd fallen into an old, poorly written black-and-white crime movie. Something like the ones that were popular before the 1939 moon landing.

"Why don't you skip all the tough guy play-acting and deliver your invitation?"

"Mr. Tate wants to see you," Hammerhand said. "Right now."

After my brief meeting with his daughter, I *wanted* to meet Mr. Tate. But I also wanted to keep that fact to myself. I drummed my fingers on my desk, vented a dubious sigh, and said, "Hm..."

The massive ex-boxer must have had more going on inside his head than I gave him credit for, because he leaned farther over my groaning desk and loomed. "You ain't thinking 'bout disappointing Mr. Tate, is you?"

"The thought crossed my mind."

"Then *un*cross it."

Slick giggled. "Yeah, uncross it."

I craned my neck back and met Hammerhand's glare. "What happens if I refuse the invitation?"

Broad shoulders shrugged. "Mr. Tate said to bring you. He didn't say you had to be in one piece."

I held fast to my role as the stubborn PI. "Are you threatening me?"

Hammerhand grinned. "Yeah."

I made a show of reluctance. "Perhaps I can spare five minutes."

"You can spare as much time as Mr. Tate wants," Hammerhand said.

"Yeah." Slick giggled and nodded at his companion. "You spare, or he strikes."

I looked at Slick. "How many hours did it take you to come up with that sad bowling pun, and how many years have you been waiting for the right opportunity to use it?"

Slick stopped giggling, and his soulless gaze met mine. "Think you're smart, do you? Why I—"

"Shaddup, Slick." Hammerhand never took his eyes off of me. "What's it gonna be, Barrett? You walking, or me dragging you?"

I'd pushed Hammerhand as far as I could, so I decided I'd shown enough reluctance. Rising to my feet, I said, "I'll walk."

We retreated to the outer office. The mouth on Rita's face screen turned down in a frown.

"Should I call someone, Boss?"

"There's no need. I'm just paying a brief call on Mr. Tate."

Rita's gaze shifted to Hammerhand, and her eyebrows changed to a pair of inward slanting lines. "If Mr. Barrett isn't back in an hour, I'm calling the cops."

"It ain't gonna do you no good," Hammerhand said.

I followed Slick out the office door, and Hammerhand fell in behind me. We marched fifty yards down the corridor to the big, blazing TATE STEELWORKS sign. Slick headed for an office door opposite the sign, and we filed through. Inside, a security guard nodded to my companions. He must have pushed a button I couldn't see, because an elevator door chose that moment to slide open. The three of us filed in, the door slid shut, and the elevator rose swiftly.

Thirty seconds later, the door opened on a lavish reception area, complete with uncomfortable designer chairs and ugly art hanging on the walls. An enormous, immaculately clean desk blocked the way to a door on the far side of the room. A gorgeous brunette sat behind the desk. At the sight of us, she tapped an intercom.

"Mr. Barrett is here to see you, sir."

The intercom crackled. "Send him in."

The receptionist rose gracefully, wiggled her way to the door, opened it, and struck an inviting pose. "Mr. Tate will see you now, Mr. Barrett."

Slick openly leered at the woman, and she pointedly ignored him. Then we were through the door and into Mr. Tate's office. Three windows, each large enough to fly a small shuttle through, provided a breathtaking view outside Carnegie Station. Hundreds of tiny asteroids tumbled and spun in the space beyond. Every few seconds, the station's energy shield flared as it deflected an asteroid from a collision course with the station.

I tore my gaze from the starkly beautiful view. Norman Tate

sat behind a desk that dwarfed the one in the reception area. Unlike the brunette's desk, Tate's held half-a-dozen screens, twice as many data pads, and even the odd piece of paper.

As the door shut behind us, Tate rose, and circumnavigated his desk. He looked like you'd expect a miner-turned-millionaire to look. Age and good living had rounded his once powerful body. But the way he moved suggested he had more muscle than fat. His working-man upbringing also showed in his practical haircut and off-the-rack suit. He smiled, and held out a scarred hand. When I clasped his hand, its softness surprised me, though it shouldn't. Tate's callouses must have faded before Trouble was born.

Tate flashed a smile that never reached his eyes. "Mr. Barrett, it's so good of you to accept my invitation."

"I wasn't exactly given a choice."

Hammerhand gave a low rumble, and his hand dropped heavily on my shoulder. I listed in that direction as a result of his heavy-handed move.

Tate gave a hearty laugh. "I have no doubt. Mr. Houlihan is quite persuasive when he wants to be." He guided me to a chair in front of his desk. "Please, sit. May I have Miss Armis bring you anything?"

"I never got around to having my morning coffee."

As if on cue, the office door opened, and the receptionist strode in carrying a tray laden with coffee and its associated accouterments. She set the tray on a corner of Tate's desk, poured, glanced my way, and raised a perfect eyebrow.

"Black," I said.

She handed a delicate cup and saucer to me. While she prepared a cup for Tate, I inhaled the aroma rising from the coffee and took a cautious sip. Heaven in a cup. Seriously.

My expression must have given away my thoughts, because Tate laughed again. "Good, isn't it? It's my personal blend. Since you like it so much, I'll have Miss Armis send a pound over to your office."

I wanted to refuse, but I took another sip instead.

Tate received his cup, and we spent a silent moment enjoying the taste while Miss Armis withdrew from the office. Apparently, that moment was all Tate could spare.

"I suppose you're wondering why I asked you to stop by, Mr. Barrett?"

"Nope."

Tate's eyebrows drew down, and he looked at Hammerhand. "What happened?"

Hammerhand fidgeted and looked at his feet. "My boys lost her when she went into the ladies' room, sir."

Tate gave a rueful shake of his head. "That girl…" He turned back to me. "May I assume she has engaged your services, Mr. Barrett?"

"Yep."

"It's a fool's errand. I have word from some of my associates on Mercury that Nick met a girl. To which I say, thanks be to God! The boy never showed much interest in the opposite sex, so you can imagine how he would react when he finally took a romantic shine to a woman."

Tate offered a wistful smile and leaned back in his chair. "Ah, to be young, foolish, and in love again. Eh, Mr. Barrett? I have no doubt that Nick is simply disregarding my rules to follow the older, deeply ingrained rule of nature."

"You think he's shacking up with this girl? That he'll wander back once he tires of her?"

"In a word, yes. I'll have to chastise the lad, of course, but I won't be too hard on him. Tina will see to that." Tate smiled broadly at me. "So, there's no need for you to gallivant off to Mercury to look for Nick. I've no doubt that he'll be back in the company office before you even arrive."

"Uh huh."

Tate looked at me.

I looked at Tate.

After half a minute of that, I said, "Isn't this where you offer me a valise full of money to drop the case?"

"There's no need to be crass, Mr. Barrett."

"I find it saves time."

Tate glanced at Hammerhand. His ham-sized hand wrapped around my arm and jerked me to my feet. "Show some respect, Barrett."

"Or what?" I asked.

"Or this," he said, and sucker punched me in the gut.

The force of the blow drove the air from my lungs and the coffee from my stomach. My knees buckled and my vision swam. I would have collapsed to my knees if Hammerhand hadn't held me up.

"Your associates from the larger investigative firms were far more reasonable, Mr. Barrett. They acquiesced with alacrity, and without mouthing off." Tate gave me a level stare. "Does Mr. Houlihan have to dispense another lesson?"

I shook my head.

"So you'll regretfully refuse Tina's case?"

Around gasps for air, I said, "I... Gave my... Word."

"And you feel you must honor it?"

"Always... Have."

"Well, there's a first time for everything, Mr. Barrett. Now, would you like me to give you a valise full of money?"

I nodded.

"Then you must give *me* your word that you will decline Tina's offer of employment."

I let my breathing settle a bit, then said, "I will refund Miss Tate's retainer, and refuse all further payment for services."

Tate sighed. "I am not a fool, Mr. Barrett. Refusing payment is not the same as refusing to take her case." His voice hardened. "Will you refuse Tina's case?"

My head drooped. "Yes."

"Good. I'm glad you've seen reason." He turned to Hammerhand. "Please see Mr. Barrett out. He may pick up his valise full of money from Miss Armis."

"What about the coffee you promised me?"

"Thank you for reminding me, Mr. Barrett. Mr. Houlihan, have Miss Armis store his pound of coffee in the valise. Tell her to remove money until there's sufficient room for it."

Tate turned his attention to one screen on his desk, and Hammerhand dragged me away.

trouble with trouble

RITA GAVE a simulated gasp as I dragged myself into the office. "You okay, Boss?"

I thought, *I will be, sometime next year when I recover from Hammerhand's gut punch.*

I said, "Doing swell, Rita. How are you?"

"Concerned."

I swung the case full of money up and plunked it on her desk. "There's nothing to worry about. I've got everything under control."

"You're kidding, right?"

I opened the valise, and the eyes in Rita's face screen grew big and round at the sight of money inside. I grabbed the bag of coffee and said, "Nope."

"You're asking for trouble, Boss."

"And I have no doubt Trouble will march through that door soon."

"You want me to tell her you're out of the office?"

"Nah, she wouldn't believe you, anyway."

"Then what should I do, Boss?"

I closed the valise and told Rita exactly what she needed to do. Then I went into my office and brewed the most expensive cup of coffee ever made. Tate's personal blend still tasted good. But not nearly as good as when it had been free, and served by a shapely brunette.

I put the cup down, scooted my chair up to my desk, and winced as I got too close and rammed my stomach into the desk's edge. Then I turned on my screen, activated its phone feature, and made some calls. By the time I remembered my half-full cup of coffee, it had gone cold.

That's when the outer office door slammed open. There were two seconds of silence, followed by the sound of expensive high-heeled shoes clicking across the floor towards the door to my office. I don't know *why* expensive women's shoes sound different from the budget brand. Maybe it's the materials. Maybe it's the way a woman walks when she's wearing designer shoes.

Still thinking about ladies' fashion, I went to open the door for my former client. The door nearly hit me as it flew open, and again as it rebounded from the wall.

Trouble stood framed in the doorway. Narrowed eyes glared at me from under lowered eyebrows. She had compressed her full lips into a stern, angry line, and her hair swung in artful disarray. A professional makeup artist could labor for hours and never match this perfect embodiment of feminine fury.

Her tone of voice matched her appearance. "There you are, you low-life piece of garbage!"

"Hello, Trouble."

"That's *Miss Tate* to the likes of you."

"You appear upset."

"You're damned right I'm upset! I can't believe I thought you were different from the other men I hired to find Nick." Her eyes frosted over. "Your offended-man-of-honor act sure had me fooled. I bet you and Father had a good laugh over that."

I resisted rubbing my aching stomach. "I didn't laugh, and it wasn't an act."

"And to think I honestly thought you wouldn't compromise your principles for any price, when it turns out, your price is much lower than I believed."

"My honor isn't for sale."

"Oh really? Father says differently. He says you agreed to renege on your agreement with me. For once, I believe him." Her eyes darted around the office. "Where is it?"

"Where is what?"

"The valise full of money. I want to see how much it costs to buy off a once-proud man's honor."

"I told you before, Miss Tate, my honor isn't for sale. And certainly not to Norman Tate. As for the money, Rita has it."

She voiced a wordless cry of irritation. "Do you even hear what you're saying, Mr. Barrett? *I'm not for sale,* followed by *my Robosec has the money your father used to buy me off.* Can you truly be that blind to your utter failure as a man?"

"That was a low blow. Especially since all I did was tell your father I would refuse your case. Which I do."

Trouble's eyes blazed again. "That. Is. Exactly. My. Point."

"Because finding your brother is now *my* case, Miss Tate."

She had already opened her mouth for another verbal volley before she realized what I'd said. Her expression flowed from fury to confusion. "What?"

"Your father is hiding something, Miss Tate. That was abundantly obvious in his ham-handed attempt to buy me off. I'll lay long odds I'll find Nick when I find his secret."

"So, you're *not* giving up on my case?"

"I am a licensed investigator, Miss Tate. That means I am an agent of law who has more freedom of action than the traditional police. If I believe someone is breaking the law, I am duty-bound to report it or investigate it. Since reporting your father will not help Nick, I choose to investigate him."

"So, you *are* taking my case?"

"No, I'm not. I'll even refund your retainer."

"At least let me pay your expenses."

I shook my head. "That would go against what I told your father I would do. And I always honor my word." I offered a conspiratorial smile. "Besides, your father has already given me a valise full of money." I remembered the coffee and amended that. "Mostly full of money. It should cover our expenses, with plenty to spare."

"*Our* expenses?"

"You said I'd need your help finding Nick, didn't you?" She nodded, and I continued, "I've always wanted to hire an assistant, but this is the first time I've had enough money to actually do it."

I watched comprehension dawn on her. "Are you offering me a job?"

"I am, Miss Tate."

"Then I accept." She flashed her troublesome, dazzling smile. "And call me Trouble, Boss."

I stared into Trouble's eyes, bright blue again and dancing. A small, rational part of my brain screamed, *Look away, Travis!* But my primitive emotions cheered me on.

From far away, I heard the outer office door open and shut.

"Boss?" Rita called. "I'm back from shopping."

Rita's voice broke the spell Trouble had inadvertently cast over me. I broke eye contact and drew a deep, nervous breath. Trouble blinked her eyes, swayed back, and drew a breath of her own. Had she been as caught up in the moment as I had?

Nah. Probably just my imagination.

Rita bustled through the door to my office, cutting off further speculation. The eyes on her face screen flicked from me to Trouble and back to me as she deposited two small suitcases at our feet. "I had to guess Miss Tate's size."

"My size for what? And, Rita, now that we're working together, you should call me Trouble, too."

Eyebrow images rose to the top of Rita's face screen. "You hired her, Boss?"

"As my investigative assistant. Just for this case, of course." I was babbling, but couldn't stop myself from adding, "It seemed like the right thing to do."

"Oh, yeah, Boss. I can *totally* see that." Rita's eyes cut to Trouble. "Welcome to Team Travis, Trouble."

With effort, I wrenched my attention away from Trouble and back to the case. "Did you get everything else I asked for?"

"I'd have said if I didn't," Rita said.

Trouble looked at the suitcase at her feet. "What is all this?"

"Clothes for our trip to Mercury," I said.

Her brows drew down in mild confusion. Or maybe consternation. "That's kind of you, Travis, but unnecessary. You must know I have closets full of clothes at home. Some of them are even practical."

"Yes," I said, "but what do you think your father will say if you leave this office, go home, and start packing for a trip?"

"I'll tell him it's none of his business. What's he going to do, ground me? I'm not a child anymore."

"Neither is your brother."

That gave her pause. "I could tell him I'm furious with him and you, and I'm going to stay with a girlfriend for a few days."

I shrugged. "That might work. But are you willing to risk it just to pack your own suitcase?"

"No, you're right, Trav—Um, Boss." She looked around my Spartan office. "So, where can I change clothes?"

"Not here. The men your father has watching my office will—"

"Father has men monitoring you?"

I glanced at Rita. "How many of them did you see loitering in the corridor as you approached the office?"

"Three, Boss, including Mr. Ham-handed and his friend, the ferret-faced guy."

To Trouble, I said, "They're watching to make sure I keep my word to your father and refuse your case."

"You kept your word to the letter," Trouble said.

"I don't think your father will see it that way."

"What do we do?" Trouble asked. "A simple change of clothes won't fool Father's men, especially since I'm the only woman in here." She glanced at my Robosec. "I'm sorry, Rita. I mean, I'm the only flesh-and-blood woman in here."

Rita patted Trouble's arm. "No offense taken, dear."

"What you're going to do is storm out of here, in the same manner you stormed in. I'll follow a few minutes later wearing a hang-dog expression, with Rita carrying the suitcases. Once we get past your father's men, we'll meet you someplace very public, and very crowded. We'll both slip into a restroom and change clothes. Then we slip off to the spaceport and catch our flight to Mercury."

Rita added, "And I'll already be there, packed in a shipping crate."

I whipped my head around in surprise. "*What*?"

Rita's face screen displayed an arch expression. "You'd be lost without me, Boss, and you know it. Besides, how safe do you think Carnegie Station will be for me once Norman Tate figures out you ran off with his daughter to find his son?"

"She's right, Travis," Trouble added. "Father can be... vindictive when someone thwarts his will."

I remembered Hammerhand's punch to my gut and the most expensive pound of coffee in the solar system and gave a reluctant nod. "That was smart thinking, Rita."

"Yeah, I know, Boss." But her face screen glowed brighter at the compliment.

"Where should we meet up, Trouble?"

Trouble suggested a large shopping arcade near the spaceport, and Rita agreed it was perfect for our needs. With that decided, Trouble took a moment to reignite her fury, and then she stormed out of the office with high heels clicking and doors slamming. A few minutes later, I slumped my shoulders, hung my head, had Rita pick up the suitcases, and dragged myself out of the office. When I turned around after locking the door, Hammerhand and Slick stood before me.

"Where you going with them suitcases, Barrett?" Hammerhand asked.

"Out."

"You get that, Slick?" Hammerhand asked. "He says he's going *out*."

"Out." Slick giggled like it was a joke. "Yeah, Hammerhand."

I didn't have to fake my exasperated sigh. "What do you two low-lifes want?"

"We's here to make sure you don't do nothing stupid," Hammerhand said.

"Yeah, stupid," Slick said.

"You have my word I am not doing anything stupid."

That didn't convince Hammerhand. "Uh huh. You wanna tell me what happened with Miss Tate?"

"Did you see her enter my office?" Hammerhand nodded, so I continued, "And did you see her leave my office?" He nodded again, so I finished, "If you saw that and think you still have to ask what happened, you're a bigger idiot than I thought you were."

Hammerhand balled up his right hand and smacked it into his left palm. "Anybody ever tell you, you got a big mouth, Barrett?"

"Yeah, all the time."

Hammerhand pulled his fist back. "I think maybe I oughta break your jaw, so's nobody gotta listen to you for a while."

"Yeah, break his jaw," Slick said.

"You realize we're in a public corridor, right?" I asked.

"So?"

I pointed a finger straight up in response.

Hammerhand barked a laugh. "You think God is gonna stop me?"

"God." Slick giggled. "Good one."

"No, you muscle-brained morons," I snapped, "the station security camera. Hit me, and I'll make sure the cops haul your ass off to jail. I bet Tate will love the publicity, especially with his son missing and him buying off firms set to investigate."

Hammerhand gave me a slow-motion chuck to the jaw. "We was just having a little fun, Barrett. That's all."

"Having fun," Slick echoed.

"I've had more than enough of your idea of fun, Hammerhand." I pushed past him and Slick. "You and ferret-face back off, got it?"

"Hey, who you calling ferret-face?" Slick asked.

I ignored his question, but in a surprisingly soft voice, Hammerhand said, "You do kinda look like a ferret, Slick. But in a good way."

Rita and I didn't wait around to find out what was good about having a ferret face. And after they exchanged a few quiet words, Hammerhand and Slick fell in behind us. They boarded the same tube train we boarded, got off at the same stop, and didn't even try hiding from us. It was the first smart thing they'd done. I mean, Hammerhand doesn't exactly blend into a crowd.

Rita and I pretend-wandered through the shopping arcade, gradually working our way to the place where Trouble would meet us. Before we got close, a girl who looked no older than thirteen stopped in front of me, struck what she thought was a provocative pose, and asked, "You looking for trouble, mister?"

"Please tell me you're delivering a message and not propositioning me," I said.

"Message, and *ew*!" the girl said.

"Then yes, I'm looking for Trouble."

"She's in the thrift shop across the way. Says you should ask for Sally."

"And Sally is...?" I asked.

"How should I know?"

"Of course. Thanks."

"Whatev," she said, and vanished into the crowd.

Rita and I crossed to the thrift shop and entered. I caught the eye of the woman behind the counter and asked, "Sally?"

The woman pointed towards the clothing section in the back. After crossing the length of the store, I spotted a dark-haired woman in a shapeless dress that even I knew was thirty years out of date.

"Excuse me," I said, "I'm looking for Sally?"

The woman turned around and, in low tones, said, "What took you so long?"

My eyes widened. "Trouble?"

She struck a brief pose. "What do you think?"

"I'm impressed," I said.

"Good. Now, let's do you."

"A change of clothes will do for me," I said.

"You hired me to assist," Trouble said, "so let me do my job."

"She's right, Boss, and take these." Rita handed me the two suitcases and turned to leave. "I'll see you when they unpack me on Mercury."

Trouble took my hand and dragged me through a door marked EMPLOYEES ONLY. Thirty minutes later, the two of us left carrying different suitcases and looking nothing like our usual selves. We walked right by Hammerhand and Slick, and they never even noticed. Trouble and I went straight to the spaceport and joined the board line for our ship to Mercury.

THE LINE for boarding moved at a crawl, and the wait worked on Trouble's nerves. She began casting glances around the loading dock, craning her neck to see how many people were ahead of in line, and otherwise drawing attention to herself.

I put an arm around her shoulder, pulled her close, drew deeply on my manly fortitude to ignore how good that felt, and whispered, "Relax, or your nervous act will draw exactly the attention we're trying to avoid."

"I can't help it," she said. "We might have given Father's men the slip, but once they realize they've lost us, this is the obvious place to come look for us. I checked the departure schedule, Travis, and the *Star of Sol* is the only passenger ship heading to the inner planets today."

"There's nothing we can do about that. But you can stop fidgeting. It won't make the line move any faster."

Trouble nodded at an entry port thirty yards away where a well-dressed couple had just walked up. The crewman at the hatch tipped his hat, had another crewman take the couple's luggage, and ushered them onboard. "Why can't we just go over there?"

"That's for first-class passengers."

"Oh." Trouble forced a smile. "This ought to be an adventure. I've never traveled second-class before."

"And you still won't have after this trip."

Her eyes widened as comprehension dawned on her. "Third class?"

I nodded. "The only way to hide on a spaceship is to merge with the biggest crowd."

"Hide? But—"

"It's just a precaution, Trouble."

She looked around again, froze, and then said, "It *was* just a precaution."

I followed her gaze. Hammerhand and Slick strode onto the loading dock, leading a small gang of Tate's henchmen. As we inched closer to the third-class boarding hatch, the men spread out and wandered through the crowd looking for us. They paid particular attention to young women, which didn't sit well with the men accompanying those women.

Hammerhand and Slick headed straight for the first-class entry and flashed a picture under the crewman's nose. He shook his head. Hammerhand pressed him and got a more vehement head shake for his trouble.

Behind us in the third-class line, a man shouted, "Get away from my wife."

The slap of a fist against flesh sounded, and one of Tate's goons stumbled backwards, flailing his arms.

"You gonna regret that, buster!" another goon said and waded into the crowd with raised fists.

Other men from the line closed in to support their fellow passenger, and the rest of the goons rallied to their associate's aid. Hammerhand and Slick hurried towards the fight as the boarding officer blew a whistle. A burly band of the ship's crew rushed out onto the dock and followed Tate's head goons.

To my surprise, Hammerhand didn't join the fray. Instead, he yanked goons away from the fight and Slick kept them out. The crewmen were less gentle with the goons, and the waiting passengers cheered the crewmen on every time they beat down one of Tate's men.

In thirty seconds, the fight was over. Tate's men dragged unconscious comrades away while the passengers jeered.

The officer marched up to Hammerhand. "Sir, this dock is for *passengers* only. You and your thugs must leave."

Hammerhand towered over the officer. "We ain't finished looking."

To the officer's credit, he didn't quail before the obvious threat. But his crewmen took Hammerhand's implied threat seriously. They gathered behind their officer, none of them looking the worse for wear after their scrap with the goons. They all pulled leather blackjacks from their pockets and began slapping them into the palms in practiced unison. It made for an intimidating show of force.

I tore my eyes away from the scene and glanced towards the third-class entry. The line ahead had vanished as people crowded closer to the confrontation between Hammerhand and the officer.

I grabbed Trouble's hand and dragged her past the watching passengers. "Come on."

I had to wave our tickets in front of the boarding officer's eyes to get his attention. Once I had it, he pasted a smile on his face and said, "Welcome to the *Star of Sol*."

I gently pushed Trouble ahead of me up the boarding ramp. Just as we entered the ship, I heard the officer facing Hammerhand say, "The *only* way you may remain on the dock is if you purchase tickets."

In his gravel-tone voice, Hammerhand said, "Then gimme two tickets for me and my associate."

In a surprised tone, the officer asked, "Which class? And to where?"

"First class, all the way to Mercury."

WE FOLLOWED the spaceliner's main corridor deep into the bowels of the *Star of Sol*. Trouble's gaze darted left and right, probably comparing the utilitarian accommodations to her accustomed first class. I prepared myself for the explosion I feared would erupt when we reached our room. That, or quiet tears of misery. But when I ushered her into our minuscule third-class compartment, Trouble quietly began unpacking her suitcase and putting the clothes away.

"Aren't you going to unpack?" she asked.

"Aren't you going to rant or rail about the room?"

She looked at me with her head cocked to one side. "Why would I do that?"

"Because, in my experience, girls who are used to traveling first class don't take well to traveling third."

"I see." She returned to unpacking. "How many wealthy women have you taken with you on a third-class cruise?"

I put my suitcase next to hers on the bed and began unpacking. "None. But—"

"So you drew on your complete lack of experience with this situation when forming your expectations?"

"*But...* In my Space Patrol days, I took part in half-a-dozen rescues of wealthy women whose yachts broke down or crashed. None of them ever understood that we weren't there to serve their every whim." I glanced at Trouble. "Each one expected six patrollers to vacate shared quarters so they could have their own cabin."

Trouble folded her arms across her chest and leaned casually against the bulkhead. "Did their demands come as a surprise?"

"No, they acted that way from the moment they boarded the Patrol ship."

"Have *I* acted that way?"

"No, Trouble, you haven't." I stood and faced her directly. "I apologize for making unwarranted assumptions about you."

She drew breath for a response but was interrupted when the narrow door to the tiny room flew open. My hand darted into my suitcase and grabbed my blaster, ready to blow a hole right through the first person who threatened Trouble. But she caught my arm.

"No, Travis."

I shoved the blaster back into the suitcase as a giggling two-year-old boy zipped past my legs and dropped to all fours, ready to crawl under our bed. Trouble caught him and scooped him up into her arms.

"Where did that boy get to?" a harried woman's voice asked. "Ian Riley Carson, you had better get back here on the double!"

The boy giggled as Trouble scooted past me with him. "He's in here."

A pleasantly plump woman with tied back auburn hair and a worried expression appeared at our door. "I am *so* sorry about this. He's usually better behaved, but the excitement of boarding, plus that fight outside, and, well..."

Trouble bounced Ian on her hip and smiled at his mother. "There's no need to apologize."

"That's kind of you to say. I'm Liz Carson."

"Connie Rollins," Trouble replied, smoothly remembering the name I used for her when buying our tickets. "And this is my husband, Jack."

From outside, a baby suddenly wailed.

"Oh dear, Trudy is hungry." Liz held her arms out to Ian. "Come to Momma, so she can feed your baby sister."

Ian flung his arms around Trouble and buried his face in her breast. Lucky kid. Trouble bounced him again and smiled at Liz.

"Liz, I don't mind keeping an eye on him for a few minutes, if it will help. We'll leave the door open."

"Oh, I couldn't impose on you, Connie."

"I offered, so you're not imposing." Trouble smiled at the boy in her arms. "Besides, what woman wouldn't want to spend a little time with a charmer like Ian?"

The baby wailed again. With a grateful smile, Liz backed through our door and darted to her cabin next door.

I finished unpacking for both of us and shoved the blaster under the mattress. Trouble settled back on the bed and hummed a melodic tune to Ian. By the time I finished, the boy was fast asleep on her shoulder and Trouble had drifted off, too. A tender smile lit her tranquil face, once again showing the girl-next-door hidden behind her glamorous image.

I don't know how long I stood there lost in thought as the pair slept, but a knock on our open door startled me so much I jumped. A powerful, compact man filled the narrow entrance to the room. "Hey, neighbor. Sorry to startle you, Jack. I'm Sam Carson, Liz's husband? I came to collect Ian."

"Oh, right." I motioned to the pair napping on the bed. "It's been a busy day for both of them, I guess."

Sam edged into the cabin and joined me, gazing down at the pair. After a moment, he said, "It's none of my business, Jack, but your wife looks much better as a redhead."

My chest tightened. "I don't know what you're talking about, Sam."

"Like I said, it's none of my business. But the big thug out on the dock was flashing her picture to everyone around. Your lady changed her hair color and she piled on some wild makeup, but she's the same woman." Sam shrugged. "Liz says I've got an eye for the ladies, so maybe those two thugs won't see through her disguise. But I wouldn't bet on it if they get face-to-face with her."

I sighed. "As if I didn't have enough to worry about."

Sam turned his gaze on me. "I won't pry, but do I have to think about my family's safety, being next door to you?"

I shook my head. "It's a drag-her-back-to-her-father kind of trouble."

I hoped I wasn't lying, but Sam visibly relaxed. "Her daddy didn't want his baby girl marrying someone from the wrong side of the station?"

"Something like that."

"So I guess you want to lie low and avoid that big guy and his ferret-faced friend?"

"More than anything."

"Then we'd better come up with a better disguise for her, because last I heard, the pair of them were working their way through the ship, looking in every room and compartment for your girl."

three
trouble onboard

"IF A COUPLE of thugs are shoving their way into passengers' rooms, why don't the ship's officers do something about it?" I asked.

"A ship's officer is escorting them. From what I saw, I don't think he's happy about it. But he's doing it." Sam's eyes darted to Trouble, still asleep on the bed. "Her daddy must be all kinds of rich to get that kind of cooperation from the cruise line."

"He is." I had a vision of Hammerhand coming through our door and pounding me into unconsciousness while Slick chloroformed Trouble and carried her away. "We have to get off this ship."

Sam shook his head. "It's past departure time."

I slumped against the cabin's thin wall. "Then I don't know what I'm going to do."

In a sleepy voice, Trouble asked, "Do about what, Travis?"

My eyes cut to Sam. "Uh, Travis is... Um..."

Sam studied the deck and said, "People with stories like yours don't use their real names around strangers like me and Liz."

Careful not to disturb the sleeping child in her arms, Trouble sat up. "I'm sorry, um, Jack? I felt so peaceful waking up from the nap that it just slipped out."

"It's okay. I think we can trust Sam. He's Liz's husband and," I pointed at the little boy in her arms, "Ian's father."

Trouble gently shifted the boy so his father could take him. But Sam just rubbed his chin and stared at Trouble and Ian. Finally, she asked, "What? Am I holding him wrong or something?"

Sam shook his head. "Not at all. You handle him just as naturally as Liz does."

"And?" I asked.

"And it gives me an idea." Sam bent over Trouble and took Ian. "Give me a minute to talk to Liz."

Sam slipped out the door. Seconds later, I heard the murmur of voices coming through the wall we shared with their cabin.

Trouble stood, stretched, and pushed our door shut. "What kind of idea is he talking about, Travis? You need to tell me what's going on."

I filled her in on Sam's news and she grimaced when I told her the ship's officers were cooperating with Hammerhand and Slick. With a sigh, she joined me, leaning against the cabin wall. "Father is probably a minority owner of this cruise line. The steelworks are his life, but he's shrewd enough to spread his investments around." She turned troubled eyes on me. "What are we going to do, Travis?"

It was my turn to sigh. "I wish I knew."

We stayed like that for what felt like hours but couldn't have been more than five minutes. A sharp knock on the door sent my heart racing. I bent over and reached under the thin mattress for my blaster.

Through the door, a voice called, "It's Sam and Liz."

My heartbeat slowed. I pulled an empty hand out from under the mattress, rose, and opened the door. Sam, holding Ian, and Liz, holding baby Trudy, stood there.

I backed up to give them room. "Come in."

Liz came in first, and she went right to Trouble and held out the swaddled infant. "Could you hold Trudy for a minute? My arm is cramping."

Trouble nodded and gathered the baby into her arms, but Liz didn't even pretend to massage a cramping arm. Instead, she stepped back and regarded Trouble and the baby. She gave a nod and said, "You're right, Sam. She's a natural. I think this will work."

"What will work?" I asked.

Sam flashed a grin at me. "Jack or Travis or whatever your name is, can I interest you in trading wives?"

I gaped at Sam. My mouth opened and closed silently as I sought, and didn't find, a response. I sensed Trouble, still holding Sam's and Liz's daughter, move so I stood between Sam and her. My hands balled into fists, driven by ancient instincts. The rational part of my brain knew I was in for a world of hurt if I fought Sam. I stood a half a head taller than him and had better reach, but Sam had the broad shoulders and muscular build common among Belt miners.

One shout from Sam or Liz would bring ship's security down on us. Hammerhand and Slick would be right behind them. They'd take Trouble back to her father and probably dump me out the nearest airlock.

"For God's sake, Sam," Liz said, "stop kidding around."

Sam raised his hands in placation. "I'm sorry, Trav- um, Jack. I just couldn't resist poking you." Despite his apology, Sam busted out laughing. "But you should have seen your faces!"

Liz shook her head. "What my comedian of a husband is trying to say is that we think Sam and Jack should swap places, but only until after the men looking for Connie finish going door-to-door."

Sam nodded. "Those thugs are searching for a couple that looks like you two. If I answer your door, maybe they won't look too closely at the woman with me."

"Especially since she'll be nursing a baby," Liz added.

"Um, nursing?" Trouble asked.

"Not *really* nursing," Liz said. "But if I loan you one of my nursing shirts and you hold Trudy under it, it might fool those men. Especially if they're bachelors." Liz shook her head. "I'll never understand how men can be so fascinated with breasts and then get so flustered when a woman uses hers for their intended purpose."

Trouble stepped out from behind me. "Won't that be dangerous for Sam and Trudy?"

Sam smacked a fist into his hand, and Liz said, "Sam is real protective of the kids and me. I don't think we have anything to worry about."

"That's because you don't know who's looking for us," I said. "The big thug is an ex-heavyweight boxer."

Sam shrugged. "If it comes to a fight, I'll go for a low blow right off. If I can hold him off for just a bit, half the guys in third class will join the fight."

I reached under the mattress and pulled out my blaster. Sam's and Liz's eyes widened as I reached around to the small of my back and tucked the blaster under my waistband.

"No offense, uh Jack, but are you properly trained with that thing?" Sam asked.

"You might as well call me Travis in private," I said. "I'm ex-Space Patrol, so yeah, I know how to handle the blaster. Don't worry, if things go wrong I'll just use it to attract the goons' attention and draw them away from you three."

"You're really ex-Space Patrol?" Liz asked. When I nodded, she leaned in close and stared hard at my face. "Oh my God! I thought you looked familiar, but I only figured out why when you said you were a patroller." She turned to her husband. "Sam, he's Travis *Barrett*."

Sam peered at me for a minute. "I'll be damned." He grabbed my right hand and pumped it enthusiastically. "I always wanted to shake your hand, sir."

Liz wrapped her arms around me and gave me a hug. "And I always wanted to thank you!"

I looked from Liz to Sam and then to Trouble. Bafflement must have shone in my expression, because she said, "They must have been passengers on the *Euphoria*, Travis."

Liz still held me in a tight hug, so I felt more than saw her head nod. "We were on our honeymoon. I can only imagine what would have happened to us if you hadn't come to our rescue."

Sam added, "A bunch of us from the ship wanted to testify at your court martial, but the Space Patrol brass wouldn't let us. They said the result of your actions was *immaterial*—their words, not mine—to the trial."

I gently pried Liz's arms from around me. "They were right. My court martial was for disobeying orders."

Sam released my hand. "Yeah, well, the Space Patrol's opinion is *immaterial* to the debt we owe you."

Trouble squeezed past me and slid in between me and our thankful neighbors. "Shouldn't we get everything ready for when Father's goons and their guide show up?"

Liz turned to Trouble and smiled. "Is that a subtle way of asking us to stop embarrassing your husband?"

"That's just part of our cover story," Trouble said. "He's not really my husband."

Liz gave us a speculative look. "Not yet, anyway." She took Trouble's arm and led her from the room. "Let's get that nursing shirt for you."

Sam backed into the hallway to clear the path for Liz and Trouble. He sidled back once they left and grinned at me. "Don't pay any attention to Liz. She's always playing matchmaker."

My mind was still reeling from the recent turn of events, so I said, "Huh?"

Sam clapped me on the shoulder. "Don't worry, Liz doesn't always succeed." He pushed the door shut. "Now, let's figure out how we're going to handle this wife swap."

Ten minutes later, Liz and Trouble returned. Trouble wore an oversized shirt and had the sleeping Trudy tucked up under it. Sam and I got out of the way while Liz got Trouble settled on the bed. "Remember, keep your attention on the baby. That will keep your head down and your face turned away from the door."

Trouble followed Liz's instructions, and it hid Trouble's face well. As Liz rose and pushed me out the door. She gave Sam a quick kiss and said, "Don't have too much fun with your new wife."

"That goes for you and your new husband," Sam said. To me, he added, "If you *do* end up running, head for the cargo section and ask for Earle. He's a buddy of mine. And don't worry about your lady. We'll keep her safe."

LIZ and I settled into their room, with her near the door and me trying to pace in the tiny cabin. Ian slept on, fortunately, so we didn't have to find a way to make a two-year-old act like I was his father. After an interminable wait of twenty minutes, we heard a commotion through the thin door. As it drew closer, I sidled up next to Liz and listened intently for the sound I wanted to hear and simultaneously dreaded hearing. Finally, and way too soon, I heard a knock next door.

"Ship's officer," a tired, business-like voice called. "Open the door."

I joined Liz at the door of her cabin, listening for Sam's response from next door. We barely fit in the narrow space, but neither of us noticed.

Then Sam, his voice muffled through the closed door, said, "Yeah, what do you need?"

In the bored tone of someone who's repeated his words a hundred times in the last hour, the officer said, "I'm sorry to bother you, sir. We believe a fugitive is hiding on board and are checking all passenger cabins."

Sam filled his voice with disinterest. "Whatever. It's just me, my wife, and my baby daughter in here."

The officer didn't reply, and I imagined Hammerhand and

Slick craning their necks to see around Sam. After five seconds, Hammerhand said, "Tell your wife to turn around so's I can get a good look at her."

"Hell no. She's nursing, and I'm not going to let you pervs stare at her. You can see there's no one hiding in here, so get lost."

I gently pushed Liz back from the door and cracked it open just enough to peer into the corridor. Without the door's muffling effect, I clearly heard Hammerhand say, "I don't give a damn about seeing her tits, just her face."

Sam's voice rose. "And I already said no. You got no right barging in on us like this."

I opened the door wide enough to peer out with one eye. Hammerhand and the officer stood less than ten feet away. Slick stood closer and had his back to me. The officer looked uncomfortable, but any backbone he possessed wilted under Hammerhand's glare.

"That's not true, sir," the officer said. "As an officer of the *Star of Sol,* I have every right to inspect any cabin and any time."

"Fine," Sam snapped, "you can look. But not him."

The officer sighed. "This gentleman is the only person who can identify the fugitive."

The baby's piercing wail cut through the argument at the door. Sam immediately said, "Now look what you've done! Are you happy?"

"Not 'til I see her face," Hammerhand said.

Slick chose that moment to turn around. He spotted me peering through the cracked door and took a step closer. "Whatcha think yer lookin' at, pal?"

Past Slick, I saw Hammerhand put a hand through the doorway, no doubt trying to shove Sam out of the way. As good as Trouble's disguise was, it wouldn't hold up under close examination from someone who knew her well.

"Hey," Slick took another step my way, "I'm talkin' to you, pal."

Without hesitation, I opened the cabin door and moved

towards Slick, drawing my blaster from the waistband of my pants as I moved. Slick's eyes widened, and he froze in place. The blaster cracked as I fired a shot between his feet and followed that with a quick punch to Slick's nose. As he stumbled back from me, I raised my blaster and fired three quick shots into the lighting panels overhead. Then I turned and ran.

"Get outta the way, Slick!" Hammerhand yelled.

Slick groaned. "My nose!"

I heard a man bouncing off the corridor bulkhead. That was probably Hammerhand shoving Slick aside so he could chase after me. Good. I wanted them to pay attention to me, and not to Trouble. I cast a quick look over my shoulder and saw Hammerhand lumbering after me, with the ship's officer and Slick bobbing along in his wake.

Hammerhand's voice echoed down the corridor to me. "I'm gonna beat you to a pulp when I catch you, Barrett!"

All along the corridor, cabin doors opened and heads popped out to see what the commotion was about. Every time they spotted me and my blaster, they jerked their heads back inside and slammed their door shut. The few people in the corridor reacted by diving through a nearby door, running down a side passage, or simply flattening themselves against the bulkhead.

Fortunately for me, The *Star of Sol* stuck to the old Space Patrol-approved layout for ships of her class. Patrollers do a lot of rescue work in space, and the less time they spend asking for directions, the better it is for everyone. That didn't mean I knew the *Star* like the back of my hand—ships always have variations—but I knew where her major corridors went and how to get from one section to another.

And I knew where to find each section's electrical fuse boxes.

Twenty seconds into the chase, I found the one for the third-class cabins. I slid to a stop next to it, ignored the heavy pounding of Hammerhand's feet as he drew closer, blasted the lock on the fuse box's cover, and opened it.

Unaware of my intentions, Hammerhand crowed, "I got you now!"

Aware of my intentions, the ship's officer cried, "No!"

I fired two blaster shots into the fuses for the lighting systems. Cries of surprise and alarm rose as darkness dropped over third class. Hammerhand checked his headlong rush my way, and I imagined him feeling his way down the corridor, hoping to find me. But I was already gone.

Trailing a hand along the bulkhead, I followed my old patroller training, built a mental map of the corridors, and set out for the cargo area. I just hoped Sam's buddy Earle was as trustworthy as Sam thought he was. Because I was about to put my life in his hands.

four
asking for trouble

DESPITE THE ABSOLUTE darkness blanketing the third class section of the ship, I ran down the corridor. I barely heard my pounding footsteps over Hammerhand's shouted curses, the officer's frantic comm to the bridge demanding help, and Slick's repeated complaints about his flattened nose.

Then my probing hand found the branching corridor I'd been looking for. I ducked down it, and just in time, too. Ten seconds after I blasted the fuse box, the section's emergency lighting activated. Harsh light shined directly down the corridor, casting everything and everyone into sharp silhouettes. With identifiable details like colors and the cut of clothing washed out, I slowed to a fast walk and casually put my blaster under the waistband at the small of my back.

A head popped out of a cabin door and a man asked, "Anybody know what's going on?"

I jerked a thumb over my shoulder and said, "I heard a ship's officer shouting into a comm back that way. Maybe he knows?"

"Thanks pal," he said, and headed in the direction I'd pointed. Just as I'd hoped, other people in the corridor trailed after him.

Hammerhand's frustration at almost catching me must have boiled over, because his raised voice echoed down the corridor.

"I'm hunting for a fugitive, so everybody better get outta my way!"

A distant thump sounded, and I imagined the boxer shoving passengers from his path. The officer's voice rose. "Mr. Houlihan, you will not treat passengers in that manner!"

If Hammerhand had a response, the shouts of passengers drowned his voice. Even better, the commotion drew more passengers towards it, further blocking his pursuit. I took advantage of the distraction and turned down the next crossing corridor I found.

For the next minute, I took every new corridor I came to, as long as it took me in the general direction of the ship's cargo hold. Normal lighting replaced the blinding emergency lights when I left third-class behind, just as third class's minimal concessions to comfort gave way to bare metal decks and gray-painted walls.

A work crew laden with electrical repair equipment hurried past me, though one member stopped before me. "This area's fer crew, sir. You lost? Cause you ain't s'posed to be down here."

I drew from all the comedy of manners movies I watched in my life and gave my best impersonation of a first-class passenger who was way out of his depth. "My goodness, that explains this atrocious decor! Am I in any danger?"

The crewman kept a pleasantly helpful expression pasted on his face, for which I felt certain he deserved a raise for superior customer service. "No, sir, not if you stick to the corridors and head straight back to your cabin."

"That is the problem, my good man." I widened my eyes and beamed a bright smile at him. "I say, *you* know your way about the ship. Why don't you escort me back to my suite?"

Passenger liners have few suites, and they're so expensive only the tiptop of the upper crust can afford them. I thought my suggestion would draw an impatient reaction from the crewman, but his only sign of impatience came when his eyes cut after his receding work crew.

"I'm truly sorry, sir, but we're responding to a power outage in third-class. But if you don't mind waiting here until the next crew member passes, tell them that Chief Robinson said to escort you back to your suite."

I compressed my lips, praying that conveyed irritation at the thought that anything associated with third-class took precedence over first-class passengers, and gave a curt nod. In a resigned tone, I said, "Very well, if I must wait, I shall do so." With a dismissive wave, I added, "Carry on, Robinson."

He hurried after his crew, and I felt certain my clueless-first-class act would be a topic of conversation when he got together with his buddies after work. I lounged against the bulkhead until Chief Robinson turned down a side corridor, then I headed aft again, towards the cargo hold. The next time a crew member stopped to direct me back towards passenger territory, I told her, "I've already spoken with Chief Robinson about this."

The crew woman's face screwed up in confusion, but then she shrugged. "I guess it's okay if the Chief says so. Do you know the way, sir?"

"I do, Miss..." I peered at her name patch. "Miss Peters. But I thank you for your concern."

I smiled.

She smiled.

We went our separate ways.

I invoked Chief Robinson's name twice more before I reached the cargo hold offices. A clerk, who looked like he doubled as a roustabout when the ship had to shift a lot of cargo, rose and barred my way. "Can I help you, sir?"

The time for acting was past, so I dropped my first-class persona. "I'm looking for Earle."

The man looked me up and down. "Is Earle looking for you?"

"No, but he'll want to see me."

"Uh huh. Why?"

"I can only discuss that with Earle."

"You better find a way to discuss it with me. Because you're not getting past me 'till I'm satisfied with your story."

I sighed. "Then could you deliver a message to Earle? I promise I'll wait right here until you return."

He regarded me critically for a moment, shrugged, led me over to his desk, and pointed at a chair. "Sit." After I sat, he activated an intercom exactly like the one Rita and I use in the office. "Hey, Earle?"

A gruff voice asked, "Yeah, Don?"

"Got a guy out here who wants to see you. Says he has a message for you."

The intercom was silent for five seconds, then Earle asked, "What's the message?"

Without waiting for Don's permission, I said, "I need help, and Sam Carson sent me to you."

"Sam, huh?" Earle replied through the intercom. "How're him and Amy doing?"

"His wife is Liz, so either Sam's cheating on her or you're testing me," I said. "It's probably testing, so let me save you some time. Their son is Ian Riley, and their daughter Trudy is still nursing."

"Okay, you've at least met Sam. But who are you?"

I glanced at Don, unsure how much he should hear. Don caught my look and said, "He's trying to figure out if he can trust me or not, Earle."

"Whoever you are, Don is as trustworthy as they come."

"I'm sure he is," I replied. "But I don't want to drag him into this if I can help it."

"If your trouble is *that* bad, I'm going to need Don's help, anyway," Earle said. "So, again, who are you?"

I took a deep breath. "Travis Barrett."

"Holy hell." The intercom was silent for two long heartbeats, then Earle said, "I'm asking for trouble, but... Don, you better bring him back here."

Don led me down a short corridor so narrow his shoulders brushed both bulkheads as he walked. It even felt tight to me and my much less broad shoulders. Don opened the door at the end and squeezed into a cramped office almost entirely filled with two desks. One held neatly stacked and labeled data pads. Two computer screens sat on the other, along with three data pads processing updates.

Earle sat in the lone chair facing the computer screens, but he spun around to face Don and me as we came through the door. Like Don, Earle had broad shoulders, massive biceps, and thighs small trees would envy. His build fit the slow-witted-freight-ape perfectly until you looked into his dark brown eyes. Intelligence shone there, just as it did in Don's eyes. I felt certain many people underestimated this matched pair of human behemoths, a mistake I wouldn't repeat.

Earle sized me up. "The way Sam and Liz used to go on about you, I thought you'd be bigger."

I folded my arms and leaned against the bulkhead. "The way dock workers act on Carnegie Station, I thought you'd be stupider."

We glared at each other. After a couple of seconds, Don said, "Okay, are you two done throwing stereotypes at each other?"

"Yeah." Earle's glare faded to intense curiosity. "You want to tell me why Sam gave you my name?"

"He said you were a buddy of his. He implied I could count on you to help me out."

"That depends on what kind of trouble you're in."

I spun the story I had concocted about Trouble and me going on the run to get away from her father, who didn't approve of our marriage. "We thought we were free and clear when we got to our third-class cabin. But her father must have leaned on whoever owns this starliner, and they leaned on the captain. Because a ship's officer personally escorted her father's two goons on a cabin-by-cabin search for us. Sam and Liz have the idea they owe me for the *Euphoria* incident, so Sam came up with a wife-swapping plan." Earle's eyebrows rose at that, so I added, "Just to confuse the goons, naturally."

"But Sam's plan didn't work?"

I shook my head. "The head goon insisted on a close look at my wife, and Sam couldn't dissuade him. So I popped out of the cabin next door, got them to chase me, and I lost them in the confusion."

Earle glanced at a data pad on his desk. "When you say confusion, you really mean firing a blaster inside the ship and frying a fuse box."

"So?"

"So, do you have any idea how dangerous that was?"

"I'm ex-Space Patrol. Of course I know. I also know where *not* to shoot."

"That doesn't excuse what you did."

I shrugged. "If your captain had shown a little backbone and stood up to whoever told him to help the goons, I wouldn't have had to do it."

Anger flared in Earle's eyes. "Captain Hughes is a good man who is just trying to do his job."

"His job is protecting the passengers."

Earle surged to his feet. "You don't know the captain, you don't know what kind of pressure he got from above, and I bet you'd have done the same thing in his place."

I tilted my head back so I could look into Earle's eyes, stared at him, and waited. I'll say this. Earle figured it out faster than I thought he would.

"Hell." He dropped back in his chair and scrubbed a hand over his face. "Lecturing a guy who lost his career, and almost his life, disobeying an order he knew was wrong. Real smart, Earle."

I gave him five seconds to work through it. "Does that mean you'll help us?"

Earle nodded. "What do you need me to do?"

"First, get word to Sam that I got here safely and tell him to bring, um..." My mind blanked on the alias I'd given Trouble. "Have him bring my wife here."

If Earle noticed my pause, he didn't mention it. "You sure about that? I mean, the cargo hold isn't exactly known for its comfortable accommodations. And now that you've gotten away, won't the pressure die down?"

I gave a humorless laugh. "I wish. If your captain thought the pressure was bad before, he's in for a rude surprise."

Earle looked askance at me. "Just how rich is your girl's daddy?"

"Rich enough, and then some."

"A girl who'd give up that much?" Earle shook his head. "At least you know it's genuine love."

I thought about the way Trouble's eyes sparkled when she talked about her brother. "It's plenty real."

"Okay, what happens after we get her back here with you?"

"I have a cargo crate in your hold. I'll need you to find it and redirect it to Marsport. That's the *Star of Sol's* first port of call, right?"

"Yeah, but aren't you going to Mercury?"

"Not on this ship, we're not." I flashed a tight smile. "Smuggle us off at Marsport, and then forget about us."

"Are you going to catch the next starliner that comes along?"

"That's my problem." And the less Earle knew about it, the better it was for both of us. "Can you do it?"

Earle looked at Don, who I'd forgotten was even in the room. "What do you think, Don?"

"Redirecting the cargo crate is easy. But smuggling people gets tricky. A lot of orbit-to-ground cargo haulers don't have pressurized holds."

I asked, "Do you have anything that has to stay pressurized? Pharmaceuticals, maybe?"

Don shook his head. "Not this trip."

That made things more difficult. "Then we're going to have to steal two spacesuits from you."

"You know we have to replace those out of our own pockets?" Don asked.

"Okay, we'll *buy* them from you."

Don gave a reluctant nod. "That will help." He looked at Earle. "Anything else?"

"No. Get word to Sam while I figure out where to hide them."

Don squeezed past me and left the Cargo area. Once we were alone, Earle looked at me. "I know some independent freight haulers who use Marsport as their home base. You want some names?"

I shook my head. "The less you know about our plans, the better it is for everyone. Besides, I know a guy."

I just hoped the guy wouldn't shoot me on sight.

EARLE and I worked on plans for smuggling Trouble and me down to Marsport. Really, Earle did the planning. I stood around, ready to answer questions that arose.

Ten minutes into his planning, Earle looked me up and down. "You're, what, six feet tall and weigh about one ninety?"

"You're spot on. I'm impressed."

"Work freight as long as I have, you get good at these things." He tapped my information into a data pad. "Tell me about your girl."

I thought about Trouble, and my lips stretched into a smile. "She's smarter than she lets on, remarkably intuitive, funny, independent—"

Earle burst out laughing. "Damn, son, you got it bad for her! But I was asking for her height and weight."

"Oh. Uh, let's see... Height is around five feet, nine inches. Weight..." I remembered picking her up when she blocked the way to my desk. God, was it only this morning? "She's about one twenty. Maybe one twenty-five."

Earle tapped on his data pad again. "Your girl sounds like quite a willowy beauty." I arched my eyebrows at the comment.

Earle shrugged. "A guy can be a freight ape *and* have a good vocabulary, you know."

"Obviously. And you're right about her."

Earle worked in silence for five minutes, then said, "You know, it might help if you told me her name. I mean, what do I call her when she gets here? *Travis's girl* seems impersonal, not to mention archaic as hell."

I'd finally remembered the alias I used when I bought our tickets, but Earle's career was toast if his employers ever found out he helped Trouble and me. Didn't he deserve to know the truth? Besides, by now Trouble had probably told Sam and Liz the entire story, and eventually they'd tell Earle everything.

Trouble was *my* name for her. Well, mine and her brother's. I said, "Tina. Her name is Tina."

In a conversational tone, Earle asked, "She got a last name?"

I drew a deep breath and said, "Tate." Earle slowly turned his head and raised his left eyebrow. So I added, "As in Tate Steelworks."

"Why didn't you say so before? Now I've *got* to help you."

"Do tell?"

Earle spun his chair around and leaned back in it. "It was thirty-four years ago, back before you were even born, Barrett. I was eighteen, all full of piss and vinegar, and cocky as hell. Five friends and I formed an asteroid mining crew. We knew just enough about mining to survive, but that didn't bother me. I just *knew* we were going to hit a big strike and get stinking rich."

He gave a rueful shake of his head. "The thing is, we made that big strike, marked our territory, and one guy volunteered to go to the asteroid management office and file our claim. Only he didn't do that. Our supposed friend sold the information to a guy with a bigger team. That guy filed our claim. He mined our asteroid. He got stinking rich. We got nothing except a mountain of useless legal bills. And the satisfaction of pounding the crap out of our so-called friend the next time we saw him."

"That sounds like something Father would do." Trouble

stood framed in the doorway. Sam stood behind her, holding our two suitcases, and Don loomed behind him. She smiled at me. "I was worried about you, Travis. I'm glad you're okay."

"He's only going to be okay as long as ship's security doesn't get their hands on him," Don said. "They've got teams out combing the ship for him, now."

Earle stood. "How much time have we got before they get to us, Don?"

"Twenty minutes, if we're lucky."

"That's not enough time." Earle grabbed a data pad off his desk, handed it to Trouble, and said, "Pass this to Don, will you, Tina?"

Don took the pad and began nodding as he read. "It's going to take close to an hour to get this set up."

"I know," Earle said. "That's why I'll stay here and do my best to stall the security team when they get here."

"What can I do?" Sam asked.

"Get your ass back to your cabin as fast as you can," Earle said. "Security is probably suspicious of you already. They'll lock down the cargo hold and tear this place apart if they see you here."

I took the suitcases from Sam, then said, "Give my thanks to Liz. And when security gets around to questioning you, tell them I used Liz and Ian as hostages against your good behavior."

Sam shook his head. "I can't throw you under the bus like that!"

"You *can*, and you *will*," I said. "If you do anything else, you and Liz will get caught up in this and risk losing your freedom, your kids, and each other."

"Listen to the man, Sam," Earle said. "Now get out of here. We've got work to do."

Trouble gave Sam a quick hug. "Thank you."

"Any time, kid," Sam said. "And you better look Liz and me up when you get to Mercury."

Trouble nodded. "Sure thing. Now get going. Ian and Trudy need their daddy."

After Sam left, Earle rooted around in a desk drawer and pulled out two comms. He handed one to Don, while sticking the other in his ear. "Keep it on, but muted. When the security team gets here, you'll be able to hear everything we say and act appropriately."

Don nodded, stuck the comm in his ear, and led Trouble and me through a different door. We went down another short, narrow corridor that opened into the *Star of Sol's* main cargo hold. Don checked the information on the data pad, and headed deeper into the hold. "Come on."

We wound our way through stacks of crates ranging from one small enough for Schrödinger's Cat to enormous ones large enough for complex mining machinery. We were still wending our way through the hold when Don stiffened and raised his hand to his comm.

He grimaced and said, "The security team just got here."

"I thought you said we'd have twenty minutes," Trouble said. "It hasn't even been ten."

"I guess we weren't lucky," Don said.

I pointed at the data pad. "I don't know where Earle planned on hiding us, but you said it would take an hour to set everything up. Do we have that much time now?"

"I think so, but..." Don's attention left us for a moment as he concentrated on his comm. "Crap. They brought *two* teams so they can finish faster, and they're asking for me to come guide the second team. I'm sorry, but it looks like you two are on your own."

Don handed me the data pad and hurried away. I wished he could leave the comm, too, but it might raise suspicion if he didn't have one after responding to Earle's comm call.

As the big man vanished behind stacked shipping containers, Trouble turned frightened eyes to me. "What are we going to do?"

I offered the most reassuring smile I could scrape together. "Exactly what we planned. We'll just have to find our hiding place without Don's help." I examined the information on the data pad, and my smile broadened. "Earle called up the data on Rita's shipping container and even changed its destination to Marsport. It still has my name on it, but I can fix that."

Trouble looked over my shoulder as I tapped the screen. "Who is Dave Hayslett?"

"A guy I know in Marsport."

"Is he a friend of yours?"

"Maybe."

I tapped an icon next to the information on Rita's container. A map of the cargo hold popped up and even provided a handy route from the pad's location to the container. I took Trouble's hand and set off.

As we jogged, Trouble asked, "Aren't you supposed to lie about your relationship with this Dave guy, so I won't worry my pretty little head?"

"Is that what you want me to do?"

"It's what all the private eyes do in the movies."

"Fine. Dave and I go way back."

"So do Hammerhand Houlihan and I. That doesn't make us friends."

"Has anyone ever told you you're too smart for your own good?"

"Has anyone ever told you you're too evasive for your own good?"

I imagined Rita laughing at Trouble's comeback, and said, "Why don't we concentrate on hiding and talk about Dave later?"

"That's two evasions in a row. You and Dave must have quite the history. But I'll allow it."

From the direction of Earle's office, a door slammed. An obvious warning from Earle or Don that the security teams were in the hold with us. I immediately slowed our pace, and Trouble hissed, "What are you doing? We should run faster."

"Running is louder than walking," I said, "and noise is a luxury we can no longer afford."

"Oh, right. Sorry."

I nodded in acknowledgement and then concentrated on the way to our hoped-for-hiding place. Two minutes later, we entered the right section of the hold, and we found Rita's container half-a-minute after that. I checked the container's information screen and verified it specified a Will Call hold for Dave Hayslett. Then I raised the lid and peered inside. Rita lay within, powered down and surrounded by packing material.

Trouble shivered. "She looks dead. I mean, I know she isn't, but she was so lively in the office and—"

I laid a hand on her shoulder. "You're babbling, Trouble."

She gave a quick nod, took a deep breath, and said, "Right. Um, what now?"

"Find someplace where we can hide all these packing peanuts. We have to take them out. Otherwise we'll never fit in there with her."

A minute later, Trouble opened a container that held machinery in a custom-made shipping harness. It had no packing material, and lots of space inside. We immediately began shifting the packing from Rita's container to the new one, but it was a painfully slow process. Then Trouble dumped the contents of her suitcase and began scooping packing peanuts into it. I did the same, and the transfer went a lot faster.

When I heard voices from the next sector, I closed the container where we stored Rita's packing peanuts. We jammed our clothes and, in Trouble's case, bundles of cash into our suitcases. I stowed them next to Rita's hover unit, climbed into the container, and stretched out next to her. I squirmed briefly, hoping to find a comfortable position, failed, put my blaster on Rita's chest plate, and then waved Trouble in with me. She took care climbing in, lay on top of me, and pulled the lid closed.

In total darkness, Trouble squirmed in a manner I'd have found delightful in less dire circumstances. When Trouble settled, she just sort of fit on top of me. I don't know how women do that or how they learn the trick to it. It's like the crossed-arms, canted-hip, tapping-foot thing that every woman can do. Are there secret training classes given to girls entering puberty, or do women just know this stuff instinctively?

I wrenched my mind away from fruitless speculation and concentrated on the parts of Rita poking me in the back. That took my mind off the feeling of having a willowy woman lying on top of me, at least. Then I heard Earle's voice from nearby.

"Are we almost done here? I have a lot of work to do, and none of it involves giving you guys a guided tour of my cargo hold."

A man's officious voice said, "We'll be done when we're done." Then it added, "Spread out and look around."

A minute later, a woman's voice sounded from outside our hiding place. "Sir? There's packing material on the floor over here, and this container doesn't look like it's been properly closed."

Trouble's breath quickened, and I felt her heart hammering in her chest. My heart matched her beat as I carefully picked up my blaster.

Outside, the officer called, "Everyone gather around that container." Five seconds later, he said, "Okay, open it up."

I squinted my eyes against the bright light that would flood the container if the security team opened it. My thumb flicked off the safety on my blaster, but I kept my finger off the trigger. I didn't want to shoot anyone just because their captain was too spineless to stand up to Norman Tate and his favorite goons. But I felt certain my life hung in the balance, not to mention Trouble's freedom.

If Hammerhand and Slick got their hands on us, Tate would surely make his recalcitrant daughter a prisoner in her own home. Odds were good that I'd get a chance to practice breathing vacuum. And Norman Tate's big secret, whatever it was, would never come to light.

That's why I knew I'd shoot if I had to. To wound, if possible. To kill, if I had no other choice.

The horrible, inescapable logic of my situation flashed through my mind in the split second after the security team leader gave the order to open the container. Immediately after my brain finished processing the situation, the security team leader asked, "What do you see?"

I released the breath I'd been holding, and I felt Trouble's body relax slightly. We weren't out of the woods yet, but at least they'd opened the wrong container.

"Some kind of machine, Sarge," a woman said. "And a lot of packing stuff."

"Make sure Barrett didn't bury himself beneath the packing material," Sarge said.

"Yes, sir."

"No, wait!" Earle said. It sounded like he stood right next to our container.

"He's not in here, Sarge," the woman called.

"Why did you want them to wait?" Sarge asked.

"Because if your guy had been hiding inside, the packing material would have conformed to his body. But now we'll never know. Unless..." When Earle spoke again, he sounded farther away. "When you first looked in here, did you maybe see a curving depression in the middle of the packing? Like something made by someone's hips or butt?"

"I don't know..." the woman said.

"He'd have mussed its shape when he climbed out, so it would have been subtle." Earle paused for a second, then added, "It would take sharp eyes to notice something like that, so don't feel bad if you didn't spot anything."

"Now that you've described it," the woman said, "I saw something like that."

"Are you certain, Dyer?" Sarge asked.

After an agonizing three-second wait, she slowly said, "Yeah..." Her tone of voice turned brisk. "I mean yes, Sarge."

Earle said, "It looks like your man hid here until we got close, then slipped away. Sounds like this Barrett guy is pretty smart. Has he got a first name?"

Sarge replied, "It's... um, Travis."

"Travis Barrett?" Earle asked. "He's not *the* Travis Barrett, is he?"

"I don't know who you mean," Sarge said.

"You ever hear of the pirate attack on the spaceliner *Euphoria* six years ago?" Earle asked.

"Barely. I was regular army and stationed on Venus back then," Sarge said. "Didn't the Space Patrol drive the pirates off?"

"Travis Barrett's ship did, but he disobeyed a direct order from his superior to do it. Saved hundreds of lives and got drummed out of Space Patrol for doing it."

"You don't say?"

"Yep. Barrett's decision made him a lot of friends he doesn't even know he has, especially among spaceliner crews. I don't know why you're hunting Barrett, but catching him will make you and your team mighty unpopular with the *Star's* regular crew." Earle paused for a heartbeat, then said, "Which container do you want to open next?"

Sarge was quiet for a moment, then asked, "Dyer, are you sure you saw a man-sized depression inside that open container?"

"I am, Sarge." Dyer's voice rang with conviction she hadn't shown earlier.

"Then I think the cargo chief is right. Barrett slipped away while we were searching other sections of the hold. He's probably gone to ground somewhere else on the ship. With his Space Patrol training, I expect he can hide from us indefinitely."

"It seems likely, Sarge," Dyer agreed.

"Let's go find the other team, and then report to the captain," Sarge said.

Earle said, "I'll get my guy on the comm and have him bring that team to the cargo office. Come on."

A minute later, all was silent around the container. I flipped on my blaster's safety and put it aside. In a hushed tone, I asked, "Are you okay?"

Trouble stirred in my arms and warm breath blew across my neck as she sighed. "I will be... I thought they were going to find us until Earle talked them out of it. Do you think the security team knows he's hiding us?"

"Hiding me. They don't know about you yet. And I'm sure they suspect, but they'll keep quiet about it because of what Earle said about being unpopular with the rest of the crew."

"Why would that matter?"

"The crew has to live together in close quarters for months at a time. Things can get tense even when everyone gets along. Now imagine how it would feel if everyone went out of their way to make your life hell."

"Yikes. Does that mean we're free and clear?"

"Only if we stay out of sight."

"For how long?"

"We're about a day from Mars, so we stay hidden until we get there and Earle smuggles us off the *Star*. So you better get cozy. You and I are going to be spending a lot of time together until we reach Marsport."

"I can think of worse people to spend my time with," Trouble said. "That reminds me, Liz asked me to give you this."

Trouble's lips pressed against my cheek in a platonic kiss of thanks. Her lips against my cheek felt as kissable as they looked, and the primitive male part of me wished she'd bussed me on the lips. The professional private investigator part of me was relieved she hadn't.

We stayed hidden for a long hour, during which my primitive and professional selves warred over what I should do with the lithe woman sharing the container with me. Civilized behavior won out, but my professional side heaved a sigh of relief when I heard Earle's voice outside the container.

"It's safe to come out, Barrett." I pushed the lid open, and Earle helped Trouble and me climb out. As we both stretched cramping muscles, Earle said, "I figured you were in there with your Robosec."

"Thanks for persuading them to move along," I said. "We owe you."

"What now?" Trouble asked. "I'd kill for a shower. This makeup is getting sticky, and the coloring is making my hair stiff."

"I can give you time for that, and get some food for you," Earle said. "Then we need to put you into spacesuits and pack you back in this container." It's what I expected, but Trouble must have looked disappointed. Earle shrugged. "I'm sorry, Miss Tate, but it's best if you two stay out of sight."

An hour later, Trouble was a redhead again after her shower. We put on clean clothes, ate a big meal, and bought two spacesuits from willing members of the cargo crew. Earle and Don packed us into Rita's container, and Earle showed me how to open it from the inside.

Twenty-two hours later, a cargo hoist lifted our container and transferred us to an orbital freight shuttle, and we were finally on our way to Mars.

five
martian trouble

AFTER SEVERAL MINUTES OF BUMPING, swaying, and manhandling, someone shoved Rita's shipping container—and our hiding place—into place in the orbital freighter's hold. The engines roared to life, but the ship's decks and the packing peanuts surrounding us softened it to a subtle background buzz. Ten seconds later, gravity vanished as the freighter pulled free of the *Star of Sol's* gravity field.

Trouble, once again lying on top of me, shuddered. I put my helmet against hers and asked, "Are you okay?"

"Where did the gravity go?"

"Little ships like this don't usually have a gravity generator in the cargo holds."

"Great," she gasped. "I think I'm going to be sick."

"Don't worry, your spacesuit's systems are designed to handle it."

She moaned. "That makes me feel *so* much better."

"That's because you've never puked in a suit that's *not* designed to handle it."

"That's not helping, Boss."

"I'm sorry, Trouble. It should only take us fifteen or twenty minutes to reach Mars' gravity well, if that helps."

"Not much." Trouble drew two deep, ragged breaths. "Tell me something to take my mind off my stomach."

"Like what?"

"I don't care!" She gulped once. "Tell me about you and this guy we're going to see."

"Dave? Okay, um..." I fell silent while I considered where to start.

"You're not talking, Boss."

"Right. Sorry." I drew a breath. "Dave and I were roommates at the academy and became the best of friends during that first semester. He's a natural-born pilot, and without his tutoring I'd have come close to failing our piloting classes. In return, I helped him get through his navigation classes.

"We did virtually everything together. Whenever we had weekend passes and went out looking for girls, we took turns acting as each other's wingman. But—"

"What do you mean by wingman?" Trouble asked.

"Have you ever been out with your friends and had a couple of guys approach your group?"

"Sure, that happens all the time."

I had no doubts about that. "Then one guy told jokes and kept your friends' attention while the other guy gave you his full attention?" Without waiting for an answer, I continued, "The guy distracting your friends was flying wingman for the guy concentrating on you."

"I never realized. Were you one of those girl-in-every-port spacers?"

"Dave was."

"Okay. It sounds like you two were inseparable. Shouldn't he welcome you with open arms?"

"He would have, if the *Euphoria* incident had never happened."

"Was he on your ship?"

"He was the *Soteria's* pilot and my first officer. Part of his job was playing devil's advocate to me if I acted against orders or regulations."

"Like when you disobeyed the order to ignore the *Euphoria's* distress call?"

"Exactly like that. Dave did his job and went on record, noting that I was intentionally disobeying orders. But he also did his other job. Honestly, his piloting is the main reason the *Soteria* avoided the pirate's blaster cannons long enough for the *Euphoria* to escape."

"I guess Space Patrol threw him out, too?"

"No, the brass did something worse. They gave him a medal."

"Why is that worse?"

"Because most of the rank-and-file Patrollers supported me, claiming I risked my men and ship following proud Space Patrol traditions. When the brass decorated Dave, it was like recognizing him because he appeared willing to turn his back on those same traditions." I sighed. "But he didn't turn his back on anyone or anything. From start to finish, he did his job to the best of his ability. When I defended his actions during my court martial, people credited me for being loyal to my back-stabbing first officer."

Trouble was quiet for a minute. "So, after the *Euphoria*, Dave faced the same situation Earle laid out for the security team that was searching for you?"

"Yes. Dave grew up dreaming of a lifelong career in Space Patrol. But one tour of duty as my first officer destroyed that dream." I sighed. "When he mustered out, no Patroller even tried throwing a farewell party for him. I would have, but he never returned my messages. I can't say I blame him, either."

As I wrapped up my story, I heard the rising shriek of a ship entering the atmosphere, a sound even the thin Martian air produced. Gravity gradually returned, though it never came close to Earth-normal. Trouble said, "Thanks, Travis."

She and I remained silent as the freighter landed and the crew unloaded their hold. They handled our container with what I assume was a casual disregard for the contents. In fairness to the guys moving us around, they didn't know the container had people in it. But it was clearly marked HANDLE WITH CARE, which they clearly ignored. They finally got us stowed in their warehouse, and I gave them two more hours to finish unloading the rest of the cargo. Then I cracked open the container's lid and peered out.

Three Martians—real Martians with deep red skin and jet black hair, not just transplanted Earthers—sat on a nearby container, munching sandwiches and watching me with curiosity. They hopped up and spread out, ready for any moves I might make. With a mental shrug, I stood up, kept my hand away from the blaster slung at my side, and twisted off my helmet. After over twenty hours of breathing canned air, even the thin Martin air smelled fresh.

One grinned. "Looks like we found that stowaway the captain of the *Star of Sol* warned us about. How big was that reward, again?"

"Big enough," the man to my left said.

"Plenty big enough," the one to my right said as he pounded a fist into his palm.

With greed glinting in their eyes, the trio closed in on me.

I could have ended the coming fight before it started by shooting the three roustabouts. But, because of the *Star of Sol's* captain and his negotiable principles, they thought they'd chanced on a criminal stowaway. In their place, I'd have believed a ship's captain over a guy climbing out of a cargo container, too. I climbed out of the container, struck a fight stance, and wished I wasn't encumbered with the spacesuit.

From the corner of my eye, I saw Trouble rise. Despite the bulky suit, she swung gracefully from the container and stood next to me. Faced with an unexpected second person, the trio of Martians paused and watched as Trouble popped open her own helmet and pulled it off. She gave her head a shake to clear the hair from her face. In the low Martian gravity, her red locks whipped around and then settled in slow motion.

Trouble ignited her gigawatt smile and said, "Hello, gentlemen. Whatever reward the *Star of Sol's* captain offered, I'll double it."

I expected the trio to rush us once they realized Trouble wasn't another man. With no room to maneuver, our fight with the Martians was going to be a straight up brawl. They had us out-numbered and out-muscled, and I had little hope we could win.

I glanced at Trouble and said, "Take off running as soon as the fight starts. I'll keep them busy as long as possible. If you can find Dave, see if you can get him to come looking for me."

Trouble met my gaze and then cut her eyes back to the Martian trio. "I... don't think that's necessary."

I looked back at the roustabouts. They stood staring at Trouble, transfixed by the sight of her. I've been on the receiving end of her smile, and it packs one hell of a wallop. But I couldn't imagine any dock worker letting a beautiful woman come between him and a sizable reward. Hell, they hadn't even responded to Trouble's counter offer. Then things got strange.

The middle man of the three took one step forward and said, "We humbly beg your pardon, Traveller." You could hear that was a proper noun in his reverent tone of voice. "We are honored to be the first to welcome you Home."

Then all three men *bowed* to Trouble.

In a hushed tone, Trouble asked, "Travis, what's happening?"

In an equally low voice, I said, "I haven't got a clue."

"Some detective you turned out to be." She visibly composed herself and turned her attention back to the three bowing Martians. "I thank you for your kind welcome. Please rise."

I'll be damned if they didn't do just that. The one who spoke before said, "Thank you, Traveller. I'm sorry about speaking as we did to your... companion?"

That was a surprisingly subtle way of asking Trouble if they could still grab me and turn me in for the reward. Uncertain she would pick up the implied question, I opened my mouth to explain my presence. But Trouble's a smart girl, and she was way ahead of me. "Travis is my protector. Without his courageous actions in my defense, I'd never have gotten here."

The Martians didn't bow, but they offered respectful nods to me. "Then Mars owes him a debt of gratitude."

Everyone was silent for a moment, so I asked, "We spent the last twenty-something hours hiding in that container. Is there some place where the, uh, Traveller and I can get out of these spacesuits and change clothes?"

"Yes," the trio's leader said. "Come with me."

I pulled our suitcases from the container. "While we're changing, could someone unpack our Robosec?"

The two roustabouts who had been silent since Trouble popped out of the container nodded and began clearing packing peanuts off of Rita. They had Rita out and resting on the floor when Trouble and I returned ten minutes later. I gave my Robosec a cursory check, then powered her up. As Rita's startup sequence scrolled up her face screen, I stood and studied the warehouse's far wall.

Trouble touched my arm. "Why did you turn away? Is something wrong with Rita?"

"No, she's fine. It's just..." I shrugged. "Rita is a person to me, but people don't have startup sequences."

"And if you don't see hers run, then she doesn't have one?"

"Something like that. I know it's stupid but—"

"Not stupid, Travis. Sweet." Trouble smiled gently. "Maybe the sweetest thing I've ever heard."

"Just don't tell Rita."

"I won't. But I bet she already knows."

A moment later, she said, "Boss, I bought tickets to Mercury. What are we doing on Mars?"

"That's a long story, Rita. Why don't we save it for later?" I gestured at the three Martians. "I'm sure these kind gentlemen need to get back to work, so we should get out of their way."

The Martians bowed to Trouble again, and we left the warehouse.

The second we were alone, Trouble said, "That was confusing as hell, Travis. Is that some kind of weird Martian custom or something?"

"I'm as much in the dark as you, Trouble."

"Your Space Patrol training didn't cover Martian lore and customs?"

"I was never stationed on Mars, so no. Besides, the Martians limit Earther access to anything except Marsport and the surrounding countryside. We don't know anything about Martian civilization that the Martians don't want us to know."

Rita sent a sigh to her vocorder. "Is there anything you *do* know, Boss?"

"I know we're in Marsport."

"And that's it?"

"No," Trouble said, "there's one more thing. We're looking for someone."

"Don't—" I began.

But Trouble kept talking. "Someone Travis served with in the Space Patrol. Dave Hayslett."

"Oh, hell no!" Rita said. She's programmed to avoid cursing, so I knew she was upset. "There is no way I'm letting you near that man again."

Trouble looked from Rita to me, then turned back to Rita. "Why not?"

Rita turned an image of wide eyes towards Trouble. "The last time the Boss and Mr. Hayslett saw each other, Mr. Hayslett swore he'd kill Travis!"

Trouble looked at me and raised one perfect eyebrow. "Your former best friend wants to kill you?"

"I wouldn't put much stock in that." I steered us into an alley between warehouses and out of sight. "He was drunk at the time."

"Travis, a drunken man is *more* likely to tell the truth, not less." She waggled her suitcase and lowered her voice. "We have plenty of money. Let's just hire another ship to take us to Mercury."

I shook my head. "If the captain of the *Star of Sol* went to the trouble of posting a reward for dockworkers, you can be sure he also filed a criminal complaint with the Marsport authorities. They'll put out an alert to all ships immediately. No one reputable will let us onboard, and someone disreputable enough to take our money will probably rob us and throw us out an airlock once we hit orbit."

Trouble rolled her eyes. "When you put it that way, Dave shooting you on sight is refreshingly straightforward." My Robosec and my assistant shared a look. Then Trouble said, "No one on Marsport is looking for *me*. I could hire a ship and—"

"I'd still have to board the ship, and no honest pilot will take off when they recognize me."

"Then I'll *buy* a ship, Travis."

"Even if we can find a ship worth buying, we'll still need a pilot."

"Why can't you fly the ship?"

"I learned just enough piloting to graduate from the Star Patrol academy and then forgot it all. I'd rather trust the shadiest smuggler in Marsport than my piloting skills."

"Travis, there has to be a better way than trusting a man who wants to kill you!"

Rita crossed her arms over her chest plate. "You're wasting your breath, Trouble. The boss has made up his mind."

Beyond our alley, I saw a cab descending towards street level. "Come on, let's catch that taxi."

Trouble let me herd her towards the approaching aircar. "We aren't done with this conversation, Travis."

"Sure, but we can talk about it after we get as far from the spaceport as possible."

We waited as the cab settled on the street. An Earther couple emerged from the backseat, while the Martian driver hopped out and got their luggage from the aircar's trunk. He bobbed his head to the couple and said, "Have a pleasant trip home."

The couple thanked him, took their bags, and walked away. Only then did the driver turn his attention our way. Like the dockworkers, his eyes widened when he caught sight of Trouble. Assuming he would bow next, I said, "The Traveller wishes to maintain a low profile. Please don't do anything that would call attention to her."

The driver settled for a respectful nod to Trouble, then opened the door for us. "The Traveller's wish is my command."

I gently pushed Trouble towards the cab. "Get in."

She slid into the backseat, but asked, "Do we even know where we are going?"

"Away from the spaceport." I climbed in after her, and we both scooted over to make room for Rita. "We'll figure out the rest later."

The driver shut the door behind Rita and returned to the driver's seat. Before he asked for a destination, I said, "The Traveller isn't sure where she wants to go yet. Please, just drive towards central Marsport."

"Of course." The cab rose smoothly into the air. "I am honored to play any part, however small, in the Traveller's Journey."

Great, the Martian mystery of the Traveller just *had* to have a capital-j Journey. It was right there in the name. Or title. Or whatever. I had plenty of questions about the traveling thing, but I pushed them aside and turned my attention to figuring out how to find Dave and persuade him to take us to Mercury. All without getting shot the minute he laid eyes on me.

Our driver looked over his shoulder. "I hadn't heard of your arrival. Have you been here long, Traveller?"

"I've only been here for an hour or two."

The driver's brow furrowed. "Word should have spread in that time. It should have spread from the moment you made your travel arrangements."

Trouble glanced at me, obviously unsure how to respond. I shrugged and waved a hand. She turned back to the driver and said, "I didn't originally plan on coming here."

The driver nodded in apparent understanding. "If Mars called you from your path, you must need something only Mars can provide. This Journey must be an important one."

"It is," Trouble said, "but my, um, Journey is supposed to take me to Mercury. We *have* to get there. Lives could be at stake."

I took a gamble and said, "What we need is a pilot with a spaceship, who can take us to Mercury."

"If your Earther governments let Martians own spaceships," the driver said, "that wouldn't be a problem."

Trouble's brows creased. "Why would the governments outlaw that?"

"Martians restrict Earther access to Mars," I said. "In retaliation, Earth governments restrict Martian access to the rest of the solar system."

The driver frowned. "You said lives are at stake, Traveller?"

"My brother's."

The driver sighed. "If you *must* go—"

"We must," I said.

"There is an Earther who lives in Marsport's Martian quarter," the driver said. "He has a ship and always needs money, but only those who are desperate seek him out."

Trouble asked, "Is his name Dave Hayslett?"

The driver's eyebrows rose. "You know him?"

"I do," I said, "and he's the person we're looking for."

The driver shook his head. "Your Journey must be perilous, Traveller, if Mars called you to join forces with the likes of *him*."

Rita turned her face screen my way. "Perilous for *some*, at least."

"Will you please help us search for Dave?" Trouble asked.

"We don't have to search, Traveller. I know where to find him."

"Thank you." Trouble flashed her bright smile. "Mars must have brought you to my aid."

The driver's posture straightened at her praise and turned his cab away from downtown Marsport. "We'll be there in fifteen minutes."

True to his word, the driver set the cab down on a street teeming with Martians. He jumped out and opened the door for Trouble. When I climbed from the aircar, I reached for my wallet. "How much?"

The driver shook his head. "I played a part in the Traveller's Journey. That is payment enough."

Around us, Martians gawked and pointed at Trouble. Some spoke in awed, hushed voices. "A Traveller!"

"Where do we find Dave?" I asked.

The driver pointed to a seedy bar nearby. "In there."

I took Trouble by the elbow and guided her towards the entrance. "Let's get you off the street."

"Thank you, again," Trouble called to the driver.

Then I bustled her through the door and into the blessedly dim interior. Maybe the relative darkness would hide whatever it was Martians saw in Trouble. Trouble wrinkled her nose at the alien odors that permeated the bar. When my eyes adjusted to the lack of lighting, I glanced around the bar's interior.

Dave was easy to find, being the only pale-skinned man among the deep red of the Martians. He slumped in a chair at a table with an older Martian woman whose black hair had faded to gray. From his dejected posture, Dave looked more needy than even our cab driver implied. The woman turned curious eyes on me when I stopped at the table, but Dave kept staring at the table.

"Hello, Dave," I said.

He looked up and blinked twice. "Damn. I thought this day couldn't get any worse."

He turned his gaze back to the table. His lack of reaction irritated me for some reason, so I asked, "Didn't you swear you were going to shoot me if you ever laid eyes on me again?"

"Can't." He gave a half-hearted wave at the woman across the table from him. "I lost my gun to her in a game of *bakar*."

"Is that a Martian gambling game?" Trouble asked in a quiet voice.

In a disapproving tone, Rita said, "It is."

"I guess it's my lucky day." I said to Dave. "Yours, too. I need to hire you and your ship."

"Can't do that, either," Dave said in a toneless voice. "I lost the *Lightning's Hand* to her, too."

Trouble dropped her head into her hands. With her face hidden from me, I couldn't tell whether she felt anger, frustration, or despair. But I knew my reaction. "I'm disappointed in you, Dave."

That got through Dave's apathy. "Disappointed? *Disappointed?* That's all you can say?"

"What do you want me to say?"

"How about, *That was stupid, Dave*! Or, *You're a bigger idiot than I imagined*! Or..." Dave gave a shrug that conveyed both disgust and a loss for words. "Anything except *disappointed*."

"Why should I tell you something you're already telling yourself?"

"And then there's that whole calm-and-collected, always Mr. Cool tone of voice!" Dave stood and got into my face. "Where is your anger, Barrett? Where is your frustration? Where is any sign that you're human, and not some emotionless robot?"

"Hey," Rita said, "badmouth robots again, and I'll show you who's emotionless!"

But Dave had worked himself into a righteous fury. "You're so desperate for a spaceship that you come to *me*," he put his hands on my chest and shoved me, "and all you can say is you're *disappointed*?"

Trouble stepped between us. "That's enough. *I'm* the one who's desperate for a ship, not Travis."

Dave leered at Trouble, then glanced over her shoulder at me.

"You might not be human, but you do have good taste in women, Barrett."

"Get your mind out of the gutter," I growled. "Miss Tate is my assistant."

Dave ran his eyes up and down Trouble's body. "Is that what the dockside dames are calling themselves these days?"

I felt my face flush with anger.

"Oooo, *that* one got through the Iceman's defenses!" Dave crowed. "She must be your special favorite, huh?"

I stepped up next to Trouble and cocked my fist. Dave just grinned at me, so he never saw Trouble move. Her left jab caught Dave in the eye, and her right flattened his nose. Dave stumbled back and tripped over the table. *Bakar* tiles went flying as the table overturned, and Dave fell to the floor. Blood streamed from his nose, and I thought he'd have a nice shiner soon.

Dave gingerly probed his nose with his hands. "Ow."

"Are you okay?" I asked.

"She flattened my nose!" Dave said. "What do you think?"

I glared at Dave. "I was talking to Miss Tate."

"Your friend has a thick skull." Trouble rubbed her knuckles and turned her own glare on Dave. "In more ways than one."

Until now, the old Martian woman watched our little drama with bemusement. But Trouble's words brought a dry, cackling laugh from her. "Mr. Hayslett understands Earther women as poorly as he does Martian women."

"Nobody cares about your opinions, Mah'Ri," Dave said.

"I care." I faced Mah'Ri and bowed. "My name is Travis Barrett."

"I guessed as much." Mah'Ri glanced at Dave. "When he is deep into his cups, he rants about *that bastard Barrett* and how you ruined his life."

Trouble shook her head. "That's just pathetic."

"Pathetic is an apt description of Mr. Hayslett's current life," Mah'Ri said.

"But he is right about one thing." Trouble gave Mah'Ri her

full attention. "We desperately need a spaceship." Her eyes cut to Dave as he sat up, and she grimaced. "And a pilot to fly the spaceship."

Mah'Ri gave a dismissive wave at Dave. "You may have the pilot."

Trouble shook her head. "He's useless without the spaceship."

Mah'Ri gave Trouble her full attention. "He is useless with the spaceship, too."

"No," Trouble said, "he's *mostly* useless with the spaceship."

Mah'Ri cackled again. "I think I like you." She stood, looped her arm through Trouble's, and said, "Come, my dear. We will talk." As Mah'Ri led Trouble deeper into the bar, she looked over her shoulder at me. "You may come, as well. And bring Mr. Hayslett."

I prodded Dave with a toe. "Get up."

Dave gave a half-hearted swat at my foot and missed. "Why should I do anything you ask me to do?"

"Do you want the *Lightning's Hand* back?"

"Yes, but there's no way *you* can afford to buy it back."

"Did you pay *any* attention to my assistant's name?"

"Miss Tate. So?"

"Miss *Tina* Tate." At Dave's blank expression, I added, "That name doesn't mean anything to you?"

Rita floated up next to me. "It didn't mean anything to you, either, Boss." She patted my arm in a bless-your-heart manner and turned her face screen to Dave. "She's one of *those* Tates."

Dave's brow creased, then his eyebrows rose to his hairline. "Tate Steelworks?"

Rita turned back to me. "He's not a complete idiot, after all."

"Barrett, has anybody ever told you your Robosec has a smart mouth?"

Dave raised his hand, obviously looking for a hand up. I ignored it, stepped around him, and said, "The rest of her is just as smart."

"Aw, thanks, Boss." Rita floated over Dave and took my proffered arm. "Does that mean I get a raise?"

"No."

I heard Dave scramble to his feet and fall in behind us. I didn't see Trouble or Mah'Ri, but I heard the murmur of Trouble's voice beyond a partially closed door. She finished speaking as I pushed the door open.

Inside, Mah'Ri sat behind a large desk, with Trouble sitting in a chair close to the door. We entered just in time to hear Mah'Ri say, "No, I will not sell the spaceship to you."

six

trouble with dave

MAH'RI'S REFUSAL hung in the air as Rita and I entered the little office, followed by a limping Dave. I watched Trouble's hopeful expression crumble as she blinked back tears.

"Please, Mah'Ri," she said, "my brother's life could be at stake."

Mah'Ri shook her head. "That does not matter."

Trouble sniffed once, then said, "Mars must have guided me to you, so you could assist a Traveller on her Journey. How can you refuse?"

Mah'Ri cackled. "I follow the ancient religion of Mars, not this Traveller foolishness the young ones invented."

Dave snorted and shook his head. "You don't even know what you're talking about, do you, Miss Tate?"

Trouble shrugged. "Not really, but I thought it was worth trying."

I turned towards the office door. "Let's go. There's no point continuing this discussion if we can't get the *Lightning's Hand* from Mah'Ri."

Mah'Ri slapped her desk with her palm. "I did not say that, Mr. Barrett. I will *give* you the ship, but you must do something for me in return."

"Name it," Dave said. "I'll do anything to get my ship back!"

Mah'Ri made a dismissive wave at Dave. "I was not speaking to you."

"Then *I'll* do anything to get his ship back," Trouble said. "I'm begging you!"

Mah'Ri's voice softened. "Nor was I speaking to you, child." She looked at me, and her voice hardened. "What of you, Mr. Barrett. Will *you* do anything to get Mr. Hayslett's ship?"

I locked eyes with Mah'Ri. "No."

Trouble turned her gaze on me, and I had to look away from the anguish clouding her blue eyes. "Travis, please!"

I shook my head. "My word is my bond. What if I give it, and Mah'Ri asks me to kill someone for her? Regardless of the choice I make, I end up compromising my principles. I will not do that."

Trouble closed her eyes and dropped her head into her hands. Dave gave a humorless laugh and said, "It's about time you revealed your inner self, you sanctimonious bastard. I can't believe—"

Mah'Ri interrupted. "I will not ask you to do anything you do not already do as part of your business, Mr. Barrett."

I chose my next words with care. "I would like to find Miss Tate's brother before doing your favor. Is that acceptable?"

Mah'Ri gave a decisive nod. "It is."

"Then I give you my word. I will return here as soon as I wrap up this case."

Without a word, Mah'Ri picked up the ship's title and keycards and handed them to me.

"What the hell?" Dave shouted. "How can you trust him? What makes you think Barrett will ever return to Mars again?"

"Mr. Barrett gave me his word," Mah'Ri said.

"He would have said anything to get the *Lightning's Hand*!"

"No, Mr. Hayslett, *you* would have said anything to get the ship back. Mr. Barrett gave his word only after I assured him I would ask nothing illegal of him."

Dave shook his head. "And that's all it took for you to believe him?"

"No, I listened to your drunken ravings about Mr. Barrett and his word of honor so often I think I understand him. I also believe he will keep his word because you believe it." Mah'Ri stared into Dave's eyes. "You *do* believe that, don't you?"

Dave met her stare for a moment, then turned a glare on me. "Yeah, death is the only thing that will keep Mr. Perfect over there from coming back here. Hell, knowing Barrett, he'd come back from the dead to keep from breaking his precious word."

Mah'Ri pointed towards her office door. "Find Miss Tate's brother quickly, so you may return to me."

"Aren't you even going to tell Travis what you want him to do?" Trouble asked.

"No. Now, go away. I have a business to run. Close the door after you leave."

We filed from the office, and Trouble and Rita headed for the bar's exit. Dave shut the door and leaned against it, a lost expression on his face. I stopped and regarded him in silence.

"What?" he demanded.

"I still need a pilot."

"Do you think you can just waltz in here, take my ship, and then expect me to come work for you?"

"I don't have time to find another pilot desperate enough to work for me."

"Then fly the damned ship yourself. You passed all the basic piloting courses at the academy."

"Only because you helped me." I tried a different approach. "Do you really want me taking the helm of the *Lightning's Hand*?"

"God, no," Dave snorted.

"Then help us." I looked towards Trouble. "Help her."

Dave sighed. "I still hate your guts."

"I can live with that."

"How much will you pay me?"

"Help us with this case, and then bring me back here so I can take Mah'Ri's case, and I'll give you the *Lightning's Hand*."

A small spark of life ignited in Dave's eyes. "I have your word?"

"You have my word."

"I lost all my money in the game with Mah'Ri."

"I'll cover your expenses."

He shoved off the office door. "Where are we going?"

"Mercury."

"Twi-Town?"

"Yes."

"I'm going to need a gun."

"Will you shoot me with it?"

"Not while you own my ship."

"How reassuring." I headed for the bar's exit. "We'll buy a gun for you on the way to the spaceport."

Two hours later, the *Lightning's Hand* rode a column of fire into space, and Dave set a course for Mercury.

DAVE REMAINED in the cockpit until the *Lightning's Hand* cleared the ships approaching and departing Mars' lone spaceport. Rita plugged herself into an unused screen and busied herself with the office bookkeeping. Trouble and I just sat in the lounge, lost in our own thoughts. But now and then, she cast glances at me. I finally grew tired of it.

I caught her gaze and asked, "What?"

She feigned innocence. "I don't know what you're asking."

"You keep looking my way. You're furtive about it, so I assume you don't want me noticing. That suggests something is bothering you, but you aren't sure if you should say what it is."

"I thought I was being subtle."

"You were."

"But you noticed."

"Noticing things is my job."

"Then I got the right man for the job." She fell silent. I watched her and waited. Finally, she said, "I think I did, anyway."

"Having second thoughts about me?"

"Would you really have refused Mah'Ri's request for a favor if she hadn't assured you it wasn't illegal?"

"Yes."

"Even if refusing ended up costing Nick's life?"

"I won't compromise my principles for anyone."

Dave sauntered into the lounge. "There's the Travis Barrett I know and loathe so well." He headed straight for the liquor cabinet. "Anybody else want a drink?"

"No," Trouble said.

"Scotch on the rocks," I said.

Dave splashed scotch into a glass, downed it in one practiced motion, poured another, and waggled the scotch bottle. "Anyone?" He looked at Trouble. When she shook her head, he said, "No?" and put the scotch back in the cabinet.

He leaned against the cabinet, swirled his liquor for a moment, drained it in a single gulp, and slammed the empty glass down on the counter so hard I thought the glass would break. Dave crossed his arms and asked, "Have you ever wondered how Truthful Travis here ever disobeyed a direct order from a superior Space Patrol officer?"

"What do you mean?" Trouble asked.

"I mean, he swore an oath when he joined the Space Patrol. One that specifically states, *I will obey the orders of the officers appointed over me.*" Dave turned his impassive gaze on me. "You did swear that, didn't you?"

"You know damned well I did."

Dave pretended to concentrate. "Now, correct me if I'm wrong, but when you *swear* something, aren't you honor bound to do that thing?"

"We've been over this before," I said. "You know—"

Dave ignored me. "So when Commodore Jacobson ordered

his squadron, including the *Soteria,* to withdraw, and you disobeyed his order, you broke your precious word of honor."

"We've been over this a dozen times," I said. "You know it's not that simple."

"Then make it a dozen and one times, Barrett. Besides, I'll bet Miss Tate would like to know what kind of man she's working for. What kind of man would let her brother die rather than accept even the slightest chance he might have to break his word?"

I glanced at Trouble and turned away from her intense gaze. "As usual, you left out the earlier part of the oath. The part where I swore to *support and defend the citizens of the solar system against all enemies*. It comes first in the oath because it takes precedence over everything else. That means disobeying a superior's order in defense of citizens of the solar system did not violate my oath."

Dave snorted. "Semantics. And an argument the court martial board didn't accept."

"What if Jacobson ordered the squadron to join the pirates and attack the *Euphoria*? Would I have been honor bound to obey that order?"

"More semantics."

"Is there *any* time when disobeying a superior's order is the honorable thing to do?"

Dave picked up his glass and peered into its empty depths. "You know there is."

"When is that time?"

"We took the same ethics classes at the academy. You know the answer."

"Yeah, but do you?"

Dave grabbed the bottle of scotch, filled his glass a third time, and sipped the liquor. "Yes, I know it."

I waited for him to explain. He took another sip of scotch. Finally, Trouble said, "*I* don't know when disobeying orders is the right thing to do."

Dave murmured something into his glass. Trouble shook her head. "I can't understand you."

Dave heaved a sigh. "It depends on the situation."

Trouble considered that for a minute. "Travis believed the pirate attack on the *Euphoria* justified disobeying his orders, so he doesn't believe he broke his oath."

"Yep." Dave took another sip. "But no one on the court martial board agreed."

Trouble rose, faced Dave, and looked him in the eye. "Do *you* believe Travis did the right thing?"

Dave broke Trouble's gaze, downed the remaining scotch, and said, "It doesn't matter what I think." He threw the glass across the lounge, where it shattered against the bulkhead, and glared at me. "Look at him sitting there, smug and secure in his righteous superiority."

Trouble looked my way. "Travis doesn't look any different to me."

"No?" Dave pointed at me. "You can't see the halo hovering over his head?" Without waiting for an answer, he stalked back towards the cockpit. "Do you ever get lonely sitting up there on top of your mountain of morality, Barrett?"

All the time, I thought. But I just watched him leave and said nothing.

DAVE SLAMMED SHUT the hatch to the cockpit, and the clang echoed down the length of the *Lightning's Hand*. I sat and stared at the closed hatch and tried to ignore the voices that called to me across the years.

"Explosion in the aft missile tubes, sir!"

"Engine three is offline!"

"Casualties on all decks, sir!"

"The pirate is coming about for another pass!"

"Drink this."

I blinked.

Surfaced from my waking nightmare.

Focused on something inches from my face.

A glass.

Scotch.

Rocks.

A hand with perfectly manicured nails.

I looked up and found Trouble standing over me. She swirled the glass. "You asked Dave for scotch on the rocks."

The cold glass felt good in my sweaty hand. I brought it to my lips and downed the liquor in one well-practiced motion. Smoky fire burned down my throat and warmed my stomach. Trouble took the glass, refilled it, and handed it back. "Sip this one."

She settled onto my chair's armrest. "Tell me."

"Tell you what?" I asked.

"You were a million miles away just now. Where were you?" When I didn't answer, she said, "Back on the bridge of your ship, the *Soteria*, right?"

I looked up at Trouble with a lie poised on my tongue. But after everything we'd been through, I didn't lie to her. "Yeah."

"Tell me your side of the story."

"What makes you think I want to talk about it?"

"Don't you?"

"No." Trouble arched one eyebrow. I sighed. "Yes."

She sat while I marshaled my thoughts. Finally, I said, "Our squadron was out in the middle of nowhere in the Belt, running through rescue maneuvers. Rescue is—*was*—the *Soteria's* specialty, so she was a hundred miles ahead of the rest of the squadron when we picked up the distress call."

"Mayday! Mayday! This is the starliner Euphoria *and we are under attack. Mayday! Mayday!"*

"Comm," I said, "put me through to the Euphoria. *Then contact Commodore Jacobson on the squadron emergency channel."*

"You're through, sir." Comm Officer Alicia Power's hands danced over her controls. "Stalwart, this is Soteria. *Put me through to Commodore Jacobson immediately!"*

I engaged the comm at my command chair. "Euphoria, this is the SPS Soteria. *What are your coordinates?"*

"Thank God! Hurry! We think it's the Bloodsword!"

My bridge crew fell silent when the Euphoria's *comm officer named the system's most feared pirate ship. He followed with the* Euphoria's *coordinates, but no one reacted.*

"Navigation!" Lieutenant Harper, the nav officer, jumped at the sound of my voice, and I continued, "Plot a course to those coordinates."

"Um, aye, sir!"

As Harper bent over his console, I turned a fierce grin on Dave. "Helm, seconds count here. Time to show us if you're really as good as you say you are."

I expected a return grin, and maybe a remember-you-asked-for-it comment. But he just stared at me for two long seconds, gave a slow nod, and turned back to the helm.

"Nav? Do you have an ETA?"

"Two minutes, sir." Harper flashed the grin I'd expected from Dave. "Ninety seconds if Hayslett really is the best helmsman in the Patrol."

"Euphoria, we're ninety seconds out. Clear out of there the second we show up. Do not stop to watch. Do not try to help. Get your people to safety. Is that clear?"

An explosion sounded over the comm. "As crystal, Soteria. *And for God's sake, hurry!"*

"Comm? Send the Euphoria's *coordinates and our planned course to the rest of the squadron."*

Lieutenant Power faced me, a stunned expression on her face. "They're not coming."

Silence blanketed the bridge for the second time since we received the Euphoria's *call. Words almost failed me but I choked out, "What?"*

"Commodore Jacobson says they're too far out to render aid in time."

"That's utter crap! Put him—"

Lieutenant Power didn't hear me. As if in a daze, she added, "And he says the Soteria *is too small to go in alone. You're ordered to withdraw."*

I blinked, drew a deep breath, and then turned to navigation. "Nav, do you have a course to the Euphoria*?"*

"Yes, sir."

"Transfer it to the helmsman."

"But sir," Comm said, "the Commodore—"

"Can go straight to hell. I will not sit idle while pirates enslave the citizens I swore to protect."

Without looking up, Dave said, "I am duty-bound to log an objection to this course of action. You are disobeying a superior officer's order."

"You're damned right, I am." I looked back at the comm officer. "Lieutenant Power... Alicia, please put my comm on ship-wide."

Eyes wide, Alicia turned to her console, tapped three keys, and said, "You're on, sir."

"This is the captain speaking. We are responding to a starliner's distress signal. They say they're under attack by the Bloodsword. *Worse, we're on our own. Our squadron is* not *coming. Jacobson issued a withdrawal order to us, too. I choose to disobey him." I paused for a moment, then said, "From all reports, the* Bloodsword *would be a challenge for the full squadron. The* Soteria *has no chance against that ship in a straight up fight. That's why we're going in fast, and only staying long enough for the* Euphoria *to get away. Then we run, too."*

I looked around the bridge, and everyone except Dave was watching me with wide, fearful eyes. I added, "Space Patrol regulations deem my order unlawful. You will not be found guilty of mutiny should you disregard my order and remove me from command. I will even testify in your defense. You have but to say the word, and I will step down. Or we can do our jobs to the best of our abilities and, God willing, save hundreds of lives from the pirates."

The weapons crew responded first. "We're with you, skipper!"

"Engineering is go, sir!"

"Medical is ready and standing by, Captain."

Alicia glanced around the bridge. "We're with you, too, sir!"

I fell silent. Realized I still had a nearly full glass of scotch. Gulped it down. I closed my eyes and drew a shuddering breath. Trouble sat quietly next to me and waited. Finally, I said, "The bridge took a direct hit. Everyone except Dave and me was killed instantly, and Dave was badly injured. I gave the order to abandon ship, dragged Dave to the nearest lifepod, waited until all surviving crew were clear, and then launched our pod."

Trouble said, "I thought pirates were a bloodthirsty bunch. Why didn't the *Bloodsword* blast the *Soteria's* escape pods?"

"Our squadron finally showed up, and the *Bloodsword* retreated. Jacobson might be a coward, but even he couldn't ignore the *Soteria's* plight. Not and keep his career." I looked down at the deck. "You know the rest."

"You saved Dave's life. Why does he hate you for that?"

"I put Dave in the line of fire, so saving him from that fire shouldn't count in my favor." I shrugged. "But it's what happened afterwards that made Dave hate me."

Trouble tapped her lips with one lovely finger. "I don't think that's right."

"Then what?"

"I don't know," Trouble said. "Not yet, anyway."

I flashed a smile, hoping to lighten the mood. "Who's the private investigator now?"

I don't think it fooled Trouble, but she played along. "Pretty soon, the office door is going to read Travis and Trouble."

I'd like that. But I didn't say it aloud.

Trouble and I sat in companionable silence for a few minutes. Then she laid a hand on my shoulder, squeezed gently, smiled at me, and then returned to her own chair.

"Boss?" Rita asked.

"Yes, Rita?" I said. "What's the problem?"

She gave a very human dismissive flip of her inhuman hand. "No problems, Boss. Not since we got all that money from Trouble's father, anyway. I got a question. But it can wait, if you don't want to talk right now."

"The Rita I know never asks permission to question me."

"The boss I know never talks about the *Soteria*."

Surprised by her reply, I groped for the usual bantering tone I used when talking with Rita. "Did you install an upgrade for polite respect while you were shut down?"

"Travis," Trouble said, "that was rude!"

The eyes on Rita's face screen cut to Trouble. "It's okay. That's just the boss being the boss." Her eye images swung back to me. "There might be an upgrade available from my manufacturer, but Rossum isn't known for giving upgrades away and you aren't known for paying for them. Maybe my circuits are just taking their sweet time warming up. Whatever the reason, you better enjoy it while it lasts, Boss."

"I will do everything possible to encourage respect from you," I said. "You may ask your question."

"You're a prince among bosses, Boss."

"I can never say no to you, Rita."

"Good. How about a raise?"

"Nope."

"I thought you couldn't say *no* to me, Boss?"

"That's why I said *nope* instead."

The eyes on Rita's face screen made an exaggerated roll. "Whatever. I'm going to ask my question now." She paused. I waved permission for her to carry on, and she asked, "You got any idea what was up with Trouble and all that Traveller stuff back on Mars?"

"Oh," Trouble said, "I'd forgotten about that in all the excitement. From what Mah'Ri said, I guess it's religious. But why me? I'd never even been to Mars before today."

I raised an eyebrow. "I thought rich girls like you had been to every planet in the inner system, and maybe even some of the floating cities above Jupiter and Saturn."

"Father never takes pleasure trips. If he doesn't have business somewhere, he doesn't go there. Martian civilization is ancient—hundreds of thousands of years old, according to my tutors—and the Martians mined all the economically accessible metal from their world thousands of years ago."

"He never went for other reasons? I hear Martian artwork is all the rage among the super rich."

Trouble sniffed. "Father has no interest in, or appreciation for, art."

"That explains the crap hanging on the walls in his office."

"Nicely done, Boss," Rita said. "You got us off the topic of the Traveller real quick."

Trouble's eyebrows rose. "You did, didn't you? Why is that?"

From the hatch to the cockpit, Dave said, "Ol' T-Square there doesn't like admitting there are things he doesn't know."

Trouble looked at Dave. "Um, T-Square?"

Dave pointed at me. "Truthful Travis."

She considered that, and asked, "Shouldn't that be T-Square*d*?"

"Nah," Dave said. "Leaving off the 'd' makes it twice as funny."

Trouble wrinkled her brow. "How?"

Dave turned to me. "She's your assistant, T-Square. You should be the one to educate her."

I sighed. "*Square* is a slang term from the earliest days of space travel. It means someone who's old-fashioned or uncool."

"Yep, and square fits him to a T." Dave forced a laugh. "God, I'm funny."

I mimicked Slick's nasal whine. "Hi-larious."

"Wow, Travis," Trouble laughed, "you nailed that ferret-faced freak perfectly."

Dave scowled. "And you let T-Square drag you away from stuff he doesn't know, again."

"Wrong, Dave," I said. "You did it that time."

"Hey, I didn't—"

"Shut up, both of you," Trouble said. She folded her arms and looked at me. "I want a straight answer, Travis. Do you know why the Martians called me a Traveller?"

I hesitated, then said, "No."

"See?" Dave crowed. "Look how much it hurt him to admit he doesn't know."

Trouble glared at Dave. "Do you?"

"Yeah."

Trouble's eyebrows rose. "You do?"

"Yeah."

We waited for Dave to say more. When he stayed silent, Trouble broke down and asked, "Please explain it to us?"

Dave shrugged. "Red planet. Red hair."

Trouble twirled her hair around a finger in a fetching manner. "It's because of my hair?"

"Yep."

"Don't redheads come to Mars all the time?"

Dave shook his head. "Ever since this Traveller stuff got popular, Earth governments keep redheads from mixing with the locals."

"Why would they do that?"

"The governments think the Martians restrict access to the planet because they're hiding technology that's thousands of years ahead of anything Earth has. Earth wants to get its hands on Martian super science—stuff they assume modern Martians no longer understand—and they figure a loyal, properly trained redheaded agent is their best bet to get it."

Trouble wrinkled her brow. "That doesn't explain why Martians all but worship redheads. Don't they have redheads of their own?"

"If they do, no one has ever seen one." Dave dropped into a chair next to Trouble. "To understand the rest, you have to know that Martians believe in reincarnation. From what I've heard, Hinduism has a lot in common with Martian religion."

"Okay," Trouble said, "but what does that have to do with redheads?"

"I'm just a guy who spent a lot of time in Martian bars talking to drunks, but I think they believe red hair marks an enlightened Martian soul that traveled somewhere else for rebirth."

"But I'm human."

"So are the Martians," I said.

"What?" Trouble asked.

"He's right." Dave grimaced, as if it pained him to admit that. "It bugs the hell out of evolutionary biologists, too, because it ruins a lot of their pet theories."

"Or it means Mars developed space travel sometime in their past," I said, "and Earth started as a Martian colony."

"Back to Travellers," Trouble said. "Even knowing all that, it doesn't explain why Martians believe redheads were Martians in a former life."

Dave shrugged. "It has to do with the first Mars landing. The ship's pilot was redheaded and knew all sorts of stuff about Mars, Martian history, and even led a mixed Earther and Martian expedition straight to a long-lost, underground city. That's the story, anyway."

"But it's so farfetched," Trouble said. "Why—?"

"I've told you what I know," Dave snapped. "It's not my religion, so I can't explain it any better than I just did."

Trouble looked at me. "What do you think, Travis?"

"I think it's time to eat something and then get some sleep."

"That's not what I meant," Trouble said.

I nodded. "I know, but I'm right."

"Of course you are," Dave said. "T-Square is *always* right."

I raised one eyebrow, because I know that irritates Dave. "Do you disagree?"

"No. Happy now?"

"Ecstatic."

"Great." Dave looked at Trouble. "Can you cook?"

"Well enough, I guess."

Dave pointed down the central corridor. "The galley is down there." He turned to me. "You clean up. Starting here."

"Who died and put you in charge?" Rita asked. "Last time I looked, the Boss owns this ship."

"Fine. Let *him* fly it."

Slanting lines drew themselves over the eyes on Rita's face screen. Before she launched into a secretarial tirade, I said, "It's okay, Rita. Dave is right. We all need to do our share of the work."

Dave leaned back in his chair. "Don't forget to sweep up the broken glass." Then he closed his eyes and pretended to sleep.

Trouble rose, cast a glance my way, and headed for the galley. I found an old non-mechanical broom in a closet and began sweeping. We were two hours into a two-day journey, and I already wondered if Dave and I could both survive the trip.

MY MENTAL ALARM clock woke me at 4:00 AM ship's time. I dressed and headed forwards. I passed Rita in the lounge recharging alcove and entered the cockpit. Dave snored gently, asleep at the controls. Just as I expected. Back in our academy days, he always felt like he had to do things personally or they wouldn't get done right. That habit stayed with him into active service and pissed off more than a few of his superior officers. Including me, when we served together on the *Soteria*.

I backed out of the cockpit and then banged around in the lounge until I heard an interruption in Dave's deep breathing. I gave him another half a minute to rub the sleep from his eyes before entering the cockpit a second time. "You ought to get some sleep, Hayslett. I can keep an eye on everything until you wake up."

"You think I'm going to trust you with my ship?" Dave stifled a yawn. "You only got through pilot training because of me, and I can't imagine your piloting has gotten any better since then."

"This is *my* ship right now, not yours. And do you think you can stay awake for the entire two-day trip to Mercury?"

"I've pulled long shifts before, Barrett."

"Yeah, when you were a twenty-two-year-old kid in top physical condition. That was over a decade ago."

"Don't remind me."

"I'll just watch the controls and call you if something comes up."

Dave gave me a sidelong glance. "I've got your word of honor on that?"

"I thought you loathed the way I keep my word."

"Priggish honesty has its occasional uses."

"Fine. You have my word."

Without another word, Dave rose, pushed past me, and headed aft. I settled into the pilot's chair and familiarized myself with the controls. Then I pulled out a datapad and finally had time to record my case notes. I hadn't realized how busy the previous two days had been until I had a written timeline. Realizing that Trouble and I had spent nearly than half that time closed up in a packing container made it worse.

As if on cue, Trouble poked her head into the cockpit as I finished with the notes. Her eyebrows rose at the sight of me. "I thought neither you nor Dave trusted your piloting?"

"I'm just monitoring the controls while Dave sleeps. I'll call him if actual piloting is required."

"That's thoughtful of you."

"Not really. I just don't want Dave crashing into Mercury because he fell asleep at the controls."

"Uh huh." She watched me for a moment, as if waiting for me to open up about my less-than-cordial relationship with Dave. When I didn't say anything, she asked, "Do you want me to fix breakfast?"

"Please. Do you mind eating with me in here? I want to ask you a few questions about your father's operations on Mercury."

"Okay."

She ducked out of the cockpit, and soon I heard the rattle of pans from the galley. Breakfast aromas followed as Trouble brewed coffee and fried bacon. My stomach rumbled, and kept at it until she returned carrying two plates with scrambled eggs, bacon, and buttered toast. Trouble handed them to me, went back to the galley, and returned with two steaming mugs of coffee. She settled into the co-pilot's seat. We tucked in and passed a pleasant few minutes enjoying the food and each other's company.

I used my last bite of toast to mop up the grease and remaining bits of egg from the plate, then put it aside. Leaning back, I sipped coffee and waited as Trouble cleaned her plate. She put her plate on top of mine and turned an expectant look my way.

"May I assume you've been to Mercury and have at least some idea of your father's business holdings there?" I asked.

Trouble nodded. "I made a few trips with him. He keeps a metallurgical research station on Mercury. I think he set it up on Mercury because the extreme temperatures on the day and night sides of the planet let his researchers test alloys in a natural setting." She shrugged. "Father never involved me in the business, so I don't really know much more than that."

"Did you ever visit the metallurgy lab?"

"No. Mr. Houlihan—the one you call Hammerhand—always suggested I stay at the spaceport hotel and mall. He said the lab was in a dangerous part of Twi-Town."

I felt my eyes widen in surprise. "I didn't know there was a safe part of Twi-Town."

"I always assumed Father had them say that, so he'd have an excuse to get me out from under his feet while he talked business. Is it really that dangerous?"

"Twi-Town is where all the losers who can't make it anywhere else in the solar system end up. It's so bad, none of the Earth govs will claim it. Space Patrol ended up policing the place because no one else would. Every Patroller knows Twi-Town is where Patroller careers go to die, so most resign rather than accept an assignment there. So the list of losers includes the people who are supposed to police Twi-Town."

Trouble screwed up her face. "Then I guess the hotel wasn't too bad. I mean, Carnegie Station is much nicer, but I felt safe on Mercury."

"The hotel and mall must have their own armed security team. And I bet you also had Hammerhand and Slick nearby when you were there." She nodded, and I added, "Whatever else I think about those goons, they were right to keep you outside of Twi-Town."

As my description sank in, Trouble asked, "If Twi-Town is so dangerous, why would Liz and Sam risk taking two kids there?"

I shrugged. "Some companies on Mercury are so desperate for skilled workers that they pay three or four times the going rate, and they usually provide secure housing for high-value workers and their families. I never asked Sam what kind of work he does, did you?"

Trouble shook her head and said, "We can always ask them when we get to Mercury. Remember, Sam told us to look them up when we got there." My face must have given something away, because Trouble asked, "You don't want to see them again?"

"Sure I do. But I don't want them getting dragged into our problems just because they know us."

"I hadn't thought about that." She slumped back in her seat. "I guess I'm not very good at private investigating."

"It's just a matter of experience." *And loss of innocence.* I hoped I could keep Trouble away from the darker end of the PI business for as long as possible, but Twi-Town was the worst place in the solar system for preserving something as precious and fragile as innocence. I pushed those thoughts from my mind and asked, "Is there anything else you know about your father's businesses on Mercury?"

"No. I'm sorry."

"Don't apologize. It's not your fault your father kept you away from the business. We'll just have to do things the old-fashioned way."

Trouble gathered up our plates and headed back to the galley.

Thirty minutes later, Dave wandered back to the cockpit, looking much better after his sleep. He jerked a thumb over his shoulder. "Outta my seat."

I got up, and Dave slid into the seat. Almost as an afterthought, he said, "Oh, hey, I looked up the patrollers stationed in Twi-Town. In case we knew any of them. And you'll never guess who's the Space Patrol commander?"

My recent breakfast turned into a lump in my stomach. "Who?"

"The one patroller who hates you more than I do."

"Jacobson?"

Dave nodded. "Jacobson."

trouble with customs

"SO YOUR OLD Space Patrol commander is stationed in Twi-Town?" Trouble asked. "How will that affect our search for Nick?"

"Jacobson isn't just stationed here. He's the Patrol's commanding officer."

"What am I not seeing, Travis? Can't we just steer clear of the Patrol?"

"I *should* visit Patroller HQ and let them know I'm working on a case, though that's more a courtesy than a requirement. And it's not like I'd put much trust in the dregs of Space Patrol, anyway. But if Jacobson finds out I'm working in his jurisdiction, he can throw a lot of roadblocks in my way and seriously impede the investigation."

"So we don't tell him we're on Mercury. Won't that solve the problem?"

"Maybe. But how much do you want to bet our old buddies Hammerhand and Slick make a beeline for Space Patrol HQ the minute they land on Mercury?"

Trouble's face screwed up in disgust. "That's exactly the kind of thing they'd do." Her face brightened. "Hey, can't we just pay this Jacobson guy to leave us alone? I have plenty of money."

"But your father will make sure Hammerhand has more."

Dave's voice sounded behind me. "Besides, Jacobson wouldn't stay bought."

Trouble looked past me to Dave. "What makes you say that?"

"Because Jacobson hates ol' T-Square here more than he loves money." Trouble cocked her head in obvious inquiry. Dave sighed, and said, "After Barrett's court martial brought Jacobson's cowardice to light, the old boy thought he saw a kindred soul in me. He tried to recruit me into the I Hate Travis Barrett Club, with the goal of getting revenge on Barrett by making his life a living hell."

In a deadpan tone of voice, I said, "I guess you signed right up."

Dave turned an expressionless gaze on me. "I told him to take his little club and shove it up his ass. I hate your guts, but I still have standards."

I finally got tired of dancing around the subject of what happened to Dave after my court martial. "Look, I'm sorry everyone in Space Patrol ostracized you after my discharge. I really am. But I had nothing to do with that. Hell, I defended your actions during my trial and lauded your courage in the face of overwhelming odds. So—"

Dave gave a humorless laugh. "Is *that* why you think I hate you? God, Barrett, I knew you were blind, but I didn't think you were stupid, too."

I blinked in surprise. "Uh, what?"

"Nobody ostracized me, Barrett. Oh, I got a few half-amused please-obey-my-orders speeches from commanding officers, but everyone else wanted to shake the hand of the Dave Hayslett you described in your testimony."

"They did?"

"Yeah, they did." Dave closed his eyes and vented a deep sigh. "They were just as blind as you are."

Without another word, Dave returned to the cockpit and gently shut the hatch. I looked at Trouble and found her casting a speculative look at me. I tried to smile, failed, and asked, "Do you have any idea what that was all about?"

"Not yet."

"If you ever figure it out, please tell me. Because I'm completely lost."

Soon after that, Rita woke from recharging, and we began making plans for the investigation when we reached Twi-Town. We had little information to go on, so mostly ended up going in circles and coming up with improbable theories. We accomplished little beyond occupying our time during the rest of the trip to Mercury.

Dave avoided us as much as possible. He took his meals in the cockpit or his cabin and limited his conversations with me to calling me to the controls when he needed a break and ordering me out of the cockpit when he returned. Trouble tried drawing him out a few times, always when I was busy with something else, but Dave rebuffed her, too. He treated her with more courtesy than he did me, but that was all.

Finally, thirty-eight hours after Dave's confusing revelation, the *Lightning's Hand* neared Mercury. We watched the approach through the lounge's viewport. The Twi-Line slowly grew from a narrow line marking where day and night met, into the broader band of perpetual twilight in which all settlements are built on Mercury.

Watching with me, Trouble said, "When I was a girl, I thought Twi-Town had to be the most romantic place in the solar system."

I snorted. "Romantic?"

"Twilight is the time for romance." She smiled. "Every man is more rugged and mysterious. Every woman is more beautiful and alluring."

"Huh." I looked through the viewport as the details of Twi-Town slowly emerged from the gloom. "I see shadows that conceal greed, avarice, and casual cruelty. A dangerous playground tailor made for thugs like Hammerhand and Slick."

"Can't it be both?" Trouble asked. "Romance has its share of danger, and danger has its share of romance."

I pushed aside Troubling thoughts of danger and romance. Romance, no matter how desirable, was a distraction I couldn't afford. Not if I had any hope of finding Trouble's brother and discovering what her father was hiding.

DAVE BROUGHT the *Lightning's Hand* down for a smooth landing at Twi-Town's spaceport. An unnatural-feeling silence fell over the ship as he shut down the engines and their subtle background buzz—our constant companion for the last two days— vanished. Within seconds, the sharp, random pings of cooling metal replaced the engine noise.

Trouble cocked her head, listened to the pinging briefly, pointed to starboard, and asked, "Why is the noise only coming from that side of the ship?"

"The starboard side of the ship must be facing Mercury's dark side." I thought about the situation for a moment, and added, "Dave must have landed on the night side of the Twi-Line, where the air is colder. Since the port side of the ship is still in the sun, it won't cool much at all."

From the cockpit hatchway, Dave clapped his hands slowly. "Bravo. Great lecture, O Learned One."

I glared at him. "She needs to understand the extreme conditions she'll find outside the ship." I turned back to Trouble. "On Mercury, everything is an extreme. If you wander just a few yards outside of the Twi-Line, you'll end up as a cinder or an icicle. And I mean those words literally."

Uncertainty filled Trouble's eyes. "Do we need to wear our spacesuits?"

"Not as long as we stay in the Twi-Line. But we will if we leave it. Not because the air is unbreathable, but because it will burn or freeze your lungs." I offered my most reassuring smile. "Got it?"

Trouble hesitated, nodded, then said, "Um, okay?"

Dave shook his head. "Are you crazy, Barrett? This isn't just any seedy dockyard. It's Twi-Town. Patrollers don't go out alone here. Hell, *I* won't go out there unarmed. You can't let her off the *Hand*."

Trouble turned a stare colder than Mercury's dark side on Dave. "Travis can't *let* me off the ship? Are you suggesting I just sit in here and dither while the *men* search for my brother?"

Dave had enough brains to backpedal from Trouble's interpretation. "No. But you don't understand what Twi-Town is like." He looked at me. "Back me up here, Barrett. You know no self-respecting guy would let a girl like her wander through Twi-Town alone."

Trouble's eyes narrowed. "What do you mean by *a girl like me*?"

Before Dave found an answer to that question, the comm in the cockpit crackled. "Twi-Town Port Control to the *Lightning's Hand*. Come in, *Lightning's Hand*."

Dave spun about and returned to the cockpit. "This is *Lightning's Hand*. Go ahead, Control."

"Everyone onboard your ship must remain there for the customs inspection."

"We're not carrying any cargo, Control."

"You expect us to just take your word on that, *Hand*?"

"No. I just thought—"

"I didn't know you rocket jocks *could* think."

"You're very funny, Control. How long do we have to wait for the inspector?"

"As long as it takes, *Hand*. It's been a busy day. Lots of ships are ahead of you."

Trouble peered out the lounge's viewport at the mostly empty landing field. "That Control guy is kidding, right?"

I shook my head. "Listen and learn, kid."

Dave said, "I understand and sympathize, Control. But I also have a hundred things I need to do while I'm here."

Control responded in a bored tone. "Do tell? The last pilot I talked to claimed he had two hundred things to do. So he's higher on the list."

"Control, now that I think about it, I have *three* hundred things to do."

"Well, that changes things, *Hand*. The inspector will be there in five minutes. She'll want to see your paperwork first thing. Just to make sure everything is in order."

"I'll have it ready and waiting, Control. *Lightning's Hand* out."

Dave strode from the cockpit. "I need a thousand bucks."

"You agreed to a bribe of three hundred," I said.

"Do you want your name and Tina's on an official port arrivals report? One that will definitely cross Jacobson's desk?"

I glanced at Trouble. "Bring a thousand."

She returned a moment later with the money. "What do we do now?"

Dave stuffed seven hundred dollars into his pocket. "You two go into Tina's cabin and shut the door. Leave the rest to me."

"What about Rita?" Trouble asked.

Dave waved a hand in dismissal. "Nobody pays attention to a Robosec."

Rita's head swiveled and her eye images locked on Dave. "That is yet another reason why I dislike you."

Dave ignored Rita and smiled at Trouble. "See what I mean?"

A fist pounded on the ship's outer hatch. Dave made shooing motions to us and headed for the airlock controls. Trouble and I retreated to her cabin and shut the door. A moment later, a woman's voice said, "Your paperwork is in order, Mr. Hayslett."

"Great," Dave said. "Thanks for stopping by."

"Not so fast. I still have to search the ship."

"Do you, though? I have some extra forms here that should answer all your questions."

The customs inspector was silent for a moment, probably

while she counted Dave's latest bribe. "I'm truly sorry, Mr. Hayslett, but I can't accept forms in lieu of this search."

"Are you certain? Perhaps if I gave you some more forms?"

"Certain parties are on the lookout for some, uh, lost cargo. They're leaning on Jacobson to find the missing items, and Jacobson is leaning on Customs. Leaning *hard* on us."

"How hard?" Dave asked.

"Hard enough that I must search your ship and report everything and everyone I find onboard."

"I see. Do you have to search the ship in any particular order?"

The customs officer was silent for a moment. "My instructions are not that specific. Why do you ask?"

"I can think of seven hundred reasons why you should start your search in the cargo hold."

"You told Control you weren't carrying cargo."

"Then the search won't take very long, will it?"

"No, it won't. Seven hundred reasons, you say?"

"Absolutely."

I turned to Trouble. "Quickly and quietly throw your things into your suitcase. We have to get off the ship while Dave has the officer in the hold."

"What about your stuff, Travis?"

"I'll grab what I can on the way out." I turned to Rita. "No one is looking for you, so stay with the ship for now."

Rita's mouth compressed to a line of disapproval and both ends of the line turned down. But her facial image bobbed in acknowledgment.

From the lounge, the customs officer said, "Lead the way to your cargo hold, Mr. Hayslett."

"Right through this hatch," Dave said. Three seconds later, the hatch slammed shut.

"Time to go!" I said.

I waved Trouble towards the lounge, popped into my room just long enough to shove my stuff into my suitcase, grabbed my blaster, and then followed her. Dave had thoughtfully left the airlock hatch partially open. We slipped through it into the cool air of the dusk side of the Twi-Line. As I'd feared, the mostly empty landing field offered no place for us to hide.

"Now what?" Trouble asked.

With trepidation, I said, "Now we walk to Twi-Town."

Without prompting, Trouble began walking deeper into Mercury's dark side. "We use the darkness for cover, right?"

"Yep."

Our feet fell soundlessly on a landing field melted smooth as glass by decades of rocket blasts. It didn't even have the usual grit and grime that you'd find on any other landing field in the solar system. None blew in from Mercury's light side because most of it tumbled into widespread molten pools before it reached the Twi-Line. Little came from the dark side, where the grit caught in pools of liquid oxygen or stuck to frozen metals. Sobering thoughts for a guy walking towards the dark-side edge of the Twi-Line. At least we weren't leaving tracks someone could follow.

The air grew cooler with each step we took, and the plunging temperature also took its toll on us. When I realized Trouble was shivering, I said, "Let's stop for a minute and add some layers."

Her head bobbed and she put down her suitcase. Trouble's hands shook so much it took her three tries to open the suitcase. I fared little better.

"Start with the tightest clothing you can fit over what you're already wearing," I said. "Then layer with looser clothes."

Trouble's teeth chattered as she said, "G-got it."

I felt warmer after I pulled three shirts over the one I already had on. My hands weren't shaking, anyway. Not much. I glanced at Trouble as she struggled with the tighter clothing currently popular with fashionable women.

I went to her and asked, "Need some help?"

"Please."

"Brace yourself."

Trouble locked her knees and hips, and then I pulled the shirt over her shoulders and down her torso. The material stretched enough to go over her breasts without me touching them. Thank God. Trouble must have noticed my caution, because she said, "You know, this is a first for me, Travis."

"Freezing on Mercury? I would hope so."

"That, too. But I meant it's the first time a man had offered to help me get dressed. Plenty of men have offered to help me *un*dress."

I turned my mind away from that intriguing notion and firmly towards the task at hand. So to speak. *Dammit, Travis, concentrate!* I pulled a pair of pants from her suitcase, bent over, and held them open at knee-level. "Put your foot in, and I'll pull the pants up over your shoes."

Trouble held onto my shoulders for balance and stuck a foot into the pants. I worked her shoe through one leg, then the other, and then helped her pull the pants over the pair she was already wearing. I thought pulling the shirt over Trouble was distracting. We only managed with the pants because she *wriggled* into them.

Finally, she said, "That's good enough, Travis. I ought to warm up once we start walking."

I nodded, closed our suitcases, and we set off again. "Where's your blaster?"

Trouble lifted the loose pajama shirt she wore as her outer layer. She had her shiny blaster tucked into the waistband of matching pajama pants. "It's in easy reach."

"You can leave it there until we leave the landing field. After that, it's probably safer if you have the blaster in your hand."

"Why? We're still a couple of miles from Twi-Town."

"There are people on Mercury who are so down and out that the idea of living inside Twi-Town is beyond their wildest dreams. Surviving in Twi-Town can be tough. There's only one way to survive *outside* of it, and that's being tougher and meaner than everyone else in the wastes."

"If you're trying to scare me, Travis, it's working."

"Good."

Trouble turned searching eyes on me for a moment. I don't

know if she liked what she saw in my expression, but she gave a slow, single nod.

"One other thing," I said.

"Yes?"

"If we *do* get into a fight, shoot to kill. Because anyone who attacks us will do their best to kill us."

Trouble was silent for a moment. "I've never killed anyone, Travis."

"I hope you never have to, but..." I left the rest unsaid. After a moment, I added, "If it helps any, killing someone who lives in the Twi-Line wastes is more compassionate than wounding them."

In a hushed tone, Trouble asked, "How can you say that?"

"There's no room for mercy in what passes for society in the wastes. A wounded person is a burden too great for its limited resources. So the healthy strip the wounded of everything useful they own, and then leave them to die slowly and painfully."

"That's horrible!"

I nodded. We trudged along for another minute, and then Trouble said, "How can places like this still exist, Travis? It's the twenty-first century, and—"

"It's the twenty-first century on Earth and in places like Marsport. On Mercury, it's more like the seventeenth century. You'll find the same on Venus, outside of a few cities, and in the Belt once you get away from Carnegie Station and the other big Belter stations."

"I had no idea."

"That's why the Space Patrol exists." I remembered Jacobson's cowardly order to leave the *Euphoria* to the pirates. "It *should* be why, anyway."

Five steps later, something crunched under my foot. I looked down and saw we'd reached the edge of the smooth landing field. I pulled my blaster out. Trouble did the same. Then we struck out into the Twi-Line wastes.

After the near-silence of our footsteps as we crossed the glassy landing field, the grit beneath our feet ground so loudly underfoot that I almost believed we walked on gravel. The logical part of my mind insisted the sound was almost inaudible, that the soft shifting of dust beneath my feet heightened my awareness of the sound. But my ears didn't believe my brain, and I wasn't the only one affected by it.

In a hushed tone, Trouble said, "If anyone is lurking out here in the wastes, they're going to hear us coming from a mile away."

"I have the same feeling, but we're not making much noise."

"How can you say that?"

I looked over my shoulder at Trouble. "Stop walking for a moment and listen to me."

She stopped while I walked on. I heard my steps plainly. From the look of surprise on Trouble's face, she didn't. I stopped walking and said, "Walk to me."

Five steps later, Trouble stood at my side. Her breathing was far louder than her footsteps had been. I offered an encouraging smile and said, "See what I mean?"

We began walking, and she nodded. "Our imagination amplified our footsteps. And now that I *know* that, they don't sound loud anymore." She was silent for a few seconds, then asked, "Is that something you learned in the Space Patrol?"

"Yeah, in the academy survival training course. In a dangerous situation, heightened awareness of your surroundings is a survival mechanism. But you have to train yourself to pay attention to the right things."

"And now that my brain understands how quiet our footsteps are, it filters them from the rest of the background sounds?"

"Something like that."

We walked in silence, gazing out at an uneven, boulder-strewn landscape cast in the perpetual shadows blanketing the dark side of the Twi-Line. The eerie, haunting silence worked on my nerves and, from the ragged sound of her breathing, Trouble's nerves. Even though Trouble and I walked next to each other, the desolation of the wastes evoked loneliness deeper than anything I'd ever experienced.

Trouble's hand caught mine. "I'm sorry. I know I should keep my shooting hand free, but this place gives me the creeps."

My loneliness retreated with the warmth of human contact, and I gave her hand a gentle squeeze. "It's okay. I feel it, too."

"What?" Trouble forced a teasing smile through her unease. "From everything Dave told me, I thought you had ice water running through your veins."

I tried matching her tone. "That's me, Travis 'the Iceman' Barrett."

"Is that why you didn't have a girl in every port?" Trouble's casual tone sounded forced, but anything so normal would sound that way in these wastes. "Because it was easy for the Iceman to love 'em and leave 'em?"

I snorted. "Yeah, right. Let's go with that explanation."

"What does that mean?"

"I was a lot more successful as a wingman than the lead."

"Meaning?"

"Dave went home with a lot of the girls he set his sights on. Me, not so much."

"I can't believe any girl would shoot you down so quickly."

"It wasn't quick, but I think it was inevitable."

"Why?"

"Dave always looked for girls he could have fun with for a night or two. Girls he could call whenever he was in port and forget about as soon as he shipped out."

"I asked about you, Travis, not Dave."

"I did fine with girls right after we met. But it always fell apart when they found out what I was looking for."

Trouble cocked her head, and a mischievous smile lit her face. "Mr. Barrett, this would go a lot faster if I didn't have to drag the information from you."

I sighed. "I was looking for *one* girl, in *one* port, who waited for me after I shipped out, and met me at the docks with a hug and a kiss when I returned. But clubs are full of girls like…" I stopped myself before I said *you*. "Like Dave was looking for.

Eventually, I stopped going to clubs during shore leave, because even a dim guy like me can take a hint."

Trouble's smile faded, replaced by a serious expression. "I think you gave up on clubs too soon."

"Why? Are the girls you hang out with any different from the ones I met?"

"No, but—"

"Then I don't see your point."

"You will if you stop interrupting me."

"Sorry. Please continue."

"My friends are like that, but *I'm* not. I want what my late mother never had—a good, honest man who will love me for who I am, not what I look like."

"I hope you find him, Trouble. I truly do."

Trouble stopped and spun me around to face her. Her eyes darted around the area, then she leaned in and kissed me quickly on the lips. She pulled back, took her place at my side again, and began walking. "I've already found him."

Emotions warred within me, as what *felt* right battled against what *was* right. "We can't do this. You're my assistant and—"

"Then I quit."

"Oh... That changes things," I said.

Trouble gave a satisfied nod. "I'm glad we settled that question. I'll show you *how* glad when we're safe in Twi-Town."

I let my searching gaze light on Trouble for a second. "Rita was right about you."

"Oh?"

"She warned me you were trouble with a capital-T."

"It's not like I hid it from you. I mean, it's right there in my nickname."

My response died on my lips as I heard the soft scrape of fabric against rock. I released Trouble's hand, swept my gaze over the landscape, and spotted half-a-dozen boulders large enough to hide people. Warned by my reaction, Trouble held her blaster at the ready and turned to face in the opposite direction as me.

Light exploded behind my eyes as something hit me on the side of the head, and I collapsed to the ground.

I slammed into Mercury's unyielding surface, and blinding pain lanced through my head as it bounced off the ground.

A blaster cracked above me.

A voice called from far away.

I looked up, but the strobing lights inside my head blinded me. The blaster fired again, its flat crack a clarion call for help. I shook my head, hoping it would clear my vision. A spike of pure agony drove through my eyes and into my brain.

The voice called again. Higher-pitched. Desperate.

I looked up. Saw nothing. *Of course you can't see. Your eyes are closed!*

I strained to lift lids so heavy I felt as if we were on Jupiter. A crack of dim light appeared. It widened, doused the flashes behind my eyes.

Blurred figures stood over me. The smaller one moved. Metal smacked against skin and bone. The larger figure stumbled back. Another blur closed in.

I blinked. The lids moved easier. The blurry shapes came into focus. I raised my blaster without conscious thought and fired at one. A blindly bright plasma bolt lit the Twi-Line's perpetual twilight for a microsecond, then it burned into a man's chest. Confusion crossed the man's face, then he fell.

I rolled over so Trouble and I faced in opposite directions again. More people came into view. I snapped off a shot at each one. Some screamed. One dropped. They broke and scrambled for cover.

Above me, Trouble's blaster fired in time with mine. More cries rose from behind me.

Silence fell.

"Can you get up, Travis?"

I pushed myself to my hands and knees. "Yeah, I think so."

"Do you need help?"

"I'll manage. You keep watch on the wasters."

Trouble grunted as something hit her. A rock dropped at her feet as she snapped off a quick shot. Trouble anticipated my question and said, "I'm okay. The padding from those extra layers of clothes helps."

I got my right foot under me and pushed myself up. I never thought of myself as tall, but six feet seemed unimaginably high as I unfolded to my full height. Trouble pressed her back against mine, steadying me and protecting me at the same time.

"What do you see?" she asked.

I waited five seconds until the Twi-Line wastes stopped spinning, then looked around me. Eight pairs of eyes peered over and around boulders. The man I'd shot in the chest sprawled nearby, eyes that would never see again staring into the heavens. A ragged woman huddled in the open twenty feet away. Fearful eyes watched Trouble and me, and filthy hands covered a blaster-burned hip.

"At least eight hiding, one wounded, and one dead." My voice sounded coolly matter-of-fact to my ears. How must it sound to Trouble? I pushed that thought aside. "What about you?"

"Um, six hiding. At least six, I mean. And, um, two wounded." The tremor in Trouble's voice worsened as she added, "I blew a man's leg off at the knee, Travis. He's... He's trying to drag himself behind a boulder, and..." She drew a ragged breath. "And..."

In a low voice, I said, "You did what you had to do, Trouble. They gave you no choice."

"I know that. But it doesn't help." She drew a deep breath and her voice steadied. "What now?"

"We get out of here." I raised my voice so the wasters could hear me. "We're leaving. If any of you makes a hostile move, we will kill every last one of you. Is that clear?"

The only sounds were the soft whimpering of the wounded woman and the scrape of the one-legged man dragging himself over the ground.

"I'll take your silence for agreement." I glanced around,

spotted my suitcase, and carefully retrieved it. Over my shoulder, I asked, "Do you have your suitcase?"

"Uh huh."

"Okay. We stay back-to-back until we're outside of their circle." I raised my voice, wanting the wasters to hear my next words. "Shoot anyone who moves toward us. Even if it's just one step."

Trouble caught on. In a loud, surprisingly steady voice, she said, "Got it."

It took us a few steps to get a feel for walking back-to-back, but once we found our rhythm, we moved faster. We cleared the ring of wasters in two minutes, but we kept our backs to each other until the ambush ground was fifty yards behind us.

"Can you run?" I asked.

"Can you? You're the one who had a big rock smack into his head."

In the tension of the moment, I'd all but forgotten my wound. I put a hand to my left temple. That hurt, so I put my hand down. A thin layer of blood covered the hand. Since there was nothing we could do about my head now, I said, "Yeah, I can run for a while."

We took off at a jog, and every step set off minor explosions of pain in my head. I kept a watchful eye on the landscape around us and ignored the pain as best I could. A quarter of a mile later, we crossed into a boulder-free plain and slowed to a walk. Once we put a hundred yards between us and the nearest rocks large enough to hide a person, Trouble stopped.

"Let me look at your head." She sucked breath through her teeth when she got a good look at the wound. "That's a nasty cut, Travis, and it's covered in dirt. Once we find a place to stay in Twi-Town, I need to clean and bandage it."

We set off again. It took us an hour to cross, but the plain stretched to the edge of Twi-Town. Entering the city, I felt something I never believed I'd feel in Twi-Town. Safer. But I felt certain the feeling wouldn't last.

eight
street trouble

EYES WATCHED us as we entered the outskirts of Twi-Town. They peered from the shadows, through the slats in boarded-up windows, and over dilapidated rooftops. I steered us to the center of the road, and the safety I'd felt when we left the wastes ebbed with each step we took. Trouble's rapid breathing showed she felt it, too.

"Breathe normally," I said, "walk with confidence, and keep your blaster in plain sight. Scavengers attack weakness. Show strength and they usually leave you alone."

"Usually?"

"We'll be fine as long as they aren't too desperate."

"Okay." Trouble's breathing slowed, and she matched her stride to mine. "Like this?"

"Yes. But keep your eyes moving, too. You're harder to ambush if you're aware of your surroundings."

We walked in silence for a minute, then Trouble said, "At least a dozen people are watching us."

"More like two dozen."

"Why don't they rush us? They have to know we couldn't shoot them all."

"They know. But they also know we'll shoot the ones who attack first."

"They're all waiting for someone else to make the first move?"

"Yes."

"So, should I shoot at anyone I see creeping forward?"

"That is an excellent idea."

Trouble's right arm rose and she fired into an alley beside us. The bolt cast stark, brief illumination down the passageway before it struck a crumbling brick wall. Five ragged figures cringed as drops of white-hot plasma splashed them and brick shards flayed their exposed skin. Howls of rage and pain erupted and quickly receded as the five would-be attackers ran away. Those who hadn't attracted Trouble's aim faded into the perpetual twilight, but others quickly replaced them.

The hum of a repulsor lift filled the temporary silence. Headlights illuminated the street as a hover car nosed from a side street and accelerated our way. A lighted sign on its roof identified the car as a taxicab.

Trouble and I faced the approaching car and raised our guns halfway. "What do we do, Travis?"

"Pray the driver is honest. Shoot if he tries to run us down."

The car sped closer. Braked just before I took aim. The driver deftly swung the cab sideways to us. The window rolled down. A brunette about my age looked at us and said, "Get in."

Trouble bolted for the car. "You heard the woman."

I stayed put. "But can we trust her?"

The driver smirked. "Dave said you'd ask that."

I half-shrugged and started for the car. "This *is* Twi-Town."

Trouble slid into the backseat as the driver's gaze swept the area behind me. "Yeah, that's why I won't wait for you if the low-lifes out there attack."

"Point taken." I picked up my pace.

As I slid into the car next to Trouble, the driver put the car in gear. I barely got the closed the door before she swung into a turn. The engine roared, and the acceleration pressed us into the seat as the car powered deeper into Twi-Town.

"Dave must be warming to you," Trouble said. "He sent a car."

"Nah," our driver said, "he just doesn't want Barrett croaking before Dave gets the *Lightning's Hand* back." She glanced at a screen showing the backseat. "But he'd sure as hell warm to *you* right quick, Miss Tate."

I frowned. "Dave told you who we are?"

"I'da known you, anyway, Barrett. But cabs don't come this far out from midtown 'less there be a damn good reason." Her eyes shifted to Trouble. "Oh yeah. You owe me a thousand bucks for coming to get you, Miss Tate."

Trouble popped open her suitcase and began counting out money. "You might as well call me Tina. Do you have a name?"

"Rachel. But everybody calls me Rach."

Trouble put a wad of money into the hand Rach held over her shoulder. "Where are you taking us?"

"Wherever you want to go, honey."

"How about a safe, discreet, out of the way hotel?" I asked.

Rach laughed. "You can get two out of those three, Barrett."

I thought for a moment. "How about safe, out of the way, with discretion for a price?"

Rach nodded. "Yeah, I know just the place. But you better make sure you got a way to make sure the guy at the desk stays bought."

Before I could respond, Trouble said, "Don't worry, Travis. I have that covered."

In unison, Rach and I said, "You do?"

"I watched my father for years. If there's one thing he knows how to do, it's buying silence."

"I thought he'd just send Hammerhand and Slick to lean on people," I said.

"He only does that when he can't buy silence." Trouble turned her attention to Rach. "How much will *your* silence cost?"

"Tempting as it is to take you for another grand," Rach said, "the first thousand buys the ride and silence."

"We're going to need someone who knows the town and has a car," I said. "Are you interested in working exclusively for me for a few days?"

"Depends," Rach said. "How much you paying?"

"How much do you want?"

She thought for a moment, then said, "Five hundred a day. Plus another five hundred every time I have to take you out of midtown."

"For that kind of money," I said, "I expect services beyond just driving."

Rach cackled. "From everything Dave told me 'bout you, I didn't figure you for a threesome kinda guy. But sure."

Trouble covered her mouth, partially smothering a laugh. I rolled my eyes and said, "I *meant* delivering messages, and maybe even doing a stakeout somewhere."

Rach heaved a theatrical sigh. "Not as much fun as a threesome, but you got yourself a driver."

Trouble yawned, and hers made me yawn, too. Exhaustion washed over me as the last dregs of adrenaline left my body. "Are we far from the hotel?"

Rach nodded ahead. "That's it at the corner of the next block."

"Thank God," Trouble said.

Agreement died on my lips and I came wide awake as adrenaline flooded my body again. Two figures stood in front of the hotel. A skinny, ferret-faced man standing next to a hulking brute. Hammerhand and Slick. And Hammerhand was waving at our taxi.

Without taking my eyes off Hammerhand and Slick, I said, "Don't stop."

"Huh?" Rach asked.

"Those guys in front of the hotel are the ones we want to avoid."

Trouble sat forward, and her eyes widened. "No, not after everything we've gone through to avoid them!"

Rach didn't waste time with further questions. She swung out of the light traffic, stopped at the mouth of a narrow alley between two buildings, and opened her door. As Rach exited, she hissed, "Follow my lead."

Rach stalked around the front of the air car, her face a mask of fury. Then Rach yanked open the rear door next to Trouble. In a loud, snarling tone, she said, "Outta my cab! I don't carry freeloaders." Trouble hesitated, and Rach reached over the door, caught Trouble by the arm, and tugged. "I said get out!"

Rach lowered her voice. "Get moving, girl. Those thugs you wanna avoid are looking this way. Stay low so the door hides you." Rach raised her voice again. "Go on. Get!"

Hunched over and hugging her suitcase to her chest, Trouble piled out of the backseat and scurried into the alley. I followed her lead. As I slunk past the door, I risked a quick glance up the street. Hammerhand and Slick strode purposefully down the street towards the cab. "They're coming this way, Rach."

Her voice returned to the low tone. "I know. Get your ass hidden before they get here."

I all but dove after Trouble. She stood ten feet into the alley, peering ahead. In a frantic tone, she said, "I can't see anything in here, Travis!"

I caught her by the arm and hurried her into the deep darkness blanketing the alley. "Good. That's what we want."

"How can we hide when we can't even see enough to find a hiding place?"

"If we can't see in here, you can bet Hammerhand and Slick can't, either."

Behind us, Rach slammed shut the cab's rear door, and then shouted, "Yeah, you bums better run! I ever see your sorry asses again, I'm gonna run you over!"

I glanced over my shoulder at the sliver of comparative brightness where Rach stood. She leaned forward, as if getting a foot closer to the alley would make it easier to see us. She straightened, gave a wave of disgusted dismissal, and started back to the driver's door.

"Stop," I said. "We'll hide here."

"Behind what?" Trouble asked.

I put my suitcase on the ground and pushed it against the nearest wall. "Behind our suitcases. Give me yours."

Trouble passed her suitcase to me, and I put it on top of mine. The suitcase balanced precariously, so I kept a hand on it, put my back to the wall, and slid down behind the makeshift wall. Pulling my legs up almost under my chin, I said, "Now you. Do just what I did."

Trouble joined me against the wall. Even in near-total darkness, I saw she was far more comfortable folded up like an origami ornament than I'll ever be.

From the alley mouth, Hammerhand called, "Hey, don't go nowhere!"

Rach said, "Why?"

"We wanna a cab."

"Yeah, a cab," Slick echoed.

"Didn't you see me waving?" Hammerhand asked.

"Nah. I was busy putting out the trash."

"What was that about, anyhow?" Hammerhand's voice grew louder, like he stood at the alley's mouth.

Rach snorted. "Did you hear me yelling?"

"Yeah."

"Then you already know what it was about."

"Where'd they go? I don't see no one down there."

In a droll tone, Rach said, "That's 'cause it's dark, genius."

"You got a smart mouth fer a cabbie," Hammerhand said.

"And?" Rach gave Hammerhand a heartbeat to reply, then said, "You wanna cab or you wanna stand around starin' into the dark?"

"Cab."

"Yeah, cab," Slick agreed.

"Then get it."

Three car doors opened and shut. Rach gunned the engine, and we heard the cab drive away. Trouble and I stayed behind our suitcase wall for five minutes as a precaution. Finally, I said, "It ought to be safe to get up, now."

My knees popped and my back ached as I stood. Trouble's body unfolded in silence, and she didn't even pretend to stretch. I returned her suitcase, we walked to the street, and turned towards the hotel. A minute later, we entered a clean, well-lit little lobby.

A short man who looked like he wouldn't last fifteen seconds on the streets of Twi-Town stood behind the front desk. The clerk's eyes widened when he saw us. He acted casual as his hand strayed towards the desk's comm unit.

I kept my tone even. "Don't even think about it, buddy."

The clerk's hand jerked back from the comm as if he'd been burned. "Think about what?"

"Calling the big guy who just left."

"Why on Mercury would I do that?"

I shrugged. "Probably because he paid you to."

The clerk drew himself to his full, unimpressive height as he pasted a look of indignation on his face. He drew a breath, no doubt to deny my charge, but Trouble said, "I'll pay you if you *don't* call them."

As if her words had thrown a switch, greed lit the clerk's eyes. "The big guy offered a lot of money for information about a couple matching your description."

Trouble marched up to the desk. "How much money?"

The clerk paused for a moment, probably to figure out just how much he could inflate Hammerhand's offer and get away with it. "Five hundred bucks."

Trouble raised one eyebrow. "That much?"

The little man must not have trusted his voice, because he gave a silent, jerky nod. Trouble put her suitcase on the desktop, opened it just wide enough to reach inside, and not wide enough for the clerk to see the contents.

I put an elbow on the desk and leaned towards the clerk, drawing his attention my way. "You got a name, buddy?"

"Archibald."

"Can I call you Archie?"

"If you must."

"What me and the lady are looking for is someone who stays bought. Is that you?"

Fussy Archibald surprised me by saying, "If it was, I'd be on the comm to the other guy right now."

I couldn't help laughing. "I do like an honest crook. But I have to tell you, things will go badly for you if you don't stay bought. By us, I mean."

Archie sniffed. "The goon who just left was far more convincing when he threatened me."

I sought after a sufficient comeback and failed. "You have a good point."

Trouble saved me from further embarrassment by closing her suitcase. "Here's five hundred dollars to buy out the previous man's contract." She held up a small stack of bills. "Here's two thousand more to shift your allegiance to us."

Archie smiled and reached for the money. "You have a deal."

Trouble pulled her hand back. "Not so fast, Archibald." She handed the bills to me. "Please rip those in half."

Archie's eyes widened as I followed her instructions. I had to separate the bills into two stacks, but soon Trouble held two sets of half-bills. She handed one to Archie. "As long as you keep your end of the bargain, I'll give you the other half when we check out of the hotel."

A genuine smile creased his face. "Well played, ma'am." He shoved the paper into his pocket. "May I assume you want a room?"

"Yes," I said.

"For Mr. and Mrs. Smith, I presume?"

"Correct."

He tapped on a keyboard for a moment and then handed me two keycards. "Room four twenty-eight. Have a pleasant stay."

"You don't want any payment upfront?" I asked.

"I believe you have as much reason to keep our bargain as I do, Mr. Smith."

I nodded, and we headed for the elevator. A minute later, we let ourselves into a clean, comfortable room with its own bathroom.

Trouble pointed to the only chair in the room. "Sit."

I sat. She examined my head wound, headed into the bathroom, returned with a soapy washcloth, and thoroughly cleaned the cut. I only hissed twice from the pain.

When she finished, I said, "You take the bathroom first, Trouble. Take as much time as you need."

"Very gallant of you, Travis." She put her suitcase down, turned to face me, and lifted her arms over her head. "But could you help me peel off the extra layers of clothes first?"

It took some work and more than a little distracting wriggling by Trouble, but I helped her out of all but the clothes she wore when we left the *Lightning's Hand*. She pulled something from the suitcase, went into the bathroom, and started the shower. While Trouble was bathing, I fought my way out of my own extra layers of clothes.

The bathroom door opened just after I finished folding and storing the extra layers I'd worn. Trouble emerged, hair damp and wearing an oversized shirt that left her legs bare from the thighs down. She flashed a smile, wrapped her arms around my neck, and kissed me gently on the lips. "The bathroom is all yours."

Trouble sauntered to the bed, and my eyes followed her swaying hips all the way. She looked back, smiled, and pointed to the bathroom. "Go."

I went. When I emerged fifteen minutes later, Trouble was fast asleep. I turned off the lights, joined her in the bed and, less than a minute later, in sleep.

I AWOKE to the feel of warm breath on my neck, heat from a willowy body pressed against my back, and with Trouble's right arm flung across me. Three years had passed since the last time I woke up next to a woman, and my relationship with her hadn't ended well. None of them ever did. The few girlfriends who weren't scared off by my desire for a serious, permanent relationship eventually got tired of me and my inflexible sense of honor, which often put my client's needs ahead of their needs.

Trouble would agree with my priorities on this case—we were searching for her brother, after all—but what about future cases? How would she feel about cold dinners, missed dates, or plans canceled at the last minute, all because of the demands of my job? Was it even me that Trouble found so intriguing, or was the heady allure of mystery and adventure driving her interest? God only knows how many romances bloom from the thrill of danger, only to wither and die when the boring, everyday world returns.

I pushed aside thoughts of a future with Trouble and turned my attention to her brother's fate. Everyone in the solar system leaves a trail as they move through life. Some leave tracks so faint that they're all but impossible to follow. Others cut such a wide swath that a blind man could trace their movements. Time to find out which type Nick Tate was. I lifted Trouble's arm, rolled carefully out of bed, and gently put her arm down.

Trouble's blue eyes fluttered open, and a languid smile lit her face.

"Good morning."

"Morning." I went to the hotel room's small dresser and began pulling out clothes. "You can go back to sleep."

She sat up and stretched. "What kind of assistant lets her boss do all the work while she sleeps?"

"A smart one?" Trouble stuck her tongue out at me. I wrenched my attention away from the gorgeous girl in my bed and said, "Besides, you're not my assistant anymore. You quit, remember?"

"You didn't give me much choice." Trouble stood and came my way. "But I will not sit around and do nothing just because you're not paying me anymore." She studied her small assortment of clothes. "What do you need from me, distraction or decorum?"

"What?"

"Do we start the investigation by talking to men at the Tate Steelworks office or finding the girl Nick was seeing? I'll dress provocatively for men. If their attention is divided between your questions and my body, they're more likely to let useful tidbits slip out. If it's Nick's girl, I dress down and go for the concerned sister or best friend look, so she'll feel more at ease and willing to confide in me."

I raised both eyebrows. "Where did you learn that stuff?"

"I learned how to make guys say more than they mean to at clubs." She glanced sideways at me. "It's amazing how much a little cleavage distracts guys." Unbidden, my gaze went to Trouble's chest. She laughed. "See?"

I yanked my eyes back to my clothing. "We'll start at the Tate facility in Twi-Town, so dress for distraction."

"Is that a good idea, with Father's goons looking for us?"

"I think so. Norman Tate doesn't strike me as a man who tells his underlings more than what they need to know to do their jobs."

"Yes, that's Father in a nutshell."

"I'm betting he told Hammerhand and Slick to keep their search for us on the down low, for that reason. Telling people to keep an eye out for his runaway daughter and a private investigator would raise questions he doesn't want anyone asking."

"What if you're wrong?"

"It'll tell Hammerhand that we're on Mercury, but that will just confirm what he already believes." An idea occurred to me. "Can you pull off both business-like and provocative dress?"

Trouble gave a dismissive snort. "Of course."

"Good. Do that."

"What's the plan?"

"Your father plays everything close to the vest with his business. I bet that's why he sent Nick here a few weeks ago, right?"

"Father wants Nick to take over the company someday, so that's probably right."

"So who would Norman Tate trust to look into his son's disappearance? He'd want to keep it in the family, wouldn't he?"

A bitter edge crept into Trouble's voice. "If he had another son, sure. He never involves me in the business."

"But how many people on Mercury do you think know that?"

Trouble said a silent O of enlightenment. "Probably just Hammerhand and Slick."

"Exactly." I waved towards the bathroom. "Go make yourself beautifully business-like. I'll call Rach and have her bring the car."

Rach said she'd be waiting out front. Then I placed a call to the *Lightning's Hand*. Dave answered with, "So you're not dead."

"Sorry to disappoint you, Dave."

"I'm used to it. My life is one disappointment after another, Barrett."

"Have you got web access on the ship?"

"Yeah, but it routes through the spaceport link. It's not what I'd call secure."

"Can you come down here and bring Rita with you?"

"I'm just the pilot, Barrett."

"I'll pay you."

"Yeah, okay."

I told him the hotel's address. "I'll get a room for you under the name Jones."

"How original."

"When you get here, have Rita connect to the web and start tracking Nick Tate's purchases in Twi-Town."

"What will you be doing?"

"Asking questions at the Tate offices."

"I still want my ship back, so don't get yourself killed."

"Your concern is touching," I said, and disconnected.

A minute later, Trouble emerged from the bathroom and struck a pose. "How do I look?"

"I wouldn't get any work done if I shared an office with you."

I pulled on my shoulder holster, made sure Trouble had her blaster inside her purse, and we left the room. As promised, Rach was waiting for us out front. I gave her the Tate office's address.

Rach grinned. "That's outside of midtown, Barrett. Driving there is gonna cost you an extra five hundred."

The drive took twenty minutes, and the city deteriorated with each block we passed. I'd hoped for a simple office building we could just walk into, but the Tate facility was a gated and guarded complex.

Rach looked over her shoulder. "Do I drive up to the gate?"

"Yes." I turned to Trouble. "You do the talking. I'm just here as your bodyguard, or maybe your assistant."

At the gate, an armed guard approached the cab. He looked at Rach, and she jerked her thumb over her shoulder at the backseat. I rolled down the window, and Trouble leaned over me.

"I'm Tina Tate. Open the gate."

trouble with
human resources

AS SOON AS the guard heard the name *Tate*, his eyes snapped from Trouble's legs to her face, and his posture straightened. He didn't quite jump to attention, but it was a close-run thing. "Welcome to Tate Steelworks, Twi-Town Division, Miss Tate. We weren't told to expect you."

"Nor should you have been," Trouble said.

The guard jumped to an obvious conclusion. "Should I announce you or do you wish to keep your arrival a secret as long as possible?"

"Do not announce me..." Trouble glanced at the guard's name tag. "Mr. Sharpe." Her lips spread into a friendly smile. "My brother mentioned an appropriately named guard. I must assume he meant you."

Trouble's smile didn't reach megawatt caliber, much less match her dazzling gigawatt smile, but it enchanted Sharpe. He grinned. "That sounds like something Ni- um, I mean young Mr. Tate, would do. Everyone here liked him a lot and we were sorry when he left."

I kept my face impassive as the guard's revelation sank in. People in the office complex didn't know Nick had gone missing. They just assumed he went back to Carnegie Station. Or they'd been told he did. I glanced at Trouble. Her smile remained fixed in place, though her eyes had narrowed. She definitely understood the implication of Sharpe's words.

"It's all right to call him Nick," Trouble said. "He never cared for such formalities and neither do I. Please call me Tina."

Sharpe glanced around, as if afraid someone was listening to our conversation. "I'm sorry, Miss Tate, but Mr. Graham doesn't approve of casual relations between management and labor."

"Then call me *Miss Tate* if the director is around." Trouble brightened her smile. "Otherwise, I expect you to use *Tina*."

"Yes, ma'am." Trouble's eyebrow arched and Sharpe said, "Yes, Tina."

Trouble nodded. "Better. And what is your first name? I can't keep calling you Mr. Sharpe while you call me Tina."

"It's Max. Now, um, where may I direct you, Tina?"

"Shouldn't you ask for my ID, Max?"

"There's no need, ma'am. I mean, Tina. Nick told me all about you and showed me some pictures. I know you're you."

And there was another revelation. Apparently, Nick Tate hung out with regular employees during his visit and got to know them well enough that he talked about his sister and shared family photos.

Despite Sharpe's words to the contrary, Trouble pulled her ID card from her purse. "I insist you treat me like any other visitor, Max."

She passed the ID to me and I handed it to Sharpe. As he studied the card, I took a shot in the dark. "Nick told us about a bar he liked going to while he was here, but I forgot the name."

Sharpe handed the ID back to me. "Forever Five is the place you want."

"Interesting name," I said.

Sharpe said, "The guy who owns it says the light outside reminded him of five o'clock back on Earth. And you know the old drinking saying."

I nodded. "It's always five o'clock somewhere. Clever." I glanced at Trouble, and then back at Sharpe. "Is it safe?"

Sharpe shrugged. "It's in midtown and on the light side of the Twi-Line. Safe enough if you keep your eyes open."

"Thanks."

Trouble added, "I hope we'll see you there, Max."

"Count on it, Tina," Sharpe replied.

"Good," she said. "Now, if you could point me to the Human Resources office? The HR director's office, in particular?"

Sharpe gave us directions and a minute later Rach parked in front of a building that looked like the compound's main office. I climbed from the cab, gave Trouble a hand up, and looked at Rach. "I'll check in with you every hour."

Rach pulled a battered book reader from her glove box. "I'll be waiting with bated breath, Barrett."

I followed Trouble through the entrance and towards the office door bearing the sign HUMAN RESOURCES then hurried ahead of her and opened the door. She breezed through without slowing and marched past the receptionist's desk. The young man behind the desk leapt up and hurried after Trouble.

"May I help you, ma'am?" he asked.

The guy tried squeezing past me to get to Trouble. I slid over and blocked his path as Trouble said, "No, thank you."

The kid cut around to my other side, and I blocked him again. He said, "Could I tell someone you're coming?"

"That won't be necessary," Trouble said.

When it became clear Trouble was heading for the HR director's office, the kid gave up being polite and tried shoving his way past me. "You can't go in there without an appointment!"

I stiff-armed the kid into the wall and pinned him there. "Maybe *you* can't go in without an appointment. Miss *Tate* can."

The kid's eyes cut to the Tate Steelworks' logo on the director's door, not so discreetly positioned above the name SANDRA HODGES and HR DIRECTOR. In a small voice, he asked, "Tate?"

"Tate," I said. "*That* Tate."

He stopped pushing against my arm. "Um, go right in?"

I released the kid. "Don't breathe a word of this to anyone while we're in there. Is that clear?"

He nodded, then watched as I joined Trouble at the office door. Without another word, I opened the door, and she entered.

The door opened into a spacious office, complete with a six-person conference table and three chairs facing a large desk. A woman in her mid-forties sat behind the desk. From the hair tightly wound into a bun to her deepening frown to her well-tailored but unflattering business suit, Sandra Hodges radiated severity. Her first words did nothing to dispel my initial impression.

In a voice sharp enough to flay skin, Hodges asked, "Frederick, what is the meaning of this?"

From the door, Frederick the receptionist said, "I'm sorry, ma'am. I couldn't stop them."

Trouble ignored that exchange, approached the desk, and rapped it with her knuckles. She looked at me over her shoulder. "It's oak. See how it makes the office pop?"

"You've convinced me," I growled. "I'll ask Santa for one next Christmas."

Frederick politely waited until Trouble and I stopped talking, then said, "Miss Tate to see you, ma'am."

I heard a finger tapping the door and had no doubt Frederick was tapping the logo painted above Hodges' name, ensuring his boss knew one of *those* Tates stood in her office. He needn't have bothered. Hodges' face paled the moment she heard *Tate* pass his lips. Hodges rose and extended her hand over the desk and plastered a false smile on her face.

"Welcome to Twi-Town, Miss Tate. I'm Sandra Hodges." She invited us to sit with a gesture, waited until we'd taken chairs, then resumed her seat. Her glance flicked to the door. "That will be all, Frederick. Close the door and see I'm not disturbed." She didn't add *again*, but from Frederick's miserable expression, she didn't need to.

I looked over my shoulder, caught Frederick's eye, and said, "Remember what I said earlier, Frederick."

His head bobbed as he shut the door. I turned back to Hodges and wasn't surprised to find her eying me. I offered a smile just as sincere as the one on Hodge's face.

The HR director returned her gaze to Trouble. "Please excuse my initial reaction, Miss Tate."

Trouble dismissed the incident with a wave of her hand. "I'm performing a surprise follow up to my brother's visit a few weeks ago. It was Nick's first solo business trip, so Father sent me to confirm the results."

Hodges' expression turned guarded and her eyes darkened in wary concentration. She might as well have shouted, *I know you're lying*. I'd give good odds Hodges knew Nick never left Mercury.

"Does your father doubt we followed his instructions to the letter?" Hodges asked.

Hodges' question made today's entire hornet-nest-kicking expedition worthwhile. Hodges definitely knew Nick never left Mercury, and her wording implied that his disappearance was on Norman Tate's orders. What Hodges didn't know was Trouble's level of involvement.

As much as I wanted to respond to Hodges, the Tate heiress had to handle this part of the conversation. During the drive from the hotel, I'd impressed on Trouble the need to choose her words with care and to imply knowledge where none existed. Trouble's a clever girl, and I prayed she remembered everything I told her.

"Father didn't get where he is today by assuming people do as they're instructed." Trouble's pleasant smile vanished. "*Especially* in matters such as this."

"Of course," Hodges murmured. "How may Human Resources be of assistance, Miss Tate?"

"Nick had two local employees working with him," Trouble said. "I need to discover what they know."

"You may rest assured they know nothing, Miss Tate."

"I wouldn't have come to Twi-Town if local assurances

sufficed." Trouble pointed to the intercom on Hodges' desk. "Have Frederick summon the employees."

"Certainly, Miss Tate." Hodges began typing on her keyboard instead of activating the intercom. "Let me just look up their names."

I rose, came around Hodges' desk, and looked over her shoulder at the screen on her desk. The screen's focus was on an internal messaging application. Hodges began deleting text as soon as she realized my intention, but *Ta*—all that was left of *Tate*, no doubt—still showed in the message box.

Hodges glared at me. "Do you mind?"

I perched on the edge of her desk. "Yes." I leaned closer, read the recipient's name in the message application, and glanced at Trouble. "She tried sending a message to the director."

Trouble stood and leaned over Hodges' desk and glared at her. "I will decide when Director Graham is informed of my arrival. Is that clear?"

"Yes, Miss Tate."

"What are the names of the two employees I requested?"

Hodges waved at her screen. "I still have to look them up."

With precise enunciation, Trouble asked, "Did you not just tell me they knew nothing? How can you know that if you do not even know their names?"

Hodges' eyes darted around, looking everywhere except at Trouble. "I have, ah, just recalled one name. Horace Lance. He'll know who else worked with your brother."

Trouble sighed, activated the intercom, and said, "Frederick?"

"Yes, Miss Tate?"

"Please summon the two employees who worked with my brother during his visit."

"Of course, Miss Tate." Frederick hesitated, then asked, "Since your associate told me to keep your presence a secret, what reason should I give?"

"Tell them the HR director wants to see them."

"Very well, ma'am."

Trouble switched off the intercom and turned to Hodges. "How is it your receptionist recalls their names without prompting, yet you do not?"

Hodges sniffed. "I assume it's because he socializes with them outside of work."

Trouble flashed a dubious expression but dropped the subject. She resumed her seat, and we waited in silence for the two employees. Five minutes later, Frederick showed a man and a woman into the office. "Horace Lance and Laura Wiggins, as requested."

Frederick directed the comment to Hodges, since the request ostensibly came from her. Without waiting for a reply, he retreated and shut the door behind him.

Laura Wiggins didn't meet any of my preconceptions. She was a pretty girl barely older than twenty, with an air of shy innocence about her that enhanced her beauty. Intelligent, hazel eyes watched us as she fiddled nervously with long brunette hair. Recognition flashed in her eyes when she looked at Trouble.

Horace Lance was her complete opposite. He was older—close to my age—blonde-haired, blue-eyed, blandly handsome, and sharply dressed. Lance also had a cocksure attitude he didn't bother hiding. Lance glanced at me in disinterest, openly ogled Trouble, and grinned at Hodges. "Are these new employees you want shown around?" Without waiting for a response, he turned to Laura. "You show the guy around, okay?"

I didn't want to give Hodges a chance to alert either employee, so said, "We're from the home office, performing a follow up to Nick Tate's recent visit."

Lance's jovial expression turned guarded, just as Hodges had. "I covered everything in my reports."

"What can I do to help?" Laura Wiggins asked.

I looked at Trouble. "Why don't you interview Miss Wiggins in here? I'll talk to Mr. Lance in another conference room."

She nodded, so I led Lance out of the office.

The minute the door closed behind us, Lance said, "Let me congratulate you, buddy."

I headed for the open door of an empty conference room. "For what?"

"Winning the secretarial sweepstakes!" Lance said. "That girl is hotter than a day on the light side of Mercury."

His words confirmed what I'd suspected from the moment he laid eyes on Trouble. Unlike Max Sharpe, the gate guard, and shy Laura Wiggins, Horace Lance didn't recognize her. That meant Lance was never around when Nick talked about his sister. Considering how close Trouble and Nick were, it seemed likely Nick didn't socialize with Lance. From my brief exposure to Lance, I couldn't blame Nick for that. But was Lance's personality the only reason Nick steered clear of him after work?

Without waiting for an invitation, Lance plopped down in a seat, leaned back, and grinned at me. "So, what do you need? Considering your hot secretary, I'm guessing you don't need help getting your hands on a girl?"

"I do not, Horace."

"Call me Race."

"No."

Lance visibly wilted at my refusal, but did his best to sound chipper. "Then what can I do for you, my man?"

Time to kick the hornet's nest again. I unbuttoned my jacket and let my shoulder holster show as I settled in a chair opposite Lance. "Tell me everything you know about Nick Tate's disappearance."

My question hung in the air between Horace Lance and me. Horace opened and closed his mouth twice, obviously at a loss for words.

"I..." Horace drew out the single syllable for five seconds, then lamely said, "Thought Nick went home."

"No, you don't."

From his expression, Horace wasn't used to people flat out contradicting him. "What?"

"My meaning is perfectly clear. You know Nick didn't go home."

"Look, I don't know who you are—"

"And you want to keep it that way." I leaned forward and caught his gaze. "Mistakes were made, Horace. It's my job to discover who made the mistakes and ensure they never make the same mistake again."

Horace's eyes darted to the conference room door and back to me twice. Horace's fight-or-flight instinct had obviously settled on flight, which should make my job easier.

I leaned back in my seat. "I'm going to level with you, Horace. A private investigator is looking into this issue, and I know for a fact that he's already in Twi-Town. This has to be cleaned up fast, and if that means breaking a few eggs..." I shrugged. "Your position is precarious. If everything hits the fan, do you think Director Graham or HR Director Hodges will take the fall when they can point fingers at someone like you?"

In a whine that grated on my nerves, Horace said, "I only did what I was told to do!"

"Which was?"

"Don't you know?"

"I'm trying to find out what *you* know, Horace. I can't help you if you won't help me."

"You'll keep my name out of any official reports to Mr. Tate?"

"There won't be any official reports."

"Right. Um, will you keep my name out of any *un*official reports to Mr. Tate?"

"I give you my word that I will not mention your name to Mr. Tate." Keeping my word would be easy, since I doubted Norman Tate would ever talk to me again.

Horace bobbed his head once. "Okay... Okay... I was just supposed to stay with Nick while he was onsite, and report his movements, who he talked to, what caught his attention. That sort of thing."

"Who did you report to?" I asked.

"Hodges."

"So, what attracted Nick's attention?"

A bit of the old Horace surfaced, and he leered. "Laura Wiggins, for one thing."

I already knew Nick had found a girl in Twi-Town. Time to find out more. "A honey trap?"

Horace's brows drew down in puzzlement. "A what?"

"It's a standard investigative technique. Dangle a pretty girl in front of a guy so she can either distract him from something or learn how much he knows about something."

"Oh." Horace tilted his head back and thought about my question for a moment. From his expression, thinking didn't come naturally to him. "I don't think so. Wiggins has been in the office for close to a year, and Nick is the first guy she's shown any interest in. I didn't think she even was into guys before he showed up."

In other words, she'd been immune to Horace's supposed charms. I said, "That could have been part of her cover."

"Maybe, but my guy instincts say no. Wiggins just doesn't give off that experienced-girl-acting-coy vibe, if you know what I mean."

Surprisingly, I did know what he meant. I'd run across more than my share of women pretending innocence during my younger days. Back when Dave dragged me to clubs looking for girls, I learned the hard way how to recognize it. Laura Wiggins didn't set off those alarms, but Trouble would figure out if my initial impression was wrong.

"What, other than Laura, caught Nick's attention?"

"Um... He liked visiting the metallurgy research area. I don't see the attraction to watching techs melt metal, but Nick sure loved watching it and writing melting point records and stuff like that in his little notebook."

"What else did he put in his little notebook?"

Horace shrugged. "Budget numbers, maybe? It's not like he showed his notes to me."

"Do you know where Nick's notebook is now?"

"No."

"Do you know where Nick is now?"

Horace offered a weak smirk. "Laura's place, waiting for her to get off work?"

The grin faded when my face remained impassive. "Can you think of anything I haven't asked about?" Horace shook his head, but I thought of one more question. "Have you seen a big guy and his ferret-faced friend around here?"

Horace brightened. "You mean Mr. Houlihan? Sure. He and his friend are up in Mr. Graham's office right now."

Damn, I'd hoped Hammerhand would still be out bribing hotel clerks. I stood. "Come with me."

Horace followed me out of the conference room. I glanced at the receptionist. "Frederick, please join us in the HR director's office."

Frederick and Horace followed in back to Hodges' office. Inside, I found Trouble had banished Hodges to the conference table and appropriated the desk, handily taking control of Hodges' web screen at the same time. Laura Wiggins perched on the edge of her seat, talking with Trouble in a voice too quiet to be heard by Hodges.

"Horace, Frederick, take a seat at the conference table." I caught Trouble's eye. "We need to get going."

Trouble picked up the urgency in my tone and rose. She hefted the desk intercom, used it to smash Hodges' screen, and strode to the office door. "Laura, come with us."

Laura fell in behind Trouble. "If you say so, Miss Tate."

"Call me Tina," Trouble said as she exited Hodges' office.

Horace's eyes bugged out when he heard Laura say *Miss Tate*. I resisted the urge to laugh at his expression, followed the two women through the door, and pulled it shut. Then I drew my blaster, set it to low power, and fired it into the locking mechanism. "That won't hold them for long."

As we exited the HR office, Trouble asked, "What's the rush?"

"Hammerhand and Slick are in this building."

She nodded, looked at Laura, and asked, "Are you sure you want to get involved in this?"

"Nick's involved," Laura said, "so that means I'm involved."

Behind us, a gruff, familiar voice bellowed, "Barrett?"

I looked over my shoulder. Hammerhand and Slick emerged from an elevator just thirty feet behind us. I gave Laura Wiggins a gentle shove in the back. "Run!"

trouble on the run

TROUBLE RAN for Rach's cab and Laura followed, slowed by her high heels. To buy time for Laura, I drew my blaster and snapped an over-the-shoulder shot down the corridor. Hammerhand and Slick jumped back into the elevator. That would slow them down, which is all I wanted. I kept my blaster drawn and ready and ran for the exit.

The automatic door trundled shut after the two women passed through. I turned sideways and slipped between the closing doors. The door's sensors finally noticed me. It reversed itself and trundled open again. But I was already outside and sprinting for the cab.

Hammerhand must have heard the door grinding as it switched directions, because I heard his feet pounding down the corridor after me. "Yer gonna pay when I get my mitts on you, Barrett!"

Even in the middle of a chase, Slick stuck to his Greek chorus role. "Yeah, pay!"

Trouble caught Laura's arm and dragged her into the back seat. When I ran for the front passenger door, she slammed shut the rear door. Rach leaned across the seat and shoved the passenger door open. It didn't open far, but Rach saved me precious time I'd have lost fumbling with the handle. I pulled the door open and hopped into the passenger seat.

"Go go go go go!"

Rach didn't need my encouragement. While I reached to close the door, she spun the wheel clockwise and floored the accelerator. The force of the hover cab's tight half spin threw me against Rach.

"D'ya mind, Barrett?" she snapped. "I'm driving here."

Hammerhand reached the car, and his huge hand grabbed the edge of the still-open door. I pushed myself away from Rach, grabbed my door's handle, and slammed it shut. Hammerhand howled as his meaty fingers kept the latch from catching. He fell from sight, releasing the door at the same time. I pulled it shut and then looked back to see what he was doing.

Hammerhand stuffed his smashed fingers into his coat pocket and used his good hand to push himself to his feet. Slick stood next to him, yelling into a comm. It didn't take a genius to figure out Slick was calling for a car, and five seconds later, a powerful car pulled up in front of them.

As Hammerhand and Slick jumped into their car, I looked ahead to the closed gate guarded by Max Sharpe. I rolled down my window. Rach slowed as she approached the barrier, and I stuck my head and shoulders out of the car. "Max! Open the gate now!"

Max hesitated, but Trouble leaned far over the seat and showed her face. "Please do as he said, Max!"

Max's doubt vanished, he tapped a control, and the gate swung open. Slowly.

I glance back at Rach. "Gun it as soon as the gate is open enough for the cab to fit through."

"I sure am tickled pink I got you around to tell me how to do my job, Barrett," Rach said, never once taking her eyes off of the gradually widening opening.

I ignored Rach and glanced at Trouble. "Ask Max to slow Hammerhand down if he can."

Trouble gave a fractional nod and said, "Max, there's a car chasing us. If there's anything you can do to—"

The cab surged forward, throwing Trouble and me back into our seats. A horrible screech sounded as the edge of the gate scraped down the driver's side of the cab. Then we were through.

In a matter of fact tone, Rach said, "I'm gonna add a new paint job to your bill, Barrett."

I turned and looked back at the gate. Relief washed over me when I saw it slowly closing ahead of Hammerhand's approaching car. "Max came through. By the time the gate cycles around—"

The other car never slowed, smashed through the gate, and roared after Rach's cab.

Shouting to be heard over the growling engine and whining repulsor, I said, "The other car is gaining on us, Rach. Can this thing go any faster?"

"Not much. The repulsors suck a lot of the engine's power." Rach glanced at our pursuer in the rearview screen on her dashboard. "That car's got a bigger engine and wheels. So no repulsor sucking power."

"At least tell me you're Twi-Town's best driver and can lose them, anyway." The cab suddenly slewed left, throwing me hard against the passenger door. "A little warning would be appreciated."

"Shut it, Barrett!" Rach snapped.

Tires squealed as the car behind us slid around the corner. The rear end fishtailed and then lined up behind the front.

"Hold on!" Rach called.

I grabbed the door handle just before the cab spun violently to the right and into a narrow alley. Twi-Town alley-dwellers leapt from the cab's path.

"Don't hit them!" Laura called from the backseat.

"Don't worry," Rach said. "Alley bums are real good at getting clear."

The larger car shot into the alley. It had less than a foot of clearance on each side, but the driver didn't slow. Bums leapt for fire escapes and squeezed into doorways. A few unfortunate souls tried diving over the car. Two made it, but three more bounced off the windshield. The car never slowed and kept its arrow-straight rush down the alley.

"Damn," Rach said, an undercurrent of admiration in her voice, "that guy's good." As an afterthought, she said, "Grab something."

I hadn't let go of the door handle, so Rach's careening right turn didn't send me tumbling into her. "Can you keep this thing going straight long enough for me to climb into the backseat?"

"It's not a good time to go cuddling with your girlfriends, Barrett."

The car carrying Hammerhand and Slick burst from the alley. A bum who'd been clinging to the hood lost his grip and tumbled away.

"I want to shoot at the car's tires, you idiot. But I'm right handed, so I need to shoot from a driver-side window."

"Can't hurt to try," Rach said. "Make your move after the next turn."

Rach spun the wheel back and forth as she dodged through the first traffic we'd encountered since the chase began. Approaching a traffic light, she laid on the horn, ran the light, cut around two cars that screeched to a stop, and shot the wrong way down a one-way street.

As Rach wove through the handful of cars and trucks out in this rundown neighborhood, I clambered over the driver's seat. Trouble and Laura scooted to the right side of the seat and then helped pull me into the back. I sprawled on top of Laura and disentangled myself with a quickly muttered, "Sorry."

Rach picked that moment to say, "Turning."

The cab whipped to the right, throwing Laura and Trouble on top of me. They slid off of me and huddled together against the right rear door. I wound down the left rear window as the other car charged into the street behind us. I leaned out and struggled to keep my hand steady as the cab wove through increasingly heavy traffic.

Rach called, "Won't be long before we run into heavier traffic and I'll have to slow down. Or maybe even stop. So get shooting already, Barrett."

"I can't get a clear shot," I called.

"Not much I can do about that," Rach said.

"You can slow down."

"Do what?"

"Ease off the accelerator. Let the other car get closer."

"Don't be stupid, Barrett! It'll shove us into a building or another car."

"Not if I can take out a tire."

Rach hesitated for two long seconds, then the cab slowed. "You better be a damn good shot."

Hammerhand's car swung out from behind the nearest car. I leaned out of the window as the pursuer clawed closer. But I wasn't the only one who thought about shooting. Slick stuck his head and arm out of the right rear window and snapped off a shot at the cab. I resisted the urge to flinch away from the shot and aimed at the other car's front tire. The other driver swerved just as I fired, and my shot slagged part of the bumper.

Slick's next shot scorched my door, causing an eruption of cursing from Rach. I pushed thoughts of having my arm shot off from my mind, focused on the closest tire, and fired. The blaster bolt grazed the sidewall. A bang sounded as the weakened right front tire blew. Sparks flew as the rim tore into the pavement and the car pulled sharply to the right. The driver fought the wheel, regained control of the car, and braked.

Rach took the next right turn at full speed and almost threw me from the car. As soon as Hammerhand's car was out of sight, she slowed to the speed limit. "Nice shooting, Barrett."

I pulled myself back into the cab, rolled up the window, and slumped back in the seat. "Thanks."

"What do we do now?" Trouble asked. "We can't keep using this cab now that Hammerhand knows about it."

"Yeah," Rach agreed, "and it sorta stands out, what with the scraped paint and the melted door. All of which—"

"Is going on my bill," I said. "I know."

Rach nodded. "Good. Just wanted to make sure we got that straight."

"We do, Rach." I looked at Trouble. "As for what to do, I'm open to suggestions."

Trouble pondered for a moment. "You don't have any ideas?"

"I have one, but I'd rather not do it until things get desperate."

Rach snorted. "Geez, Barrett, you got some warped ideas if you don't think things aren't already desperate."

Trouble nodded. "I agree with Rach. What's your idea?"

"We get local help." I caught Trouble's gaze. "We call Sam and Liz Carson."

Laura Wiggins looked back and forth between Trouble and me. "Sam and Liz Carson? Who are they?"

"A couple we met on the spaceliner, before we trip veered off course," I said. "Sam said to look them up when we got to Twi-Town."

Rach looked over her shoulder. "When folks say that, they're offering dinner, not help fighting killer goons."

"I won't ask them to fight," I said. "We just need a place to lie low for a while."

"Still gonna be some danger," Rach said.

"The Carsons won't mind," Trouble said.

"What makes you think that?" Rach asked.

"They were on the *Euphoria*," Trouble replied.

Rach gave a slow nod of understanding. But Laura cocked her head and asked, "What's the *Euphoria*?"

I looked out the passenger window. "A spaceliner I helped defend against pirates when I was in the Space Patrol."

Trouble heaved a sigh. "What Travis is leaving out is that he defied a direct order to leave the *Euphoria* to its fate. It cost him his career."

Laura turned eyes shining with admiration on me. "Really?"

"It also cost the lives of twenty-four members of my crew," I said.

"But you saved all those people!" Laura said.

"My crew saved all those people," I said. "I just gave a few orders."

In a soft tone, Rach said, "That ain't the way Dave told it to me."

I turned back to the shadowy city outside my window. "If he made himself out to be the big hero, it's because he was. Without his piloting, I'd have lost the entire crew."

Rach shook her head. "That's not what he said."

I kept staring out the window, but Trouble asked, "What did Dave tell you, Rach?"

"He said the *Euphoria* woulda been a pirate prize if anybody 'cept Barrett was in command."

"Because I'm the only man stupid enough to take on the *Bloodsword* with a search-and-rescue ship?"

"No," Rach said, "because you were the only man with the guts to do the right thing."

I didn't know how to respond to that, so I said nothing. In the silence, Laura asked, "The *Bloodsword*? I heard even big navy ships are scared of it."

"They should be," I muttered.

Trouble must have sensed my unease. "That's enough about the past. What we need now is Sam's and Liz's number." She pulled out her comm and tapped a number. A few seconds later, she said, "Hi Rita. It's Trouble with a capital T." I heard an outraged squawk from the other end, and Trouble flashed a smile at me. "Yes, he told me... No, you can't kill him. But you can get a comm number for me... Sam and Liz Carson. It should be a new listing... Uh huh... Got it! You're the best, Rita... Bye."

Trouble disconnected and immediately tapped in a new

number. "Hi, Liz? This is Connie Rollins, from the *Star of Sol*... Yes, it took some work, but we finally got here... I know you're just moved in and you've got a lot of unpacking to do, but Jack and I need some help. Could we come by with a couple of friends?" She glanced at me and nodded. "What's your address?"

A moment later, Trouble gave the address to Rach, who whistled. "Nice neighborhood. *Great* neighborhood for Twi-Town. What's your buddy do to rate a place there?"

"I don't know," I admitted.

Rach snorted. "What *do* you know, Barrett?"

"I know Horace Lance is a sleazeball."

Laura said, "*Everyone* knows that, Mr. Barrett."

Despite everything that had happened in the last few hours, I felt my lips quirk up in a smile. "Does everyone know it was Lance's job to report whatever caught Nick's eye to the HR director?"

In a dry tone, Laura said, "*I* knew that, Mr. Barrett."

I raised one eyebrow. "Oh?"

"Nick and I hit it off from the beginning. I didn't think it was such a big deal until my manager had a private chat with me about Nick. She said his constant questions were taking people from their real work and suggested I could use my 'special relationship' with Nick to distract him. She even told me that Mr. Graham would consider it a personal favor if I found 'something' that kept Nick away from the office compound." Laura crossed her arms and glared straight ahead. "She even said I could stay away from the office as long as I wanted, provided Nick stayed away, too."

Trouble's eyes narrowed, and her lips compressed. "Did Nick know they offered to pay you to have sex with him?"

"I told him the first chance I got," Laura said. "I didn't want company rumors ruining something so beautiful."

Trouble's eyes widened. "So, you and Nick were...?"

"I love your brother, Miss Tate."

"I told you to call me Tina, but considering your relationship with Nick, maybe you should use the nickname he gave me."

"You mean I get to call you Trouble?"

"Of course," Trouble said. "And knowing Nick told you about my nickname tells me more about your relationship with him than anything else I've heard so far."

"Touching as this sisterly moment is," I said, "could we get back to what I learned from Lance?" Laura nodded, so I continued, "Lance also told me that Nick was interested in the metallurgy lab, so much so that he kept notes on everything they did in the lab."

Laura nodded. "Nick was always writing stuff down in his little notebook."

I looked at Laura and asked, "I don't suppose you can tell me exactly what was in the notebook?"

"No, Mr. Barrett, but I can show you."

"What? How?"

"Before he le—." Laura bit her lip, obviously remembering Nick hadn't left Mercury, as she originally thought. "Before he disappeared, Nick gave the notebook to me."

I glanced past Laura to Trouble. "It sounds like Nick knew he'd stumbled onto something people didn't want getting out. Something so hot that they'd..."

I stopped myself before I said, *kill for it*. But Trouble is a smart girl. She said, "Something they'd kill to keep silent?"

"*Or* kidnap," I countered.

Laura looked at the car's floor and, in a quiet voice, said, "This is Twi-Town, Mr. Barrett. People kill for many reasons and for no reason at all. Nick obviously gave someone a reason to get him out of the way." She shrugged. "It's how they do things here."

Trouble caught and squeezed Laura's hand, offering comfort to the woman who loved her brother. Knowing Trouble, she also sought comfort from Laura.

Disbelief colored my voice. "I can't believe *I'm* the optimistic one, here, but..." I switched to my matter-of-fact private investigator's voice. "Trouble, do you believe your father would order Nick's murder?"

It said a lot about Trouble's relationship with her father that she considered my question for five seconds. "I don't think so."

"Okay, think about it another way," I said. "Would your father actively squash attempts to investigate Nick's disappearance if he *had* ordered him murdered?"

"No," Trouble answered immediately. "It would make Father appear too suspicious."

"Exactly." I switched my gaze to Laura. "If Norman Tate didn't order Nick's murder, do you think anyone in the Twi-Town office has the guts to kill the boss's only son?"

Without hesitation, Laura said, "No. Not a chance."

"Would they drop hints to convince someone like Horace Lance to do the job for them?"

Again, Laura didn't pause for thought. "And give that person leverage over them? Again, not a chance. Besides, Lance might be a sneak and a snitch, but he's not even a lady killer, much less a real killer." Laura sighed. "But this *is* Twi-Town. It's possible some random bum killed Nick."

I smiled and tossed Laura's words back at her. "Not a chance. Because Norman Tate wouldn't sit idly by if Nick's disappearance had nothing to do with Tate Steelworks."

Trouble gave a slow nod. "Travis is right. Father would tear Twi-Town apart if that was the case. He'd do it to make sure people learned not to mess with him and his stuff, but he'd definitely do it."

I said, "Now that we all agree Nick's still alive, let's get back to finding him. Laura, do you have Nick's notebook with you?"

Laura shook her head. "It's back at my apartment. But we could go get it. It's not far from here."

"That's not a good idea," I said. "Your apartment is the best place for Hammerhand and Slick to get back on our tail. They'll have someone watching it by now." I leaned back and vented a sigh of exasperation. "I wish I could read that notebook, though. Do you remember what Nick wrote in it, Laura?"

"No, it was a bunch of metallurgic notes, all of it over my head. But if all you want to do is *read* Nick's notebook, get me access to the web and I can get a copy for you."

My eyebrows arched. "You can?"

"Nick told me people might try to take the notebook away. So I scanned its contents and then emailed the files to myself. Using my personal email address, not my work address."

"Brilliant and beautiful, just like Nick's older sister," I said. "No wonder he fell for you."

Laura's cheeks reddened, and she ducked her head. "That's kind of you to say, Mr. Barrett—"

"Travis."

"Travis," Laura corrected. "But I just used common sense."

"Spend a few more years traveling the solar system," I said, "and you'll see just how *un*common common sense is."

Rach looked back at us. "We're approaching that neighborhood where your friends live. You got a way to get past the guard?"

I looked at Trouble. "Did Liz say anything about a guarded gate?"

"No, but maybe she forgot? They just moved here, after all."

"Pull up to the gate, Rach," I said. "I'll talk to the guard."

Rach did as I instructed, and I rolled down my window as a guard approached. A second guard stayed inside the little guardhouse, watching us closely. The first guard leaned over and looked through my window at Trouble and Laura. He touched the brim of his hat. "Ladies. Sir. What may I do for you?"

I dredged up the upper crust accent I'd used ages ago on the *Star of Sol* when I was on the run from Hammerhand. "Good day, my good man... Or should I say, good evening? This constant twilight is damnably confusing to me, don't you know?"

The guard smiled. "It took me a while to adjust to it, too, sir. It's actually late morning."

I arched my eyebrows and widened my eyes. "Morning, you say?"

"Indeed, sir."

"Well, Mercury certainly has done a number on my internal clock, eh what?" Without waiting for another platitude from the guard, I forged on. "Well, good *morning*, my good man. What assurances must I provide to assuage your protective vigilance?"

The guard spent two seconds parsing my question, then said, "Just tell us who you're here to see, sir. My fellow guard will comm them. Once they confirm your identity, we'll let you in."

"I see." I turned to Trouble. "What was the name of that lovely little family you met on the *Star of Sol*?"

"The Carsons," Trouble said. "Sam and Liz."

"That's them," I agreed. Turning back to the guard, I said, "Tell them Jack and Connie Rollins are here with a friend."

"Very good, sir." The guard stepped back from the cab and watched us while his partner commed the Carsons. A moment later, the second guard disconnected the call and flashed a thumbs up. As the gate swung open, the first guard said, "Enjoy your visit, sir."

I waved, rolled up my window, and said, "Rach, can you tell what the second guard is doing?"

Rach tapped a button next to her rearview display a few times. The image zoomed in on the guardhouse. "Looks like he's making a second comm call."

I sighed. "It was too much to hope that Hammerhand hadn't paid them to be on the lookout for us."

"What do you think he'll do?" Trouble asked.

"If we're lucky, he'll wait at the gate for us to leave."

"Patience isn't one of Hammerhand's strong points," Trouble said.

"I know. His impatience is a big reason he never won the heavyweight boxing title." I shrugged. "We have to tell Sam and Liz they're about to become very popular."

trouble with patrollers

RACH PULLED up in front of a small, two-story house. Other than the street number, the house was identical to every other one in the neighborhood. I saw the value of assembly line houses like this, but scenery isn't their strong suit. Then again, I lived off a steel corridor that's just like every other residential corridor on Carnegie Station, so who am I to talk about scenery?

"This is one of Twi-Town's best neighborhoods?" Trouble asked.

"You seen houses anywhere else, Red?" Rach asked.

"No," Trouble admitted. "And please don't call me Red. I'm not fond of it."

Where I grew up, that admission would have cemented 'Red' as her permanent nickname. But there was something about the calm way Trouble made her request that made even a wise-cracking cabbie take her seriously. "Whatcha want I should call you?"

"We've already been through a lot together," Trouble said. "So you should call me Trouble, too."

Rach's eyes widened, and I got the idea she was used to being treated more like a servant than a friend. "Um, okay... Say, Barrett, want me to park the cab in front of a different house? That

Hammerhand guy knows what it looks like, so leaving it here is a dead giveaway to your location."

"Thanks for the offer, Rach, but the gate guards know which house we're visiting. You can bet they'll tell Hammerhand." I looked down the street, noticing how few houses had cars parked in front of them. "How do people get to work without cars?"

"By bus," Laura said. "Traveling around Twi-Town is safer in a big group."

"That," Rach agreed, "and most buses got armed guards."

I forced my attention back to the moment. "Rach, why don't you park so you can't get blocked in by a single car? Do you mind keeping watch for Tweedledee and Tweedledumdum?"

"Sure thing, Barrett. I'll honk the horn if I see 'em."

The front door opened, and Sam Carlson said, "Are you going to spend all day out there, or are you going to come inside?"

"Come inside, of course," Trouble said.

Sam did a double take at Trouble, and I realized this was the first time he'd seen her without wild makeup and dyed hair. "The picture your father's pet goon was showing about on the *Star of Sol* didn't do you justice, Miss Tate."

"Thank you, Sam," she said, "but is that formal name any way to greet your temporary wife?"

"His *what*?" Laura asked.

Trouble launched into an explanation of the wife-swapping incident onboard the spaceliner as the women entered the house. Liz gave a cry of welcome to them as I shook Sam's hand. "Hey, Sam. You should have told me to go to hell when I called."

"And you should have told Jacobson 'Yes, sir' when he ordered you to ignore the *Euphoria's* distress call."

"I'm serious, Sam. One of the gate guards made a call to someone right after they let us in. I think they're on Hammerhand's private payroll."

"I'm serious, too, Travis. I owe you more than I can ever repay, so I will *always* do everything I can to help you and yours." Sam dragged me inside the house. "Now get over there and give

Liz a kiss before she gets mad at me for keeping you all to myself."

Inside, I found Trouble bouncing a happy Ian on her hip while a smiling Liz held baby Trudy. Laura sat in front of the family web station, typing quietly on the keyboard. I gave Liz a quick peck on the cheek, which widened her smile.

"It's good to see you again, Travis," she said.

Laura stopped typing and looked over her shoulder at me. "You wanted to read Nick's notebook, Mr. Barrett." She pointed at a document on the screen. "Here it is."

I bent over her shoulder and scanned the text and numbers. The words were standard English with steel industry jargon mixed in, and they obviously described columns of numbers on the page. But they made no sense to me.

A low whistle sounded next to me as Sam bent over and read the notes. I asked, "Do you understand this, Sam?"

"Not entirely. I know what it all *means*, but I don't understand how those numbers are even possible." Sam reached past Laura and scrolled the document, but didn't elaborate.

Liz gave her husband a gentle kick. "Sam, honey, your eyes kept moving, but your lips stopped."

Sam blinked and looked back at Liz. "What was that, dear?"

"None of us has your background in mining and metals, Sam." Liz nodded at the screen. "You need to explain what that stuff means."

"The notes are for some new alloy steel. The numbers are the melting points, tensile strength, rate of heat conduction, and stuff like that."

Sam fell silent and returned to studying Nick's notes. Liz sighed and kicked her husband harder. "Mercury to Sam. Come in, Sam!"

"What?" Sam asked. "I answered your question."

"You only *think* you did, Sam. We *know* you didn't, because we still don't know why those numbers have you enthralled."

"Didn't you read the numbers?"

"Yes, honey, but we don't know what they mean."

Apparently, that thought hadn't occurred to Sam. "Oh... Did those notes come from the Tate metallurgy lab?"

Laura nodded. "Nick Tate recorded them during his visit."

"My brother disappeared a few days after he recorded those notes, Sam," Trouble said. "Please tell us what they mean."

Sam shrugged. "They mean Norman Tate is about to become very rich."

"Father is *already* very rich," Trouble said.

"Not like this, he isn't," Sam said. "If those numbers are right, your father is about to become the richest man in the solar system."

Everyone except the two children stared at Sam, while his eyes never left the screen filled with Nick's notes. Silence hung in the air as we waited for Sam to explain further. Finally, Trouble gave up waiting and asked, "How is that possible?"

Sam kept scrolling through the document. "Hm?"

Trouble caught Sam by the jaw and gently turned his head towards her. Ian gave a delighted laugh at the sight. His son's reaction caught Sam's attention where Trouble's question had not. Sam smiled sheepishly. "Sorry, it's just the information your brother recorded is incredible."

"So I gathered," Trouble said. "But none of us have your expertise in the field. Could you please explain *how* that information will turn my father into the richest man in the solar system?"

Uncertainty crossed Sam's face. "You're a smart girl and a *Tate*. If anyone in this room should understand, it's you."

Pain flashed in Trouble's eyes, coming and going so fast I doubt anyone except me saw it. In an impassive tone, she said, "Father always kept me at arm's length from the business. Eventually, I gave up trying to learn how he earned his money and just concentrated on spending as much of it as possible."

I thought I understood Trouble well enough to comprehend the motivation behind her spending habits. Most parents of profligate children take pains explaining where their money comes from and often insist the child get involved in the family business. In yet another example of Norman Tate's poor parenting, he didn't bother reining in Trouble's spending, much less bring her into the business.

From the look on Sam's face, he figured out some of that. But he just shrugged. "His loss, I guess... The simple explanation is that your father's new alloy steel has all the benefits of other alloys —high melting point, high ductility, it's easy to weld, resists corrosion—"

"What is ductility?" Trouble asked.

"It can be drawn out into a thin wire or molded into new forms without losing its toughness." Trouble nodded her understanding, so Sam continued, "This new alloy also has the strength of carbon steel. According to these numbers, your father's new alloy steel is so superior to anything the steel industry forges today that no one will want anything else."

Trouble's gaze slid to the notes on the screen. "How long would it take Father to run all the other steelworks out of business?"

"That depends on the scarcity of the unknown element that goes into this alloy and how much of it he needs per metric ton. Tate Steelworks made about a billion metric tons of steel last year. If he can make that much of this new stuff..." Sam's eyes unfocused as he considered the question. "Give it five years and Tate Steelworks will control at least ninety percent of the solar system's steel market. For comparison, your father's company has about nine percent of the market right now."

Her tone faint, Trouble said, "Oh."

"I have to be honest with you about something," Sam said. "Rumors of your father's new alloy steel are circulating through the steel industry. I'm working for Astra Steel, and they brought me to Mercury to join a research project that's trying to match your father's alloy." Sam looked at the floor and shuffled his feet. "I should have told you earlier but—"

"It's okay, Sam," Trouble said. "Besides, it's not like we gave you a chance to say anything."

"But—"

Trouble interrupted him. "I have to be honest with you about something, Sam. If I can find the formula for Father's new alloy steel, I will give it to you."

Sam's head jerked up, and his eyes widened. "Why would you do that?"

"Because the *last* thing I want is my father holding that kind of power." She waved a hand at the screen. "I feel certain Nick discovered a secret about that new alloy, one my father thinks is so important he ordered Nick's disappearance. I also feel certain Father will order Nick's release if that secret comes out."

Sam didn't meet Trouble's gaze. "Are you sure about that last bit? Norman Tate is a ruthless businessman."

"Father is also practical. I think he'd release Nick because too many people already know Father is behind Nick's disappearance, and he can't have them all killed. A trail of bodies leading back to Father would be more inconvenient than anything Nick could tell."

I hoped Trouble was right, but in my experience even the most ruthlessly practical men in the solar system can panic when they feel threatened. But that was all moot if we found and freed Nick. His notes held clues to his disappearance, but they didn't explain it. Not yet. But I felt certain I knew where to find the next piece in the puzzle.

I tapped Nick's girlfriend on the shoulder. "Laura, you accompanied Nick on his visits to the metallurgy lab, didn't you?"

Hazel eyes met my gaze. "Yes, Mr. Barrett."

"How hard is it to get inside the lab?"

"It's on a restricted access floor, sir. The only reason I got inside was because of Nick. Mr. Graham wasn't happy about it, but Nick wouldn't take no for an answer."

"How is the restriction enforced? A keycard or code? Maybe an armed guard?"

"All three, Mr. Barrett."

My first thought was that it was overkill. Then I remembered Sam's prediction of the fallout if Tate Steelworks had a monopoly on the new alloy steel, and changed my mind. "Assuming I can figure out a way to get us past those three roadblocks and into the lab, can you recognize a sample of the new super alloy?"

"Sure," Laura said, "if you can unlock the safe they're stored in."

"This just gets better and better," I muttered.

"You're thinking of breaking into the lab, aren't you?" Trouble asked.

"Do you know a better way to get our hands on a sample of the alloy?"

"Yes," she said. "Let me get it."

I shook my head violently. "No way! It's too dangerous."

Trouble bristled at that. "Too dangerous for me, but not for Laura?"

"I wouldn't take her if I didn't have to."

"You have to take me, too, Travis."

"Give me one good reason I should."

Trouble folded her arms and glared at me. "I'll give you two. Nick is *my* brother, and it's *my* name on the business."

I searched my mind for a good refutation to her rationale. But a blaring car horn derailed my thoughts. It was Rach's signal. We were about to have company.

Sam looked towards the door, his gaze drawn by the car horn sounding outside. "What the heck?"

I ignored his question and headed for the front window. But Trouble said, "It's a signal from our driver, telling us Hammer-hand and Slick have arrived."

"After Mr. Barrett shot one of their tires?" Laura asked. "How did they change it *and* drive here so quickly?"

I pushed aside the curtain covering the front window and peeked out. A Patrol cruiser rolled to a stop in front of the house, its front grill inches from the grill of Rach's cab.

"They didn't." I glanced back at Trouble. "Your father's bully boys must have called in the Space Patrol, because one of their cars just pulled up."

I turned back to the window just in time to see a second cruiser come up behind Rach's cab, neatly boxing it in. "Make that *two* Patrol cars." I glanced down the street and saw two more cruisers approaching. "Make it four."

I turned from the window. "Laura, close that copy of Nick's notes and log out of your personal email. Sam, can you purge the machine's temporary storage? There's no reason to make things easy for Patrol investigators."

Laura logged out and rose from the chair. Sam plopped down and began hammering on the keyboard. I turned my attention back to the window in time to see a Patrol officer pull a struggling Rach out of her cab.

I heard an undertone of fear in Liz's voice as she asked, "What will happen to us?"

"You'll tell the officers the truth," I said. "Connie Rollins from the *Star of Sol* called you and asked if she could drop by for a visit. You had no idea she'd bring the husband who caused so much trouble. Then you'll lie and tell them you didn't know the pair had been traveling under assumed names. How could you possibly know that?"

I glanced at Laura. "You tell them you didn't know Miss Tate's companion would drag you into a car chase or start shooting at the Tate Steelworks security personnel who gave chase."

Outside, one officer shoved Rach into the back of a cruiser, six others spread out in the yard, and the remaining officer started towards the Carsons' front door.

"What's our story?" Trouble asked.

I shrugged as I fished my comm from my pocket and dialed. "Rita? It's Travis... Shut up and listen. I'm about to get dragged in by the Patrol... Yeah, her, too... Tell Dave and have him come down to Patrol HQ to bail us out... He wants his ship back, so he'll do it… There's cash in Trouble's suitcase in our room… Get Archie at the front desk to let you in."

Knuckles knocked firmly on the Carsons' door, leaving me no choice but to wrap up the call. "One last thing, Rita. If anything happens to me, sign the *Lightning's Hand* over to Dave… No, I haven't lost my mind." The Patrol officer knocked again, louder and longer. "Gotta go, Rita. Take care of yourself."

I disconnected just as Sam reached the door. He glanced my way. I nodded, and he opened the door.

"May I help you, officer?" he asked.

"We're looking for Travis Barrett, a dangerous fugitive, and have good reason to believe he's inside your home."

"Whoever told you that is wrong," Sam said.

"Then you won't mind if we come in and verify that for ourselves." It wasn't a question, and I saw the door move slightly as the officer pushed on it.

Under his shirt, Sam's miner's muscles rippled as he held the door firm. "Do you have a search warrant?"

"No," the officer growled, "do you have something to hide?"

"Let him in, Sam," I said. Hoping Sam and Liz would catch the hint and play along, I said, "I'm the man the officer is looking for."

Liz played her part perfectly. She gasped and then took Ian from Trouble's arms. Sam wasn't as convincing as he delivered a wooden protest. "But your name is Jack Rollins."

The Patrol officer pushed into the room as I raised my hands. In a scornful tone, I said, "I lied, you moron." I looked at the officer. "I have a blaster in a shoulder holster."

He fumbled for his own gun, finally drew it, and pointed it at me. "Drop it on the floor."

Moving with deliberation, I used two fingers to pull my blaster from the holster and put the gun on the floor. Then I carefully kicked it to the officer. "Don't worry, I'll go peacefully."

The officer moved away from the door and then jerked his head towards it. "Lead the way and keep your hands where I can see them." He glanced at Trouble. "I've been told to bring you in, too, Miss Tate."

Trouble headed for the door. "Am I under arrest, too?"

"Not as far as I know, ma'am."

"Then why do you want me to come with you?"

"I'm just following orders, ma'am."

Trouble hardened her voice. "Whose orders?"

"Commander Jacobson gave the order, ma'am," the officer replied. "From the commander's tone of voice, he's looking forward to seeing Mr. Barrett again." In an ominous tone, the officer added, "May God have mercy on your soul, Barrett, because Jacobson sure won't."

A patroller handcuffed me and shoved me into a cruiser's back seat with Rach.

"You okay?" I asked Rach.

"Just peachy," she said. "This sort of stuff happen a lot when you're around?"

"It's a recent development."

"Yeah, well, it's gonna cost you another five hundred bucks, and you better be plannin' on paying my fines."

"Of course."

An officer escorted Trouble to the car and held the door for her. "Please have a seat, Miss Tate."

As Trouble joined us in the back seat, Rach leaned over her and glared at the officer. "You coulda asked me nice like, too, you know."

The officer grunted. "Why? It never worked before."

Trouble raised an eyebrow. "Have you arrested Rach before?"

"You might say that," he said. "She's a regular guest at HQ."

Rach flashed a false smile. "Repeat customers oughta get treated something special."

"You've got your own cell in the lockup, Rush. Isn't that enough?" The officer turned his attention back to Trouble. "Watch your hands, Miss Tate." Then he shut the car door.

Rach flopped back in the seat and sighed. I asked, "Rush? Is that a nickname?"

She shook her head. "My last name. I figured with a name like Rachel Rush, I had to be a driver. Helps that I'm real good at it."

"Why does the Patrol arrest you so often?" Trouble asked.

Fire ignited in Rach's eyes. "Ain't nothing I do." Two officers climbed into the front seat. Rach glared at them through the grill separating the front and back seats. "It's 'cause I won't pay Jacobson to keep his guys off my back. Ain't that right, boys?"

The officer in the passenger seat glanced over his shoulder. "No talking."

Rach seemed inclined to ignore the order, but I caught her attention and shook my head. I was the one Jacobson really wanted. If she didn't overly antagonize officers, she'd probably get off with a fine. Rach held my gaze for a minute, gave a fractional shrug, and remained silent for the thirty-minute ride.

Unlike the Carsons' neighborhood, Patroller headquarters was about as deep into the dark side of the Twi-Line as it could be and still be habitable by humans. Land is cheap on the fringe. Like many bureaucracies, Twi-Town's city government had only considered their upfront costs when they'd had the headquarters built. I'd lay long odds that the cost of heating the building far exceeded the savings they got buying the cheapest land available. I'd lay longer odds that someone in the budget office griped about the monthly heating bill, too.

As with our trip out to the Tate Steelworks compound, the surrounding buildings deteriorated as the light faded. Scattered street lights created small islands of illumination in the deepening darkness. Ragged men and women hunched against the cold that stole warmth through their too-thin clothing. They scanned their surroundings with sullen eyes, and their heads never stopped moving as they did their best to watch everyone around them. Already-tense bodies stiffened as the Patrol cruiser approached and relaxed marginally as it rolled by without stopping. Their reactions just confirmed my assumption that Jacobson used his position to cow the populace and line his pockets.

Space Patrol Headquarters formed the lone bright spot in the never-ending darkness surrounding it. Powerful lights pointing out from the building's rooftop lit the area around it as brightly as if it were on the light side. Razor wire coiled atop a high boundary wall sparkled in the light.

Trouble eyed it with consternation. "What a grotesque sight."

"Shut it," the driver growled. His partner gave him a backhanded smack on the arm, and the driver's tone changed. "Sorry, Miss Tate. *You* are free to speak."

"Why aren't my companions equally free?" she asked.

The officer in the passenger seat turned and looked back at Trouble. He plastered a false expression of concern on his face and said, "It's for their own good, Miss Tate. We don't want suspects incriminating themselves with careless talk." His mouth stretched into a rictus that he obviously thought was a friendly smile. "At least, not until they've been advised of their rights."

Trouble nodded as if she believed his explanation, and said nothing more. A moment later, the driver parked the cruiser in a spot reserved for official vehicles. One officer helped Trouble out of the back seat while the other all but dragged Rach and me out through the other door. He grabbed our arms and marched Rach and me up the stairs into the building.

After the near-silence outside, the noise inside all but deafened me. Officers and civilians talked and yelled, gesticulated and lounged, sobbed and cackled. The clack of fingers pounding on keyboards made a weirdly syncopated addition to the noise. The two officers with us ignored the cacophony and headed for a door on the left side of the lobby. When the door shut behind us, the decibel level dropped by half.

The officers dragged us down a long hallway, past half a dozen grimy men seated on a bench. The men hooted when they caught sight of Trouble, and one called, "Hey baby, you as high-priced as you look?"

Another added, "Whooo, lookit the midtown whore! Businessman's special, amiright?"

A third stretched his hand towards her. "How 'bout a free sample?"

My kick hit the reacher's wrist. He howled in pain, jumped to his feet, and shoved me. "You lookin' fer a beatin', buddy?"

I'd have punched him if my hands weren't cuffed behind my back. So I settled for a sweep kick that shoved him back onto the bench. As the punk fought to regain his balance, the patroller escorting Rach and me pushed him down onto the bench.

"This is way out of your league, kid," the patroller said.

The punk snarled and stood again. The men on either side of him on the bench grabbed him and pulled him back down. One added, "It ain't worth it, Sem."

We left the scene behind, and no one rushed us from behind. I guess the punk's friends stopped him from doing something stupid. At the far end of the hallway, they put us into different interrogation rooms. I don't know how they treated Rach, but they left the cuffs on my wrists. When he left me, the officer shut the door behind him, cutting off all sound from outside of the room.

Great. They'd put me in a soundproof interrogation chamber. That wasn't ominous or anything.

In typical fashion, the patrollers let me stew for a while. The room had no clock, so I couldn't say how long I sat alone with my thoughts. Everyone who's watched a cop show knows why they do it. I was supposed to spend the time worrying about what they would do with me, and that would make me an easier nut to crack when the interrogation began. Sometimes the technique even works, but I was determined it wouldn't work on me. Besides, I knew what was in store for me.

My guess proved correct when the door finally opened and a grinning Hammerhand entered. As always, Slick bobbed along in his wake.

"Lookee what the patrollers got for us, Slick," Hammerhand said. "It's like Christmas come early."

"Yeah, Christmas," Slick giggled. "And we get to break the toy."

Hammerhand laughed. "Good one, Slick." He loomed over me and smacked a fist into his palm. "You think I'm gonna hurt my knuckles breakin' our new toy?"

Without waiting for Slick's answer, Hammerhand hit me with a right cross that knocked me out of the chair. Hammerhand grabbed my jacket lapels, pulled me up, and put me back in the chair. Then he hit me with a left cross, knocking me out of the chair again.

We went through four rounds of that before Hammerhand got tired of returning me to the chair and started kicking me instead. After snickering Slick joined in, I got it from both sides. Darkness was a long time coming, but I welcomed it when it took me.

THE PAIN from my beating increased as the darkness from the same beating receded. My head pounded. My gut ached. My shoulders screamed. My wrists chafed. I breathed through my mouth because something blocked my nose. Probably dried blood.

A young-sounding man said, "I think he's coming to, sir."

The voice rang with the toadying enthusiasm Commander Jacobson always liked in his subordinates. That could only mean that the great coward himself was in the room with me.

As if on cue, Jacobson said, "Let's have a little illumination, shall we, Warren?"

A bright light pierced my eyelids and set fire to my optic nerves. I turned my head away from it, but whoever held it moved the light so it kept shining directly on my eyelids. I jerked my head away, and that hurt even worse than the photons lancing into my brain.

I tried speaking. Couldn't. Coughed and hacked gunk into my mouth. Spit it towards the light.

"That's disgusting!" the toady cried.

"Turn off the damned light," I rasped.

In a prim tone, the toady said, "I have my orders."

I assumed Warren and the toady were the same, so personalized my next comment. "You know the first thing I'm going to do when I get free, Warren?"

"That won't happen as long as *I* hold the key to your cuffs," Warren snapped.

"I'm going to shove that light up your ass so it can shine in your eyes for a change."

"That makes no sense," Warren said, his tone snippy.

"I'm saying you already have your head stuck up your ass, you twit." I turned away from the light yet again. "Geez, Jacobson, this one's a real moron. Your taste in yes men is even worse than it was six years ago."

"Shut up, Barrett," Jacobson snapped.

"Go to hell, Jacobson."

Thin, bony fingers grabbed my chin and forced my face back towards the light. "I'm already *in* hell, Barrett. And it's all your fault."

I yanked my head from Jacobson's grip, opened my eyes, squinted at Jacobson through the desk lamp Warren the Toady waved in front of me, and forced my cracked lips to stretch into a grim grin. "I know. Ruining your career is my proudest achievement."

"Hit him!" Jacobson snarled at Warren.

Warren's voice cracked as he mewled. "What?"

"He told you to hit me," I said. "It sounded like an order, Warren, so you'd better hop to it."

Warren put down the lamp, giving me my first good look at

him. The man was milquetoast personified, with thin features almost as sharp as Slick's, but he lacked even Slick's reedy muscles. Warren cocked his fist awkwardly and threw a lame punch at my shoulder.

Without inflection, I said, "Ouch. The pain. The agony. I beg you, stop this torture." I cranked up my grin—that hurt worse than Warren's punch—and turned to Jacobson. His gaunt, gray visage pleased me. The last six years had obviously been harder on Jacobson than they had been on me. "This guy is pathetic, Jacobson."

A bit of Jacobson's old bullying tone entered his voice. "At least *he* knows how to obey orders."

I nodded and fought not to wince at the pain it induced. "True, he punched me. At least *he* isn't a sniveling coward."

Jacobson went rigid and his face paled. "Warren, summon Mr. Houlihan and his friend."

"Yes, be a good boy and do that, Warren," I said. "We wouldn't want Jacobson the Cowardly Commander to get his hands dirty."

Warren turned an earnest and imploring expression on Jacobson. "Sir, Mr. Tate ordered us to find out what Barrett knows about his son's disappearance."

Jacobson backhanded Warren's cheek. "Watch what you say, imbecile."

I gave a rasping laugh. "Like I didn't already know Tate was deeply involved in this."

Warren rubbed his cheek. "Of course Mr. Tate is involved. He wants his son found and safely returned to him."

I leaned as far forward as the restraints allowed. "If that's the case, why has Tate done everything in his power to block an independent investigation of Nick's disappearance?"

Warren stammered, "Because... Um... He, uh..."

I heard a click as the doorknob turned.

"Be quiet," Jacobson snapped, "and go get Mr. Houlihan."

A strong, female voice said, "That won't be necessary."

All eyes turned to the door. An athletic blonde woman in her mid-thirties stood framed in the light from the hallway, a briefcase clutched in her right hand. Without waiting for an invitation, she strode into the room. In the dim recesses of my mind, I recognized the same confident clicking of high heels I'd heard ages ago when an enraged Trouble confronted me in my office.

"Go away, Winters," Jacobson said. "This doesn't concern you."

"It most certainly *does* concern me. I'm Mr. Barrett's attorney." The woman's eyes widened as she neared me. "What happened to my client, and why haven't you summoned a doctor to attend to him?"

"He... had a violent episode," Jacobson said. "My men had to forcibly subdue him."

The woman stopped next to me. "I'm Allie Winters. Miss Tate engaged me to represent you." Cool, gentle fingers raised my hands and my unexpected ally examined them with a critical eye. "Commander Jacobson, Mr. Barrett must have landed many powerful punches to deserve such a severe beating. Would you care to explain why his hands have neither abrasions nor bruises?" She raised her head and leveled a glare at Jacobson. "Give me the names of the officers involved, so I may bring them up on charges of brutality."

Jacobson ignored the question and turned to Warren. "Go find out why that doctor *I told you to summon* isn't here yet."

Jacobson's ploy was so obvious even Warren caught it. He rose and started for the door. "Yes, sir. Right away, sir."

"Don't bother," Allie said. "I'll take him to a doctor when we leave."

Jacobson turned a triumphal smile on Allie. "I'm afraid that's impossible, Winters. Barrett must face charges for his actions onboard the starliner, *Star of Sol*."

Allie put her briefcase on the table, opened it, removed a small stack of papers, and slid them across the table. "Miss Tate repaid the starliner's parent company for the damages, and they withdrew their charges."

Jacobson's shoulders sagged, but he tried another tack. "There's still the matter of the traffic violations this morning."

Allie tossed another sheet of paper on top of the others. "I took the liberty of attending traffic court in my client's stead, pleaded guilty for him, and paid his fine." She glanced at me. "Is that acceptable, Mr. Barrett?"

"Yes," I replied.

Allie snapped her briefcase shut. "Release Mr. Barrett from these manacles."

Stunned at their sudden reversal of fortune, Warren and Jacobson just stared at Allie. So I said, "Warren told me he had the keys."

Allie extended her hand, palm up, to Warren. "Give me the keys." Warren's eyes twitched from Allie's hand to Jacobson and then back to her hand. Allie leaned over the table, stared into Warren's eyes, and snapped, "*Now!*"

The little man jumped, shoved a hand into his pocket, withdrew the keys, and tossed them in Allie's general direction. Allie caught them in midair, and deftly unlocked the cuff holding me to the chair.

I stood, wobbled, and almost dropped into the chair again. Allie caught hold of my arm and steadied me. "Can you walk out of here, Mr. Barrett?"

"I think so."

She kept hold of my arm and guided me out of the interrogation room, down the hallway, and into the station lobby. Trouble and Rach waited for us there, and both rushed to my side when they caught sight of me.

Trouble looped an arm around my waist. "My God, you're in worse shape than I imagined."

She turned her head and glared at someone nearby. I followed her gaze and spotted Hammerhand and Slick reclining on office chairs. Slick studiously ignored us, but Hammerhand smiled into

Trouble's glare. Her expression hardened briefly, then she turned a solicitous expression my way. "Let's get you to a doctor, Travis."

We walked out of Space Patrol headquarters, where we found Sam leaning against Rach's cab. Without a word, he helped the women load me into the backseat. Rach slid behind the wheel and drove us onto the streets of Twi-Town and back to midtown.

twelve
dave's trouble

AS THE CAB left Space Patrol HQ behind, Rach asked, "Where to?"

Allie Winters rattled off an address that meant nothing to me. But Trouble asked, "Is that the address of the closest emergency room?"

"No one in Twi-Town goes to the emergency room if they can avoid it," Allie said.

"You got that right," Rach agreed.

"It's the address of a doctor friend of mine." Allie turned and flashed a professional smile at me. "You'll be in good hands, Mr. Barrett."

I leaned back in the car seat, closed my eyes, blocked out the pain as best I could, and tried to figure out what to do next. Trouble took my hand.

In a soft voice, she said, "I'm sorry, Travis."

I cracked my eyes open and looked at her. "For what? You didn't do this to me."

"Maybe not, but I brought it down on you when I hired you to find Nick."

"That's the life of a PI, Trouble. If it wasn't your father's goons beating me up, it would be someone else."

"I don't think you realize how vindictive Father can be, Travis. He's more ruthless than anyone you've ever faced before."

I shook my head, winced from the fresh pain that caused, and said, "Are you seriously suggesting Norman Tate is more ruthless than the pirates on the *Bloodsword*?"

"When you put it that way, it sounds silly," Trouble said. "But once your battle with the pirates ended, they left you alone. Father will never do that."

"That depends on what we discover when we find Nick."

"How can you be so optimistic after everything you've been through? The beating you got—"

"Means we're getting too close to the truth," I said.

"It does?"

"There's a saying that came out of the Great Interplanetary War. *You know you're over the target when you start catching flak.* In this case, flak means the beating and Jacobson's direct involvement."

"I hadn't thought about it that way." Trouble rested her head on my shoulder. "Thank you, Travis."

"Now that we've got that out of the way," I said, "would someone tell me what happened after Jacobson's men put me in that interrogation room? That was fast work."

"Fast?" Laura asked. "It's been four hours."

I thought about it and decided I must have spent more time cooling my heels than I realized. Then Hammerhand and Slick came in and spent what felt like forever beating me up. I was unconscious for who knew how long before my confrontation with Jacobson and his sycophant. But I left all that unsaid, "There's no clock in the interrogation room. I guess I lost track of time. So, what happened?"

"Rita happened," Trouble said. "The second you ended your call to her, she started searching for attorneys, cross-referencing the results with historical records, news stories, and public case files."

"Typical Rita," I said. "She ignored my instructions to send Dave down with bail money and did things her way."

"Be happy she did," Allie said. "If she'd sent Mr. Hayslett, he would still be trying to get Miss Tate out and you'd be in the middle of a second beating. Your Robosec realized you needed someone who knew the law, not a hotshot pilot with a pocket full of cash."

"Why did she choose you?" I asked.

In a matter-of-fact tone, Allie said, "I was on the prosecution team for Jacobson's court martial, and resigned from Space Patrol when the lead prosecutor accepted the plea deal that let Jacobson keep his rank in exchange for accepting the Twi-Town posting."

"It doesn't sound like you're one of Jacobson's fans," I said. "Why the hell did you hang your shingle in his little fiefdom?"

Allie shrugged. "*Someone* has to defend the citizens of Twi-Town from Jacobson and his cronies."

In a tone of soft reproval, Sam said, "Travis knows that better than anyone in the solar system."

"You're right," Allie said. She took a deep breath, released it, and continued, "Anyway, I accepted your case, came to Patroller HQ, and insisted they charge Miss Tate or release her. Then it was simply a matter of dealing with the complaint from the starline and the traffic violations."

I sighed. "When Rita hears how this turned out, she's going to make another demand for a raise."

"You should give it to her," Trouble said. "And maybe call *her* Trouble. Because she caused a lot of it for Jacobson."

"I already have more Trouble in my life than I can handle. Besides, that would just encourage her to ignore my instructions again." I looked at Sam. "Mentioning ignoring instructions, you're not doing a very good job of distancing yourself from me."

"You're damned right I'm not," Sam growled. "So quit asking me to do it."

"Does *anyone* follow my instructions?" I asked.

"Dave does," Trouble said.

I vented a sigh of pretend exasperation. "That's just great. The only person I can count on to do what I ask him to do is the guy who hates me the most."

Allie shook her head. "Mr. Hayslett doesn't hate you, Mr. Barrett. Not really."

"You could have fooled me," I said. "How do you know Dave?"

"He was the only officer from the *Soteria* crew who could credibly testify against Jacobson in the court martial. I worked closely with him, preparing for it."

"And he told you why he hates me?"

"He told me what his issue is, if that's what you mean."

"Would you care to enlighten me?"

Allie shook her head. "That's not my tale to tell."

"Then I guess I'll never hear it," I said, "because Dave sure isn't telling it."

In a tone of absolute conviction, Allie said, "He will."

"I wish I shared your conviction, Allie."

Rach pulled up in front of a doctor's office in midtown. "We're here."

Sam and Trouble helped me into the office, Laura came with us, and Rach stayed with her cab. Meanwhile, Allie went ahead and dealt with the receptionist. I limped through a half-full waiting room and straight back to an examination room. A nurse chased Sam out, but Trouble insisted on staying with me.

The nurse shrugged. "Then you can save me some work and help him get undressed."

"How undressed?" I asked.

She gave me an appraising look. "Where do you hurt?"

"Everywhere."

"Then Doctor Chalmers will need to examine you everywhere."

The nurse strode from the room as Trouble helped me remove my jacket. I fumbled with my shirt buttons until Trouble gently pushed my hands aside and quickly unbuttoned the shirt.

Breath hissed in through her teeth when she got a look at the scrapes and bruises on my chest and back. She did it again as she pulled my pants off.

Trouble eyed my underwear, cocked an eyebrow, and flashed her devilish smile. The concern in her eyes belied the sentiment, but I played along and said, "I think I'm naked enough for now." The door knob turned. "If the doctor wants me to take my underwear off, he can tell me."

A steel gray haired-woman on the far side of middle-aged entered. "She. And trust me, you don't have anything I haven't already seen a thousand times." The doctor looked me up and down. "Someone really did a number on you, didn't they?"

For the next twenty minutes, Dr. Chalmers poked, prodded, bandaged, stitched, and otherwise put me back together again. When she finished, the doctor turned to Trouble. "He should avoid strenuous activity for at least three days." In a stage whisper, Dr. Chalmers added, "But it's still okay to have sex."

Trouble helped me get dressed as the doctor bustled out to get some medications for me. She returned just as Trouble helped me slide into my jacket and handed two pill bottles to Trouble. "See that he takes them."

Trouble opened her purse and dropped the bottles inside. "Thank you, Dr. Chalmers. How much do we owe you?"

"Nothing. Allie and I have an arrangement. She takes care of my patients who need legal representation, and I take care of her clients who need to see a doctor." She went to the door, but looked back at me. "Please don't be a repeat customer."

I slid from the examining table and only wobbled a bit. "I'll do my best, Dr. Chalmers."

"Thank you," Trouble added.

The doctor nodded once and left.

Trouble wrapped a supporting arm around my waist. "You're not going to take it easy, are you?"

"And let the bad guys get their bearings?" I asked. "Not a chance."

She sighed. "What do you want to do now?"

"How about I buy you a drink?" I tried smiling, discovered it didn't hurt much anymore, and widened it. "After all, it's five o'clock *somewhere* in the solar system."

"What do you hope to find at Forever Five?" Trouble asked. "That *is* where you want to go?"

"Any place your brother likes is good enough for me. And I'm looking for a *who*, not a *what*."

When we entered the waiting room, our three friends rose and followed us out. I caught Laura's eye. "You know Max, the gate guard, right?"

"Sure, he's a good friend."

"Would you call and invite him to join us at Forever Five for a drink? I need to ask him a few questions."

"Questions about what?" Allie asked.

"You don't want to know," I said.

"Probably not," she agreed, "but tell me anyway."

"I want his advice on crime, Counselor, and the best way to commit one."

"What kind of crime do you want to commit?" I'd half-expected an outburst of objections from Allie, so her conversational tone surprised me. The corners of her lips quirked up. "Did you expect hysterical protests, Mr. Barrett?"

"Hysteria? No." I said. "Protests? Yes."

"Will well-reasoned protests—of which I have many—deter you?" She asked.

"No."

"Then why should I waste my time and yours offering objections you will ignore?"

"That is an excellent point," I said.

Allie nodded. "I know."

I opened the rear door to Rach's cab. Laura, Trouble, and I slid into the back seat, while Sam and Allie climbed into the front seat. Rach looked over her shoulder at us. "Where to?"

"Forever Five," I said.

Laura pulled a comm from her purse and tapped a code. "Hey Max, it's Laura... We're okay." Her eyes darted to my battered face. "Mostly okay, anyway... Mr. Barrett has some questions... What? Oh, right. Mr. Barrett is the gentleman who came with Trouble, um, I mean Miss Tate, to the office today... Anyway, can you meet us at Forever Five? Mr. Barrett wants to ask you some questions... Yes, it has to do with Nick. Max, Nick didn't go home like we thought. He's dis..." Laura's voice caught, and she blinked furiously. "Nick disappeared. Miss Tate and Mr. Barrett came here to find him... Okay, we'll see you soon."

Laura disconnected the call. Took a deep breath and said, "He'll meet us there."

I extended my hand towards Laura. "Could I borrow your comm?" As she put her comm in my hand, I gave her own hand a gentle squeeze. "We're going to find Nick."

She gave an uncertain nod. "If you say so, Mr. Barrett."

"You know you can call him Travis." Trouble looked at the front seat. "The same applies to you, Allie."

"Hey, what about me?" Rach asked, glancing at the rearview screen.

Trouble arched an eyebrow. "Do you think you need permission to call Travis by his first name?"

"Hell no." Rach grinned. "Heh. I gotta say, you ain't nothing like the usual rich bitches I get ridin' in my cab."

I tuned out the chatter around me as I entered the code for Dave's hotel room. "Hello, Rita."

"Boss!" she said. "You've been out of touch a long time. Are you okay?"

"I'm a little banged up, nothing more. Hey, good job finding Allie Winters, by the way. That was a stroke of genius."

Rita fed a sniff sound effect to her vocoder. "It's about time you figured that out, Boss. Does that mean I finally get a raise?"

"Yes, that means you get a raise."

"What?" A suspicious tone entered her voice. "You're not joking, are you?"

"I'm serious, Rita. You earned it."

"Are you sure Tate's goons didn't break your brain or something, Boss?"

"My brain is as good as ever, Rita."

"That bad, huh?"

"I love you, too. We'll discuss details of your raise later. Have you had any luck tracking Nick's spending?"

"Yes, and no. His credit expenses are easy enough to trace. But he withdrew a thousand dollars in cash the day before he disappeared. It's going to be tough finding out what he did with the cash."

"Do the best you can, Rita."

"I will, Boss."

"I need to talk to Dave. Can you put him on?"

Five seconds later, Dave's surly voice said, "What?"

"I need you for a planning session."

"Lucky me."

"We're meeting at a bar called Forever Five."

"You buying?"

I sighed. "Yes, Dave, I'm buying."

"I'm on my way."

The sky brightened as Rach drove us from the depths of Twi-Town's dark side and into the city's light side. Fifteen minutes after we crossed into the light side of town, Rach pulled up in front of Forever Five. Garish neon sculptures dotted the front of the bar, their blinking lights all but invisible under the sun's glare.

The long ride across town made my abused muscles feel stiff. I winced, climbing from the cab. Once clear, I gave a cautious stretch, and said, "Rach, please park the cab and join us inside?"

Surprise registered on her face. "Uh, sure. Be there in a minute."

The five of us entered Forever Five. The interior lighting was dimmer than outdoors but brighter than your typical bar. Four-person tables dotted an open floor, and high-backed booths lined three walls. A long bar made of what looked like genuine wood stretched across the fourth wall. An impressive array of liquor bottles filled a line of shelves behind the bar. Above the shelves was a display of several dozen clocks, each one labeled with a planet and time zone. Small spotlights shined on the clocks displaying the five o'clock hour.

Since the display wasn't new to Laura, her gaze swept the room and locked on a booth in the far corner. "Max got here ahead of us. He's got the biggest table in the place."

We threaded our way through the tables to the far corner, where Max sat. He must have come straight from work, since he still wore his guard's uniform. Max stood as we approached enveloped Laura in a friendly hug, and then turned his attention to us. "Hello again, Miss Tate."

"Didn't I tell you to call me Tina?" She glanced at me. "But you should probably just skip that and call me Trouble. Because I think we're going to cause a lot of it for you."

As Trouble slid into the booth, Max extended his hand to me. "Hello, Mr. Barrett. It's good to see you again, sir."

I shook his hand. "You should skip the mister and the sir and just call me Travis like everyone else."

Max nodded and, without a hint of irony, said, "If you say so, sir."

Rach joined us as I introduced Sam and Allie, so I included her, and we all settled into the booth. We tapped drink orders into the interactive menu, and just before I submitted the order, Dave showed up. I gave him an inquiring look. "Scotch on the rocks?"

He slid into a seat next to Sam. "What else?"

"For those who don't know him," I said, "this is Dave Hayslett."

Sam's eyes widened. "The pilot from the *Soteria*?" When I nodded, Sam grabbed Dave's hand and pumped it enthusiastically. "After Travis here, you're the man I most wanted to meet. Thank you!"

Dave stared at Sam in confusion, so I said, "Sam and his wife were on the *Euphoria*."

Sam beamed a wide smile. "I can't thank you and Travis enough for your heroism and—"

Dave yanked his hand from Sam's grip and stumbled from the booth. A haunted look filled Dave's eyes before he turned and ran for the door.

A stricken expression spread over Sam's face. "What did I say wrong?"

"Nothing, Sam," I said, standing. "I'll go talk to Dave."

Sam rose, too. "I'll come with you. Maybe if I apologized—?"

Allie caught Sam's arm and pulled him down. "No, that will only make things worse. Let Travis handle this."

I offered what I hoped was a reassuring smile to Sam, then followed Dave. Pushing through the door, I squinted into the perpetual late afternoon glare outside. I shielded my eyes with one hand while my gaze swept the surrounding area, looking for Dave. Five seconds later, I spotted him heading for the bar's small parking lot. With his head down, his hands jammed into his jacket pockets, and his shambling stride, Dave looked like dejection personified.

I ran after him, and Dave obviously heard me approaching. He stopped, tilted his head back as if he was looking at the sky, and asked, "How could you do that to me?"

I stopped five feet from him. "Do *what* to you?"

Dave spun, pointed at Forever Five, and glowered at me. "How could you let that man ambush me like that? Or was that your idea of a joke?"

"I don't know what the hell you're talking about, Dave."

"Do you honestly expect me to believe that?"

"Yes."

"God, Barrett, are you truly that stupid?"

"Apparently."

Dave snorted in disgust, turned, and resumed walking. "Some detective *you* turned out to be."

I hurried after him and matched strides when I caught up. "It's hard to detect anything when I don't have any clues." Dave remained silent, so I forged on. "Six years ago, I had the closest friend a man could hope for, one I could trust with my most guarded secrets. We did everything together, and he even served as my first officer when I landed my first command.

"Then I defied a direct order to withdraw, lost half my crew, lost my ship, lost my career in Space Patrol, and lost my best friend." I glanced at Dave, looking for a reaction. He kept his eyes locked on the ground and said nothing. With a mental shrug, I continued. "I understand and accept the reasons most of those things happened."

We walked in silence for another ten seconds, then I said, "I know you hate me more than anything in the solar system. I just don't understand *why*. Maybe if I knew that…" I almost choked on my suddenly dry throat. "I might not miss my friend so much."

Dave stopped walking, and his breath came in gasps. I stood next to him, unsure of what to do next. The answer to my greatest unsolved mystery felt tantalizingly close, and my breath quickened as I racked my brains for the words that would unlock the answer Dave kept bottled up inside him.

A soft, feminine voice spoke from behind us. "You have to tell him, Dave." Trouble was quiet for a moment, then continued, "It's bad enough that you torture yourself, Dave. Do you have to torture Travis, too?"

Dave shook his head, and Trouble said, "Good. I'm going back inside now. I hope you'll *both* join us when you finish talking."

I looked over my shoulder at Trouble's receding figure, then looked back at Dave. After a long wait, he said, "I don't hate you, Barrett. At least, not the way you think I do."

A glib response popped into my head. I forced it down and waited for Dave to continue. Finally, he said, "I hate what I see whenever I see you."

"Since it's me you're seeing—"

Dave gave a violent shake of his head. "I'm saying it wrong. Whenever I see you, it reminds me of just how pathetic *I* am."

I opened my mouth, realized I didn't know how to respond to Dave's statement, and said, "I don't understand."

Dave vented a long sigh. "Do you know what I would have done if I'd been in command of the *Soteria* instead of you six years ago?"

With absolute conviction, I said, "You'd have done the same thing I did."

In a voice so soft, I barely heard him, Dave said, "I'd have obeyed orders."

Certain I'd misheard, I asked, "What?"

Dave looked at me with anguish and self-loathing shining in his eyes, and shouted, "I'd have obeyed Jacobson's order to withdraw!"

I shook my head. "No, you wouldn't, Dave. Don't you remember all those late night bull sessions at the academy, when we hashed out how we'd respond in situations like that? You and I were always on the same page."

"We were just stupid cadets, Barrett."

"Sure, but I saw the look in your eyes back then. You weren't lying."

"No, I was just *wrong*." Dave looked into my eyes. "Don't you get it, Barrett? I thought we were the most fearless pair of cadets to go through the academy. Heroes in waiting. Legends in the making. And *you* were." He closed his eyes. "But not me... I was such a coward, I was too afraid to even know myself. It took the *Bloodsword* to show me my true self."

"No, that can't—"

"Dammit, Barrett, I was about to get up from the helm and relieve you of command. Then the gunnery crew said, *we're with you, skipper*, and I was so afraid I'd look like the coward I truly was that I didn't do it."

Still unwilling to accept Dave's word, I said, "Then how do you explain your piloting? Everyone knows more people would have died without it. Space Patrol even gave you a medal for heroism!"

In a voice tight with emotion, Dave said, "I only cared about two things during that battle—saving my own skin and not looking like a coward. I wasn't heroic. I didn't care about the *Euphoria*. I didn't even care about the rest of the crew."

We stared at each other for a long time. Then I asked, "And when you see me?"

"You forcibly remind me of what I am." Dave hung his head. "I don't hate *you*, Travis. I hate who you make me see whenever you're around. And that guy I see? Oh God, I hate him. More than anything else in the solar system, I hate him."

I stared at Dave for what felt like hours, resisting the impulse to apologize for how I made him feel. Finally, I said, "Could I borrow your comm?"

Dave looked up in surprise. "What?"

"Your comm. Could I borrow it?"

He shrugged and handed it to me. I tapped in Rita's code. When she answered, I said, "Hi Rita, it's Travis. I need you to do something for me."

"Sure thing, Boss. Whatcha need?"

"Sign the *Lightning's Hand* over to Dave. He'll be there in a little while to collect it."

"Are you crazy, Boss? We still need a ride off this crummy world."

"We'll book passage on a spaceliner. Just... Just do as I asked, Rita."

"If you're sure you wanna do that, Boss."

"I am. Give him two thousand dollars for wages, too."

"I think you're going too far, Boss."

"Just do it, Rita." I closed the connection and handed the comm back to Dave. "You're free to go."

He stuffed the comm in his pocket. "Good."

Without another word, Dave Hayslett turned and walked out of my life.

trouble in the lab

I **DON'T KNOW** how long I stood outside Forever Five staring after Dave, because my mind wasn't on Mercury anymore. I remembered the long-ago day when a brash Space Patrol Academy plebe burst into my dorm room and introduced himself as my roommate.

I remembered Dave's certainty that every woman in a club wanted him, and every guy envied him. And most of them did.

I remembered the way his fingers danced over a spaceship's controls. Our instructors called him a once-in-a-generation talent.

I remembered my elation when he accepted my offer to join me on the *Soteria* and serve as my first officer. How his incredible piloting during a dozen space rescues tipped the balance from death to life for more travelers than I could count, including the four hundred and seven souls on board the *Euphoria*.

And through it all, the spark that made Dave the man he was blazed ever brighter. Until I disobeyed orders and smothered Dave's spark.

Arms wrapped around me and pulled me back to the present. "It's not your fault, Travis." Trouble rested her head on my shoulder and squeezed me. "I don't know what Dave told you, but I know the look in your eyes. You're blaming yourself for it."

"I broke my best friend, Trouble."

"No, you didn't... If you had known everything Dave just told you, when the *Euphoria* called for help six years ago, would you have acted differently?"

"No." A thought crossed my mind. "Maybe I'd have put someone else on the helm instead of Dave."

"Would that have helped Dave?"

"I... don't think so."

"Would it have helped the *Euphoria* or the *Soteria*?"

"No."

"How about the *Bloodsword*? Would it have helped the pirates if Dave wasn't at the helm?"

I nodded.

Trouble lifted her head and leveled her blue-eyed gaze at me. "You did the best you could with the situation you had. So stop beating yourself up over things that were beyond your control."

I sighed. "I'll try."

"I'll help." Trouble leaned in and kissed me gently on the lips. "Let's go back inside and figure out how to make trouble for my father."

I turned my thoughts from Dave. "You forgot about finding Nick."

"No, I didn't. Because finding Nick will cause more trouble for Father than anything else I can imagine."

A moment later, Trouble and I rejoined our friends in the corner booth. Sam still wore a hangdog expression and asked, "Is Dave coming back?"

No matter what Dave thought of himself, I refused to tarnish his reputation. So I did something I swore I'd never do. I lied. "No, but it's not your fault, Sam. You resemble a chief petty officer who took Dave under his wing during Dave's first posting. He died in a training accident."

Sam's brows furrowed. "Oh, I see..."

I felt certain he was giving my lie more thought than my lie could withstand, so I changed the subject. I forced my lips into a conspiratorial smile. "I suppose you're all wondering why I called you here?"

My cliché line drew polite laughs, which was more than it deserved. I turned to Sam and asked, "Do you have access to a metallurgy lab, and do you know how to analyze samples?"

"Yes, to both. Why?"

"Hang on." I turned to Max. "Did anyone fill you in on the situation while I was outside?"

Max nodded. "Laura and Miss- um, and Trouble told me everything. I'm on board for whatever you're planning."

"Even if my plan will cost you your job?"

"It wouldn't be the first time I've lost a job." Max flashed an infectious grin. "Why do you think I ended up on Mercury?"

I shook my head in mock disapproval and, curious if Max would take it, fed him a straight line. "And here I thought you were a smart young man."

Max took it. "No, sir, I'm a smart*ass* young man. Employers don't seem to value that in their employees."

"Their loss." I turned serious. "Before you agree to help, just remember that losing your job on Mercury won't be like losing your job elsewhere. You could end up living in a dark side alley or, God forbid, in the Twi-Line wastes."

Max shook his head. "Not me. If everything goes to hell, I've saved enough money to buy passage off this rock."

I glanced at Laura, Sam, and Allie. "The same applies to the three of you. Especially you, Laura."

A determined expression spread over Laura's face. "I'm not leaving Mercury until Nick can leave with me."

Sam growled, "You already know my answer, and it's not going to change. So stop asking."

I turned to Allie. "Attorney-client privilege only goes so far, and I'm pretty sure it doesn't include the commission of crimes."

"It doesn't," Allie said. "Am I correct in assuming you plan on taking something from the Tate Steelworks compound?"

I nodded. "A sample of a new alloy steel."

Allie turned to Trouble. "Do you own a percentage of Tate Steelworks?"

"Twenty-six percent, the same as Nick. Father owns the rest." Trouble shrugged. "Father did it for tax purposes."

Allie turned back to me. "Unless Miss Tate signed confidentiality agreements, I can make a quite compelling argument that, as a minority owner of the company, she is entitled to remove items from company grounds."

"I've never signed anything associated with the business." Trouble looked at me. "Now that you've tried to run us off and failed, what are you planning on doing?"

"I want to take a sample of the new alloy, give it to Sam, and have him analyze it."

"Yes, we already figured that part out," Trouble said. "What *else* are you going to do while we're in the compound?"

"What makes you think—?" I broke off when Trouble cocked her head and gave me an are-you-kidding-me expression. I sighed. "I'm going to search the company records for property it owns outside of the compound."

"Do you think that will tell us where they're holding Nick?" she asked.

"Your father strikes me as a micromanager, at least in matters like this. Do you agree?"

Trouble nodded. "He'd want to keep Nick somewhere he controlled."

"Good." I leaned forward, more for dramatic effect than anything else, and said, "Here's what we're going to do."

WE LEFT FOREVER FIVE, and went to Rach's cab. Everyone except Allie and I piled into the cab.

Allie shook my hand. "I hope you don't need me again, but your Robosec has my direct number if you do."

"Trust me, the last thing I want is to find myself back in

Jacobson's custody." I resisted the urge to massage my still-aching ribs. "Are you sure we can't give you a ride somewhere?"

"I'll catch the next bus." She turned away, but glanced back over her shoulder. "As your attorney, I advise against this course of action. As your friend, I say go get 'em."

I flashed a thumbs up, then joined the others in the car.

Rach drove towards the Tate Steelworks compound. She stopped just out of sight of the gate into the compound. Max climbed out and vanished into the perpetual gloom of the Twi-Line's dark side. Trouble and I took advantage of the stop to switch places. I slid into the middle seat and she took the seat next to the door. While we gave Max five minutes to get into position, Trouble straightened her clothes, checked her makeup, hiked her already-short skirt up, and opened her blouse halfway down to her navel.

Trouble looked at me through lidded eyes and quirked the left corner of her mouth up in a seductive smirk. She pulled her shoulders back, emphasizing her already-enticing cleavage, and, in a husky voice, asked, "How do I look, Travis?"

My eyes roamed over Trouble's body. It took willpower to force my gaze up to her eyes. "I, ah, wanted you to distract the guard, not strip for him."

Trouble turned off her smoldering expression, relaxed her posture, and laughed. "Really, Travis, this is conservative compared to what I usually wear to clubs."

I inclined my head and offered a faint, "Oh."

In the front seat, Rach cackled. "From the expression on Barrett's face, I think you got the right look going on, Troub."

Trouble turned her attention from me and to the front seat. As large parts of my brain began working again, she asked, "Troub?"

"I ain't whatcha call big on using full names. I went from Rachel to Rach, so you go from Trouble to Troub. Same sound dumped both times. S'all right?"

Trouble nodded. "S'all right."

Sam checked his watch. "Isn't it time we moved out?"

Without waiting for confirmation, Rach put the cab in gear and drove the remaining quarter mile to the Tate Steelworks compound. As before, a single guard stood just inside the closed gate. His hand went to the blaster at his side as the cab pulled up to the gate, but he didn't draw it.

Trouble rolled down her window, stuck her head out, smiled brightly, and said, "Open the gate, please."

The guard's hand dropped away from his holstered blaster, but shook his head. "I can't do that, ma'am."

Trouble's eyebrows drew down, and her voice sharpened. "Do you know who I am?"

Tension made the guard's nod jerky. "Yes, ma'am."

"I don't think you do," Trouble said, "or you'd have used my name."

With reluctance, the guard said, "You're Miss Tate."

"Tate, you say?" Trouble tapped her lips with one finger. "Now, why is that name so familiar? Oh yes, because it's on the company sign over the gate!" Trouble pointed to the company logo. "You *can* read, can't you?"

I almost felt sorry for the guard, as he gave a miserable nod. "Yes, ma'am."

"Then I demand you open this gate and let me into *my* company."

"I have orders not to, ma'am."

"From whom?"

"The director, Mr. Graham."

Trouble looked up at the sign again. "*His* name doesn't appear on the sign. *Mine* does. What does that suggest to you?"

"I'm sorry, ma'am, but—"

Trouble gave an imperious wave of summons to the guard. "I tire of shouting at you. Come over here."

"Mr. Graham ordered me to stay inside the fence and keep the gate closed, ma'am."

Trouble growled in frustration, threw open the car door, and climbed from the cab. Behind the cover of the door, she tugged her skirt higher, and then strode to the gate. When she got there, Trouble put her hands on her hips and bent over from the waist to bring her face as close as possible to the guard's face. And to give the guard a clear look down her blouse.

The guy wouldn't have been human if his eyes hadn't snapped to Trouble's chest. Most men would have immediately dragged their gaze back to her face. Since we didn't want him doing that, Trouble gave an angry bounce. Breasts jiggled. The guard's gaze remained riveted down Trouble's shirt.

So he never noticed Max run his employee ID past the badge reader at the employee entrance next to the gate. He never heard the soft beep as the door unlocked. He never saw Max slip through the door. He never heard Max glide up behind him. He never knew Max was even there until Max pulled the guard's blaster from its holster and pressed it into the his back.

"I think you should open the gate, Tom."

Two minutes later, we had Tom bound and gagged on the floor of the gatehouse, and Max standing in his place. Max gave me Tom's blaster and his building keycard. "This will get you through any door in the compound. But I don't know the code for the lab, much less the combination to the safe inside."

I slid the card into my pocket. "One problem at a time, Max."

Max shook my hand. "Be careful in there. I'm going to need good references to land another job. So don't get killed or anything."

I gave a short laugh. "I'll do my best."

We left the gate and headed deeper into the compound.

———

THE TATE COMPOUND'S administration building blazed with lights, a warning beacon in the forever-twilight found on the wrong side of the Twi-Line. I turned to Laura and said, "Please tell me the metallurgy lab isn't there?"

"Director Graham can't abide the odor of smelting metal," she said. "Moving the lab far away from the admin building was the first thing he did after he got here. It had to be done fast, because Mr. Graham wouldn't adjust the lab's schedule, so almost everyone on the payroll pitched in and worked through all three shifts for two days to get the move done." She grimaced. "We got some sleep, then had to work three more shifts just to catch up on the work we put on hold to move the lab."

"Was the HR director out there cracking a whip to get you to work faster?" I asked. "From my one run-in with Hodges, that seems like something she would do."

"And risk getting her hands dirty?" Laura asked, as her lips spread into a sardonic smile. "No way."

"That's a stupid way to run a business," Trouble said. "I can't believe my father allowed that. He is many things, but stupid isn't one of them."

Laura shrugged. "Mr. Graham said his orders came directly from Mr. Tate, and getting the metallurgical research project back on schedule was his number one task." She leaned over the front seat. "Take the next left, Rach."

Rach did as Laura instructed and we left the admin building behind. Two turns and three minutes later, Rach backed her cab into a dark alley between a warehouse and the building housing the metallurgy lab. She looked over her shoulder at me. "You want me to stay here and keep the engine runnin'?"

"That sounds like a good idea."

"I'll blow the horn if anyone unwanted turns up, too."

"Sure. It worked well enough last time."

"Don't bother," Laura said. "Graham had the lab sound-proofed, in case another steel company tried listening in with some kind of super spy tech stuff. It's paranoid, I know."

"Not really." Sam spoke for the first time since the cab entered the Tate compound. "According to my new boss, Astra Steel already tried it and failed."

We climbed from the car, and Laura led us to the lab's

entrance. Trouble walked beside Laura, so Sam and I fell in behind them. Laura ran her employee keycard through the reader. It flashed red, and the door remained locked.

She turned wide eyes on Trouble. "My card doesn't work anymore."

"I'm sorry, Laura," Trouble said. "Talking to me may have cost you your job."

I pulled out the card Max gave me and held it to the reader. It worked when Max used it at the employee entrance next to the gate, and he said it would get me through any door in the compound. I still breathed a sigh of relief when the reader flashed green. Laura opened the door and we filed inside.

A hallway stretched out before us, and Laura set off down it. There were three doors on the left side—Laura said they led to clerical offices—and then the hall took a right turn. In a quiet voice, she said, "The entrance to the lab is around that corner, about fifty feet down."

I kept my voice low. "You said it's guarded. Is the guard in the hallway?" Laura nodded, and I asked, "I assume he's armed?" She nodded again. I drew the blaster Max had given me. "You'd better let me take the lead."

Trouble put a hand against my chest when I started around Laura and her. "Let me lead the way, Travis. I'm one of the company owners, after all."

"That guard will have the same orders as the one at the gate. There's no way he's going to let you into the lab."

"Maybe not, but he won't shoot me, either." She turned a pointed look on the blaster in my hand. "Or he won't if he doesn't feel threatened."

I took the hint and put the gun away. "Okay, but all bets are off if he draws his gun."

Trouble's hand dipped into her purse and emerged holding the blaster she'd pulled out in her long-ago first visit to my office. She flashed a tight smile. "Then we'll see which one of us shoots him first."

I nodded, watched Trouble return the gun to her purse, and didn't tell her that the first thing I'd do was shove her and Laura out of the line of fire. Shooting the guard came in a distant second to ensuring their safety.

Then we rounded the corner and got our first look at the entrance to the metallurgy lab. The guard lounged in front of a steel door and stared at the wall in front of him. His head snapped our way, and he examined us with a sharp-eyed stare. He didn't go for his gun, but he pushed away from the door, turned our way, and let his right hand drop next to the blaster holstered on his hip.

Recognition flashed in the guard's eyes when he saw Laura. "You're not allowed in here anymore, Laura."

Laura's pace faltered, but Trouble never slowed. I guess that helped Laura steel her nerves, because she hurried back to Trouble's side, and even matched Trouble's stride.

"She is here at my request," Trouble said.

The man's eyes widened when he realized who was with Laura. "I'm sorry, Miss Tate, but you're not allowed in here either."

"On whose orders?"

"Mr. Graham's."

Trouble stopped five feet from the guard, cocked her head, and said, "Graham is an *employee*. I am his *employer*."

The guard's expression remained neutral. "I understand that, Miss Tate. But Mr. Graham is speaking for your father."

Trouble crossed her arms. "Did my father tell you that, himself?"

The guard shook his head. "No, ma'am."

"Did Graham show you a vid of my father giving that order?"

"He didn't, ma'am."

"How about a voice recording?" When the guard shook his head, she continued, "Did he even show you an email?" When he shook his head again, Trouble began tapping her foot. "Then how do you know my father gave such an order?"

"Mr. Graham told me he had."

"Oh, come on, Art," Laura said. "Do you remember all the stuff Graham told us when he first got here last year? He fed us a load of crap about why this lab had to be moved, then it turned out he just didn't like the smell! Are you really going to take his word over the word of an actual Tate who's *standing right in front of you*?"

Indecision entered Art's expression for the first time. "Mr. Graham—"

"Is a jerk," Laura said.

Art ignored her interruption and pressed on. "He said you were trying to undermine the company's work, Miss Tate."

"I'm *trying* to find my brother," Trouble said. "If doing that means undermining the company's work, so be it."

Confusion filled Art's eyes. "Nick went home nearly two weeks ago, Miss Tate."

Trouble shook her head. "No, Art, he didn't. He disappeared, and I know he never left Mercury." She pointed at the steel door. "And I think whatever is behind that door will tell me *why*."

Art looked at Laura, who said, "I haven't had a comm from Nick since he supposedly left to go home. Does that sound like him?"

"No." Art turned introspective. "I mean, why would he ignore the woman he's going to marry?"

Laura's posture stiffened. "Marry?"

From his casual shrug, Art didn't realize how big of a bombshell he'd just dropped on Laura. "He told me he was going to ask you before he left. Didn't he do it?"

"No, Art," Laura leaned forward, "because he *never left*!"

Trouble stepped up to Art, put a hand on his arm, and said, "Will you please let us in, so we can find Nick?"

Without another word, Art ran his keycard, entered the code, and opened the door.

THE FIRST THING that hit me after the guard opened the door to the metallurgy lab was a wave of nostalgia. The odor of molten metal mixed with Trouble's perfume and took me back to that ancient time six days ago, before all this began.

When I was beneath the notice of the Norman Tates of the solar system.

When Hammerhand Houlihan was just another failed boxer.

When my ribs didn't grind and grate with every breath.

When I led a Trouble-free life.

When I was an emotional pauper, so impoverished I didn't know what my life lacked.

I swallowed the lump in my throat, forced my attention back to the present, and followed Trouble through the door.

A dozen people wearing burn-resistant lab coats, thick gloves, and goggles bustled about the lab. All but four of them hovered over miniaturized equipment—smelters, industrial drills, and even a welder encased in a vacuum chamber. The remaining four stood around a cluster of four screens. Those four weren't wearing goggles or gloves, and three of them listened intently as the fourth, an older man with graying hair and a demanding manner, lectured them. The noise inside the lab made it impossible to understand his words, but I had no trouble picking up his sharp tone of voice.

No one noticed our entrance, nor heard Trouble ask, "Who's in charge here?"

I glanced around, spotted a bank of light switches next to the door, and flicked the lights off and on again. That got everyone's attention, and a dozen pairs of eyes turned our way.

"Thank you, Travis," Trouble said, without looking my way. "Now that I have—"

The older man's face reddened. He turned an icy glare on us and snapped, "Get out of my lab this instant!"

Trouble folded her arms, which is never a good sign, and said, "Excuse me?"

"Guard?" the man called. "I don't know why you let these

people in, but if you want to keep your job, you'll escort them out this instant!"

Trouble's hips canted to the left. "I'll have you know—"

Still unaware of his danger, the man interrupted her again. "I doubt you possess any knowledge which I would find remotely interesting." He glanced back at the door. "Guard!"

"Dr. Garrison," another man said, "I think—"

"There's a first time for everything, Zelinsky," Garrison snapped. He turned back to Trouble. "I am in charge here, and—"

Trouble followed Garrison's lead and interrupted him. "Not anymore, you're not."

Garrison's eyes narrowed. "What?"

"You're fired."

"You can't do that!"

Trouble looked over her shoulder. "Art, please escort Dr. Garrison from the premises."

Art entered the lab and, in a loud voice, said, "Yes, of course, *Miss Tate.*"

I'll say this for Garrison. Trouble's name did not cow him. In a pedantic tone, he said, "I answer only to Director Graham."

Trouble's foot began tapping. "Are you seriously suggesting that a facility's director outranks an owner of the company?"

Garrison sniffed. "Your *father* owns the company."

"No, Father owns forty-eight percent of the company. My brother and I each own twenty-six percent."

"I have a contract!"

"I'll buy it out."

Art took Garrison by the arm. "Please come with me, Dr. Garrison."

The reality of the situation still hadn't gotten past Garrison's arrogance. He swatted at Art's hand. "I demand you release me at once!"

Art tightened his grip. "What should I do with him, Miss Tate?"

"Relieve him of all company equipment, including his badge. Then escort him to his car and see that he leaves the compound."

"I do not own a car," Garrison snapped.

The man who tried to warn Garrison muttered, "He makes *us* pick him up and take him home every day."

"For that," Garrison said, "*you* will drive me home, Zelinsky. Get your things."

"Mr. Zelinsky has better things to do than play taxi for you," Trouble said. "As does everyone else here."

"How do you expect me to get home?" Garrison asked.

Trouble waved off Garrison's complaint. "Call a cab or wait for the next bus."

"But I never carry money."

Trouble shrugged. "Then you can walk."

Art rubbed the back of his neck. "This part of town is more dangerous than normal, Miss Tate."

She stared at Garrison for five seconds, then said, "Fine. He may wait in the hallway with you, Art. If he gives you *any* trouble, drag him to the gate."

"Yes, ma'am," Art said, and led Garrison from the lab.

Trouble's gaze swept the lab's remaining occupants. "Does anyone else have any objections?" Eleven heads shook, so Trouble looked at Sam. "Sam, what do you need to perform your analysis?"

Sam considered her question. "Some of the new alloy steel, obviously. And if we can get a sample of the unknown element, that would be great."

Trouble turned back to the lab workers. "You heard what my friend needs. Please provide it."

Pieces of the alloy were easy to come by. Chunks of the stuff were scattered over every flat surface in the lab.

Sam happily gathered four or five pieces of the steel. "These should do." He glanced around the room. "Where's the element that makes this stuff so special?"

Zelinsky pointed to a large safe in the far corner. "It's all kept in there. And Garrison is the only one of us who knows the combination."

A woman who had been running an industrial drill raised her goggles and looked at Sam. "What do you want the sample for?"

"I want to analyze it." Sam shrugged, "It may not help—"

"It won't," the woman said. "I already analyzed it, and am more confused now than I was before the analysis."

The remaining lab workers stared at the woman, and one said, "Garrison gave strict orders not to analyze that stuff!"

The woman shrugged. "I know."

Sam asked, "What did your analysis tell you? Can you identify the element?"

"That's what's so confusing," the woman said. "It's not an element."

Trouble raised her eyebrows. "What kind of mineral is it, then? Please spell it out for those of us without your background."

"It's not a mineral at all," she replied. "It's biological."

The blood drained from Trouble's face. "You're sure the sample was organic?" The woman who had dropped the bombshell nodded. Trouble drew a shuddering breath, closed her eyes as if steeling herself, and asked, "Is it... human?"

"No, definitely not," the lab tech replied.

"It couldn't be," another tech said, "because the samples look and feel like a rock."

Trouble opened her eyes, blinked twice, and then turned to me. "Travis, would you bring Garrison back in here?"

Fifteen seconds later, Art and I held the still-defiant former lab manager in front of Trouble. She pointed at the safe. "Open it."

Garrison flashed a supercilious smile. "No."

Trouble's eyes ignited. "Do as I ask, or—"

Garrison sneered. "Or what? You'll fire me?"

"There are worse things than merely losing a job."

"And you have already balked at doing them," Garrison said, "otherwise I'd be outside the compound's gate right now."

Trouble's gaze turned imploring. "I'm just trying to get my brother back."

Garrison sniffed. "I couldn't care less about your brother." Garrison's smile turned triumphant. "You simply aren't ruthless enough to do anything worse than you already have."

I shook him. "*She* isn't, but *I* am." Garrison ignored me, so I turned to Trouble. "Would you and the others please wait outside for a moment?"

The techs immediately began filing out, providing mute testimony to their feelings towards their former boss. Trouble put a gentle hand on my arm. "Please don't sink to Hammerhand's level."

I patted her hand. "I think he deserves a good beating, but I promise I won't give him one."

With a hesitant nod, she followed the others into the hallway. Art closed the door behind him, leaving Garrison alone with me.

He immediately declared, "You can't frighten me. The Tate girl is too soft to let you do anything truly dangerous to me."

I pointed at a door labeled EMERGENCY EXIT, in the far corner of the lab. "That goes outside, right?"

Confused by the change in topic, Garrison said, "What difference does—?"

"Does it, or doesn't it?"

"Yes, but—"

"Good. That way, we can leave without Miss Tate's knowledge or objections." I pulled out my comm and made a call. "Hi Rach... Yeah, we got in. I have a quick question for you. How much would you charge to drive me out to the Twi-Line wastes to drop someone off?" Garrison's eyes widened. I smiled at him, covered the comm's mic, and murmured, "Good news. She's charging less than I thought she would." I removed my hand from the mic. "Uh huh... Sounds good, Rach. There's an emergency exit from the lab that opens to the outside... One minute?"

Garrison gave an inarticulate cry and ran to the safe. With shaking hands, he tapped the combination into the electronic keypad. A mechanical *thunk* sounded, and Garrison pulled the door open.

"Never mind, Rach," I said. "It looks like I won't need that ride after all... Yeah, sorry about the lost income."

I walked to the safe, propped the door open with a stool, dragged Garrison back to the door to the hallway, and opened it. I pushed Garrison in Art's direction. "He's all yours again, Art." I smiled at Trouble. "The safe is open."

"He's a madman!" Garrison cried. "He threatened to take me to the wastes and leave me there! *Me!*"

Zelinsky laughed. "I've dreamed of doing that to Garrison."

"Me, too," said the woman who analyzed the sample.

As the other techs added their own daydreams for doing away with their former boss, Trouble looked at me. "What would you have done if Garrison hadn't given in?"

I met her gaze. "Just what I said I'd do. I wouldn't have enjoyed doing it, but this situation got a lot more serious when I learned the alloy's secret ingredient isn't a mineral. There's a lot more at stake than a missing brother."

"You can say that again," Sam said.

Trouble looked back and forth between us. "I don't understand what you're getting at."

I turned to the woman who performed the analysis. "Miss, um...?"

"Taylor," she said. "But call me Debra."

I led the way to the safe. "Debra, the samples look more like rocks than anything biological. Do they burn at high temperatures?"

"No, they melt," Debra said. "At two hundred and forty-six degrees, to be exact."

"Have you ever heard of a biological sample that did that?" I asked.

"That melts? No, but biology isn't my field, either." She

paused, then added, "The earliest samples we got came pre-melted, though." She grimaced. "They came packed in portable ovens that were heavy, hot as hell, and just a colossal pain in the ass to deal with."

"Why bother with portable ovens at all?" I asked. "I mean, you could just melt them here, right?"

Debra shrugged. "We asked Garrison, but he just told us to do our jobs and leave the questions to those intelligent enough to understand the answers. That pissed me off no end, which is why I went behind his back and analyzed the samples."

Trouble said, "I know my father. He would never waste money on the portable ovens when you could just melt the samples here."

I thought I knew what had happened, and asked, "Did your sample shipments switch from liquid to solid all at once?"

Debra shook her head. "We got one mixed shipment, tested the liquids, melted the rocks, and then ran the same tests on the melted rocks."

"Did you get identical results?" I asked.

"Essentially, yes. After that, we just got shipments of rocks." Debra shrugged. "I still don't understand why they melted the rocks before shipping them, though."

"What if they didn't melt them at all?" Trouble asked. "What if they... Froze doesn't seem like the right word, but..."

I hoped Trouble had reached the same conclusion I had. "But what?"

"What if the samples were liquid to begin with," she said, "and they only started shipping frozen samples exclusively after your testing proved that freezing didn't damage the sample.

I nodded. "I had the same thought."

Debra shook her head. "That doesn't make sense. There's no plant or animal known that could survive having something that hot coursing through it."

"Which means... it must be an *unknown* plant or animal," Trouble said.

"That makes little sense, either," Debra said. "Whatever those samples came from, they'd be rocks on any planet except Mercury. And everyone knows Mercury is a lifeless wasteland."

Trouble pointed into the safe. "Those samples say everyone is wrong. As crazy as it sounds, Mercury must support some kind of native life."

fourteen
hostage trouble

DEBRA STRUCK me as the smartest one of the lab techs, so it didn't surprise me when she asked the obvious question. "Then why keep it secret? Life on Mercury? I mean... God, that's *huge*! Just think of the prestige and accolades that would come from such a discovery!"

"But it wouldn't make money for Father, and that is all he cares about." Trouble sighed and blinked rapidly. "Along with the power that money buys."

Debra slowly shook her head, obviously incapable of believing anyone could hold that mindset. "That can't be. Not even Garrison would do something like that."

Trouble turned an imploring glance on me, so I said, "We believe Miss Tate's brother discovered the source of these samples, and Norman Tate is holding his only son prisoner to keep the secret. Does that sound like the actions of a man who gives a damn about accolades?" Without waiting for a response from Debra, I asked, "Do you think Garrison knows where the samples come from?"

All eleven techs shook their heads, and Debra said, "No way. He'd have made a public announcement and claimed credit for the discovery. Mr. Tate may not care about prestige, but Garrison wants it more than anything."

"There has to be a way to find out," Trouble said. "Nick must have discovered it, otherwise he'd have come home two weeks ago."

"I think there is, but the knowledge is obviously dangerous," I said. "That's why I think I should do the next part by myself."

Trouble stared into my eyes. "I came here to find my brother, not play it safe."

"I know, but one of us *has* to play it safe."

"Why?"

"Because your father discovered life on Mercury, and he's using it for his own gain."

"We don't *know* either of those is true."

"You don't believe that," I said.

"No," she whispered, "I don't."

"For the sake of Mercury's newly discovered life, one of us must stay free to spread the news."

"Why can't you do that?"

"Because my last name isn't Tate."

Trouble's shoulders slumped. "What do you want me to do?"

"Take Laura and Sam, and get out of here." I glanced at the techs. "You should all play it safe and head home, too."

I called Rach and had her come around to the lab's emergency exit. Laura and Sam slipped out, giving Trouble and me a moment of privacy. She slid into my arms, melted against my body, and kissed me with passion the likes of which I'd never felt before.

"Come back to me, Travis Barrett."

I caressed her cheek. "I'll do my best."

"I'll come find you if you don't."

I smiled. "Trouble has a way of finding me."

"You're damned right, I do," she said, and kissed me again. She took my hands, looked deep into my eyes, and said, "Be careful."

I held her gaze. "Don't let your concern for me stop you from doing the right thing."

Trouble nodded. Her fingers slipped from my grasp, and she was gone. I felt her absence the moment the emergency door closed behind her. But I did what I've always done, ignored my feelings and got on with the job.

I walked away from the lab, and, five minutes later, used Max's keycard to enter the admin building. I felt safer taking the stairs up to Director Graham's third-floor office and was almost to third floor when my comm buzzed. "Yeah?"

"Hey Boss."

"Rita, you're just the bot I was looking for!"

"I bet you say that to all the Robosecs, Boss."

"All the ones I know, which means just you." I paused on a landing between floors. "Trouble and some friends are coming your way. Keep an eye on them, okay? And don't let Trouble do anything foolish."

Rita was silent for a minute. "That means *you're* doing something foolish. Right, Boss?"

"Necessary, not foolish."

Rita filled her vocorder with doubt. "Uh huh."

"Enough about me, Rita. Why did you call?"

"I found out what Nick Tate did with his thousand bucks in cash."

"You're a wonder, Rita!" I meant every word, too. "How did you do it?"

"Space Patrol records, believe it or not. A vehicle rental place filed a report for a missing sun-shielded crawler, rented to one Nicholas Tate. The crawler turned up the next morning, refueled, unharmed, and with enough cash in the cab to cover the extra days, so the company withdrew the report. But it was already in the system."

"And those records are public. Like I said, Rita, you're amazing!"

"You said I was a wonder, the first time, Boss."

"You're an amazing wonder."

"That's better, Boss."

"Is there any chance you can get your claws on the crawler's trip log?"

"I'm working on that now, Boss."

"Good girl! You and Trouble probably won't even need my help solving this case."

"Probably not," she said, "but your name is on the door, so you'll get all the credit."

"I swear by all that I hold holy, I will give credit where credit is due." I glanced up the final half-flight of stairs to the third floor. "Got to hang up now, Rita. With any luck, maybe I can find out where Nick drove that crawler without cracking the rental place's computer security."

"Okay, Boss. You be careful!"

"I'm always careful, Rita."

I disconnected the call, slid the comm into my pocket, and climbed the final few stairs. I pressed my ear to the door, half smiling at the progress we'd made on the case. No sounds came through the door, so I carefully opened it and stuck my head into the hallway to look around.

Something hard struck my right temple, pain exploded in my head, and stars danced before my eyes. I looked to my right just in time to see Horace Lance take another swing at my head with a blackjack. It connected, and everything went black.

___

I CLIMBED from darkness towards the light. Fiery agony rushed in and replaced the receding darkness. I almost retreated from the scarlet pulses that pierced my mind, but I felt certain I'd already done that at least once. And, awful as they were, the red flashes reminded me of something wonderful in my world.

Of fiery hair.

Of an even temper at odds with the hair.

Of cool blue eyes.

Of a passionate soul lurking behind the eyes.

I knew I must defy the agony if I wanted to feel wonder again.

I cracked my eyes open. Winced as light assaulted them. Shielded them with my hand. Blinked away tears.

A human-shaped shadow fell over my face. A man's voice said, "It's about time you woke up. I was getting worried."

I blinked some more as my eyes adjusted to the terrible brightness. The dark silhouette of a young man hovered over me and details gradually emerged as my vision returned. A shock of red hair. An encouraging smile. Troubled blue eyes.

I tried speaking, but only managed a dry-throated croak. The man put an arm around my shoulders and helped me sit up. Then he brought a bottle to my lips. Tepid water dripped into my mouth.

"Sorry it's not cold," he said, "but nothing stays cool around here for long."

"S'all right... More?"

I felt the water flow down my parched throat and hit my stomach. It almost came back up, but I kept it down.

"Better?" the young man asked.

"A little." I took a good look at the man, and there was no doubt as to his identity. "Nick Tate, I presume?"

Red eyebrows rose. "Yeah. How'd you know?"

"You and your sister bear a strong resemblance."

"You know Tina?"

I nodded. Winced. Stilled my head. "Yeah."

"How is she?"

"Troublesome as ever."

"That's my big sister." The ghost of a smile played across Nick's lips. "If you know my nickname for her, I guess you know her pretty well?"

"Almost as intimately as you know Laura."

"You've met Laura? Is she safe?"

"She's with Trouble."

Nick's smile turned wry. "That's a no to safety, then?"

Despite what I assumed was a dire predicament, I gave a short, painful laugh. "I hope they're safe, but Trouble isn't exactly the demure type."

"Laura isn't, either. So, um... I don't even know your name."

"Travis Barrett. I'm a PI from Carnegie Station."

"Is that where you met my sister?"

"She hired me to find you. Then things got... complicated." I gave Nick an abbreviated version of events since Trouble entered my life. "The last thing I remember before waking here was getting sapped by Horace Lance."

"That sounds like something he'd do."

"Enough about me." I said. "What's your story?"

"It sounds like you've pieced together most of it."

"Up until you rented the crawler."

"There's not much to tell after that. Something about the whole situation in the metallurgical lab struck me as fishy, and that was before I got the anonymous note."

"A note?"

"It was written on a small piece of paper, and the author somehow slipped it into my notebook. It said the samples they mixed with the steel lab were biological."

"Laura didn't say anything about a note."

Nick shook his head. "I destroyed the note and didn't tell her. I was afraid she'd be in danger if she knew." He looked around the fifteen by twenty foot cell we shared. "I'm a Tate, and look how well that protected me. Someone like Laura could just disappear."

"The note was from Debra Taylor. She went behind Garrison's back and analyzed the samples."

"Good for her. Anyway, I figured out that the samples had to be coming from somewhere on Mercury, so I began quietly searching the company records for other Tate Steelworks facilities on the planet." He shrugged. "I found the coordinates for this place and decided to take a look for myself."

The idea struck me as brash in the extreme, but Nick was only twenty-two. I remembered my actions at that age, and sometimes marveled that I survived my early career in the Space Patrol. So I limited myself to saying, "I gather your search wasn't as quiet as you thought?"

"No. Some of Father's security guys ambushed me when I got out of the crawler. I've been here ever since."

"Where is here?" Nick rattled off the coordinates, and I spent fifteen seconds fighting through my headache to place them on a map of Mercury. "So we're... Um... A thousand miles sunward from the Twi-Line?"

"Yeah, that's about right."

"Have you talked with your father since his thugs captured you?"

"He calls every day and calmly tries talking me into seeing things his way." Nick grinned at me. "Every time, he ends up losing his temper and yelling at me. He wraps up by calling me stupid and telling me the Tate name won't protect me forever." The young man's face turned somber. "Honestly, I think Father might have done away with me if Trouble wasn't so worried about me."

"She's afraid of something like that happening." I struggled to my feet and face Nick. "How are you handling this? It can't be easy knowing your father is—"

"From Father's point of view, Trouble and I are irksome possessions of limited value and considerable liability." Nick turned away from me. "I'm used to it."

"Maybe it's not my place to say—"

"It isn't," Nick interrupted. His head dropped, and he sighed. "I'm sorry, Travis. I didn't mean to take this out on you."

Nick lifted his head, straightened his shoulders, and walked towards the far end of the cell. "Come here and let me show you something."

I followed, trailing a hand along the wall just in case my sense of balance suddenly abandoned me. We stopped in front of the far wall and, looking to lighten the mood a bit, I said, "It's a wall. Fascinating, and totally worth getting concussed so I could see it."

"Actually, it *is* worth it." Nick reached for a button on the wall. "The light is about to get extremely bright. I suggest covering your eyes with your hands."

I did as instructed. "Okay."

I heard a soft click as Nick pushed the button. Light far brighter than anything I'd experienced before found its way through my hands and hit my eyes. I squeezed them shut, but that only helped a little. My eyes adjusted, but not nearly enough. Finally, I decided I could brave the light pouring through the formerly opaque wall, parted my fingers, and peeked through them.

The wall had a polarized look to it, and I realized it filtered the light and screened us from its full impact. A massive sun hung in the sky above us, and sunlight streamed through a glass rooftop. A huge, rock-strewn floor stretched at least a hundred yards away from our see-through wall.

I turned to Nick. "What am I looking at?"

Nick pointed at a nearby rock. "Watch."

He raised a hand and knocked on the wall. And the rock *moved*. Something rose from its top, and I realized it must be a head.

In a quiet voice, Nick said, "I call them Mercurians."

THE MERCURIAN FINISHED RAISING his head. Or her head. Or, hell, maybe its head. Two points set deeply in the head reflected a bit of the bright light streaming through the transparent ceiling. Eyes, I guessed.

Nick flattened his hand against the polarized glass that protected us from the sun's full force. He wiped his hand to the right as far as he could reach, turned the hand perpendicular to the window, and pulled the hand back to its original position in front of himself.

He turned to me. "They have trouble seeing into the dim light inside our little cell. That's probably because their eyes evolved for bright light on Mercury."

"Why did you do that with your hand?" I asked.

"It's a hand signal I worked out with him," Nick said. "It means *come here*."

Outside, what I'd originally thought were cracks and crevices on a rock gradually resolved into arms, legs, and a torso. "Are you saying he's *sentient*?"

Nick shrugged. "He's smart enough to figure out my hand signals."

Humans have already made contact with sentient people on Venus, Mars, and Saturn. There's a lot of mystery and even more debates about who built the floating cities in Jupiter's clouds. One explorer even got as far out as Neptune and swore he met an advanced underwater civilization there. Given how many planets have sentient species, I shouldn't have been surprised that Mercury has one, too. But I was.

The Mercurian finished standing and began walking our way. At first, I thought his tottering walk resulted from rock-hard skin and joints with little range of motion. But then I spotted a discolored spot on his left leg and realized he favored that leg when walking. "Is he limping?"

In a tight voice, Nick said, "Yes."

"Is it because of that discoloration on the left leg?"

"It's not a discoloration," Nick growled. "That's a... Call it a concrete band aid."

"What happened to him?"

"My father happened to him." Nick rested his head against the glass and closed his eyes. "Once he learned about the properties of their blood—"

I interrupted him and asked the question that had been forefront in my mind since my visit to the metallurgy lab. "How did anyone even figure that out?"

"I don't know, but I assume it was an accidental discovery." Nick shook his head in disgust. "Father had his goons capture my friend and all the others you see out there, imprisoned them, and every day or two they drill through their skin so they can draw samples to send to the metallurgy lab. Every Mercurian out there has similar wounds."

Too appalled to think of any response to that, I turned and watched the Mercurian limp closer. He stopped a foot shy of the window, his massive form blocking much of the window. He stood at least eight feet tall and looked to be six feet wide. God alone knew how heavy he was, and I wondered how long the window could hold out if he began pounding on it. The Mercurian lifted his left hand, and I feared he was going to do just that. Instead, he placed his massive hand over the same place where Nick's hand was, flattened it gently against the glass, and spread three fingers and a thumb, matching Nick's hand.

I swallowed a lump as the two prisoners communed silently. "How do your father's men even do that?" I gestured to the Mercurian at the window. "He must weigh at least a ton, and has to be incredibly strong."

In a hoarse whisper, Nick said, "The bastards spray their intended victim with freezing cold water. It immobilizes them long enough for the crew to get their sample." Nick turned a haunted expression my way. "Have you ever heard a rock scream, Travis? I have."

I had no words of comfort for Nick, so I clapped a hand on his shoulder. "Don't worry. We'll find a way to get them all out of here."

Nick gave a laugh that was far too bitter for such a young man. "How?" He looked at me. "Don't you get it, Travis? We're never going to get out of here. I've seen too much for Father to ever let me go free."

"Your father is not the Tate I'm counting on to get us out," I said. "But your comment brings up a question. Why didn't your father's people put you somewhere where you can't see what they're doing? I mean, it's pretty stupid letting you watch them commit atrocities."

"There aren't that many rooms in this facility, and the others are all common rooms and dormitory housing." Nick pointed at the vast, Mercurian-strewn room beyond the window. "That room was designed for testing steel at extreme temperatures, and this is simply an observation room. But it only has one door, so it wasn't hard for Father's bullies to add a lock to the outside."

"Your father *could* have simply had you taken back to Twi-Town and put on the next starliner back to Carnegie Station," I said.

"He probably wishes he'd done that. But he believed I'd support this horrid project." Nick gave a humorless laugh. "He never took time to get to know Trouble and me, but I never imagined he could be *that* blind to who I am."

I remembered Trouble's desire to be more involved in running Tate Steelworks and realized her father had actually done her a favor by keeping her away from the business. "I wish I could say something that would make you feel better, Nick."

He shrugged. "Don't worry about me, Travis. I'm okay."

The lie came easily to Nick's lips, and I wondered if he'd told it to himself so often that he had almost convinced himself it was true. Despite his words, I sought for something useful to say. But something rattled behind us.

We turned in time to see the room's door swing open. My old friends Hammerhand and Slick stood outside. Slick held a blaster and had it pointed at me.

"Mr. Tate wants a talk," Hammerhand said.

"With me?" Nick asked.

"With both of you." Hammerhand pounded his right fist into his left hand and glared at me. "And don't think of doing nothing smart, Barrett, 'cause Mr. Tate said I could rough you up if'n you need it."

Nick and I filed out, and we took a short walk to one of the common rooms Nick told me about. It held a video comm, and the screen showed a smiling Norman Tate gazing out at us.

"Here they are, sir," Hammerhand said.

And then we stood there for nearly half an hour, while our images made the thirteen minute trip to the asteroid belt, and Norman Tate's words made the return trip to Mercury.

"Well, Mr. Barrett, this is an unexpected pleasure. I admit I hoped I'd never set eyes on you again, but that was before you corrupted my daughter and caused no end of trouble for my operations on Mercury." He paused for three seconds, then added, "I understand Tina thinks she's fallen in love with you, or some such nonsense."

I opened my mouth to make a smartass reply, remembered it would take thirteen minutes to reach Tate's office, and closed it again. Hammerhand's looming presence behind me and my still-painful ribs might have affected my decision as well.

Tate's image kept speaking, just as he had thirteen minutes ago. "Regardless of Tina's foolish infatuation, you've stumbled onto our operation at just the right time. My team in the Twi-Town compound has spent the last week performing final tests on our new alloy steel. Would you like to know what they discovered? We cannot harvest sufficient quantities of the samples to make a commercially viable product. We'd need somewhere in the neighborhood of a billion of the native life forms, and my xenobiologists doubt there are more than a million of them scattered across the sun-side of Mercury."

Tate leaned back in his chair. If he'd had a beard, this is when he would have stroked it. "I'm going to shut down this line of research, Mr. Barrett."

"Thank God," Nick murmured.

"Furthermore, I'm going to bring Nick back to Carnegie Station." Norman Tate's eyes switched to where Nick had been standing half an hour ago. "But don't get the idea that you can spill your guts about this project, my boy. *You* won't be a prisoner any longer." Tate's eyes switched back to me. "But if you care for your sister, you'll remain silent. Because the man she thinks she loves is taking your place."

THE IMAGE of Norman Tate fell silent for a moment and, without giving thought to the long transmission lag between Mercury and Carnegie Station, Nick said, "No, Father, you can't do that to Tina!"

Tate's face twisted into a wry smile. "I do hope I paused speaking long enough for your knee-jerk reaction, Nick." The smile broadened. "I'm not as blind to your ill-considered values as you think, my boy. Now, if you'll give me your full attention and refrain from further outbursts for a moment longer, I'll finish explaining the situation.

"I will hold Mr. Barrett for..." Tate stroked his chin, pretending to consider his options. "Let's say one Earth year. I'll release him at the end of that year. But *only* if this little experiment of mine remains a secret. Should word of it get out," Tate's face hardened, "I'm afraid Mr. Barrett will have an unfortunate heat-lock accident. Without protection from the sun's full force, he won't survive more than a few minutes. I imagine those last minutes will be... unpleasant in the extreme." Tate's smile returned. "But if the facility and its purpose remain our little secret, I'll release Mr. Barrett unharmed and won't even stand in his way if he still wishes to pursue a relationship with Tina."

Nick turned a confused expression my way, and I read an unspoken question in his eyes. *What's to stop me from spilling the secret after you're released?*

Again, Norman Tate showed he knew his son better than Nick thought he did. "Nick, unless I miss my guess, you're thinking you'll just wait out the year and, once Mr. Barrett is safe, spill the beans to the Space Patrol, the press, and the governments of Earth."

Nick turned wide eyes back to the comm screen, and his father said, "I suspect Mr. Barrett has thought through the ramifications and knows why I'm not concerned about that." Norman Tate's image turned his eyes my way. "Perhaps you would explain to my son why his notion is so ill-conceived, Mr. Barrett? I'll wait a moment while you do so."

Nick looked at me. I sighed, and said, "After a year of your silence, the public will assume you were deeply involved in the project, and are only speaking out to assuage guilt, avoid prosecution, to weaken your father's position as head of Tate Steelworks so you can push him aside and take his place, or any of a dozen other self-serving reasons why you might open up a year after the project ended. Then there are millions of people who will believe the worst simply because you're rich and they're not."

Denial filled Nick's eyes. "No one who knows me would believe that for a moment!"

"People are depressingly willing to believe the worst about someone, especially where a lot of money is concerned. But even if all your close friends believe you, most people will assume they're sticking by your side because you paid them—directly or indirectly—to do so."

"They'll realize the truth when I *don't* do any of those things, though."

"No, they won't. They'll just assume your power play didn't work out as you hoped." I closed my eyes for a moment, opened them, and delivered the argument Norman Tate and I both knew would seal Nick's lips. "But even if you believe you can take the scorn that will come your way, a year of silence won't just implicate you. As bad as the blowback will be for you, it'll be worse for your sister."

"Why would it even involve Tina, much less be worse?" Nick asked.

"Everything she's done since you disappeared can be cast in a poor light. Under that harsh glare, the sister concerned for her brother becomes the power-hungry woman who used public proclamations of concern to hide more sinister motivations. Even if no one pushes that story, she'll be tarred as a shallow party girl who didn't care that her father supported her lavish lifestyle with blood money." I sighed. "Your father will have a year to concoct evidence that supports whatever narrative he wants. Even if the story eventually falls apart, it'll be too late for Tina's reputation. And yours."

Horror spread over Nick's face. "That's how Father will ensure your silence, too."

I nodded. "And he'll use *us* to keep Tina quiet."

A few seconds later, Norman Tate's image said, "I trust Mr. Barrett explained the situation adequately, Nick? If you give your word that you will remain quiet, Mr. Houlihan will have you taken back to Twi-Town." Tate pasted a mockery of a fatherly smile on his face. "If you behave yourself for the next year, we'll announce the discovery of Mercury's native life form. You can even take the lead on that, Nick. What do you say, son? Will you give your word?"

Hammerhand looked at Nick and raised his eyebrows. Nick looked at me, and I gave a small nod. Shoulders drooping, Nick said, "You have my word."

Hammerhand said, "Mr. Tate said you gotta have an excuse for disappearin'. He figgered you'd see things his way, so he set up a good alibi. You been spendin' the time with a high-class hooker." Hammerhand grinned. "Your daddy sees her every time he comes to Mercury, so you know she's good. Anyway, she don't know nothing 'cept Mr. Tate paid her a lotta money to say you was with her the whole time. Got it?"

"Yes," Nick whispered, "I understand."

"Good." Hammerhand glanced at Slick and jerked his head towards the door. "Let young Mr. Tate's driver in."

Slick opened the door. "We's ready fer ya."

After everything I'd heard and seen, it didn't surprise me when Jacobson entered the room. Hammerhand pointed to Nick. "The boss says to take him back to town. Drop him off at Miss Yummy's place."

Jacobson's spine stiffened. "This is why you kept me hanging around for hours after I brought Barrett to you? I am the Space Patrol commander, not some errand boy!"

Hammerhand ambled over to Jacobson and poked him with a forefinger. Jacobson stumbled back a step, and Hammerhand said, "You're whatever Mr. Tate says you are. Got it?"

Jacobson's defiant pose crumbled. "Yes."

"Good. Take young Mr. Tate and get outta here." Hammerhand glanced at his partner. "Slick, you make sure they get to Jacobson's ship safely."

"Yeah, safely," Slick giggled. He used his blaster to wave Jacobson and Nick towards the door. "Get goin', boys."

Hammerhand turned off the comm screen and then escorted me back to the makeshift cell overlooking the Mercurians. I kept waiting for him to give me another beating, but he never touched me. Finally, I asked, "Aren't you going to impress upon me the gravity of my situation by pounding me into a pulp, again?"

"Nah. Mr. Tate says we gotta treat you okay as long as you do what you're told."

"How magnanimous of him." I looked around the small room. "So, this is home for the next year?"

"Nope. We got another spot for you. Now that he's shuttin' the project down, Mr. Tate says we gotta get rid of this place." Hammerhand winked and mimed an explosion with his hands. "Don't wanna leave no evidence laying around, doncha know."

Of course. Blow the place up, collect insurance for it, and let Mercury's harsh environment destroy any remaining evidence of Tate's crimes against the Mercurians. With a sense of dread, I asked, "What about the Mercurians?"

Hammerhand's face screwed up in confusion. "Who?"

I walked to the far wall, pushed the button that made the wall transparent, and pointed through it. "Them. What will happen to them?"

Hammerhand keyed the door mechanism. As it slid shut, he grinned and mimed another explosion. "Boom."

fifteen
trouble with goodbyes

I DON'T KNOW why Tate's willingness to slaughter the captive Mercurians surprised me. I mean, he'd been forcibly draining their blood—or whatever it was his people drew from them—just to create a better alloy steel. By his own admission, his sole reason for giving up on that macabre plan was because the supply of Mercurian blood did not meet his needs. Even so, why kill the ones he'd experimented on? It's not like they would report him to the Space Patrol.

But *why* didn't matter. I needed to know *when*. And whether I could find a way to save the Mercurians before time ran out.

I walked across the room and pressed the button that made the wall transparent. A big Mercurian sat fifteen feet away. Was it the same one Nick communicated with after I regained consciousness? Even if it was, would he react to me in the same manner? There was only one way to find out.

I knocked on the wall. The Mercurian raised his head and looked my way. I put my right hand flat against the wall and then moved it as far to the right as I could reach. I turned my hand perpendicular to the wall, just like Nick did, and pulled it back to me.

After what felt like a thousand years, the big guy slowly rose and limped to the wall. I flattened my hand against the wall, and he put his huge, three-fingered hand opposite mine. The glass between our hands warmed quickly. No surprise, since the Mercurian's normal body temperature had to be hotter than two hundred and forty-six degrees just to keep their blood from freezing. But I'd bet a fortune their bodies were far hotter than that minimum. Temperatures under Mercury's perpetual noon-day sun topped four hundred degrees. If the Mercurians are even remotely similar to the other races in the solar system, their normal body temperature would be hotter than that.

I held my hand against the wall until it grew too hot to bear. When I took my hand down, the big guy did the same. He began a shuffling turn, probably to go back to his usual spot, but an idea popped into my head. I knocked on the wall again.

He turned, and watched as I flattened my right hand against the blazing hot glass, and then moved it quickly to the right. Then I bent my arm at the elbow, and then extended it to point at a huge, overhead door I'd just noticed in the right-hand wall. I hoped the door opened onto the surface of Mercury and was the way Tate's goons brought the Mercurians into the chamber. If I was right, and the Mercurians could batter down the door, they'd have a chance to escape before Hammerhand and his friends blew up the facility.

But first the big guy had to figure out what I wanted of him. And he hadn't gotten it yet. But he leaned in close to the wall to better see into my cell. I repeated the gesture five times, but his eyes never left me.

How could I get him to understand what I meant? Maybe I could show him?

I moved my right hand along the wall again, cocked my arm just as I'd done before, but extended it towards the door on the far side of my cell. Then I walked across the cell to the door.

Bob—I decided the big guy needed a name, and that was the first one that came to mind—pressed his face against the wall and watched me intently. God only knew how long it had taken Nick to get the concept across to Bob, but it was a good thing he had. Because I spent the next two hours alternating between gesturing to the overhead door inside the vast room and to the door inside my cell. Whenever I pointed to the cell door, I always walked to it.

I almost wept when Bob finally turned his head towards the overhead door when I pointed at it. And that's when I heard the door in my cell rattle. I slapped the button to turn the wall opaque again, spun around, leaned against the wall, and twisted my face into a scowl.

Hammerhand and Slick entered the cell, and Slick held a tray of food. I'd been so wrapped up working with Bob, I had forgotten about eating. But the aroma of food awoke my appetite. To my surprise, the beef stew with mashed potatoes looked edible.

"You're ruining the prison-like ambiance of this place," I said as I took the tray and a bottle of water from Slick. "Shouldn't this be a bowl of greasy gruel or something equally disgusting?"

"You get the same stuff we get," Hammerhand said. He flashed an amused smile. "But I can put in a special request if you really want gruel."

"Yeah," Slick said. "Gruel."

I settled onto the floor against a side wall, realized there were no utensils, and asked, "No knife and fork?"

Hammerhand shook his head. "I ain't stupid enough to give you a weapon."

"Ain't stupid," Slick giggled. "Nope."

"How about a spoon, then?" I asked. "Or are you afraid I'll use it to dig my way out of here?"

Slick gave Hammerhand a sidelong glance. "Toldja he'd ask."

"Yeah, yeah," Hammerhand grumbled. He dipped a hand into his pocket, pulled out a twenty-dollar bill, and handed it to Slick. "You win. Give him the spoon."

Slick took the twenty, fished a spoon from his pocket, and threw it to me. I caught it and tucked into the stew.

Hammerhand folded his arms, leaned against the wall, and said, "Don't get too used to this place. Soon as Mr. Tate's guys get the explosives placed and wire 'em to go boom, we're catching a spaceship outta here."

"Gee, I can't wait to see my new cell," I said. "Will you and ferret-face be there to keep me company?"

Without answering my question, they left. I finished eating, drained the water bottle, and turned the wall between Bob and me transparent again. I had a lot to teach him, and his time grew shorter by the minute.

I REPEATED my gestures over and over. The need to walk to my cell's door and back whenever I made the gestures for myself slowed my progress. I lost track of time and despaired of ever getting my message across to Bob. But he finally turned away from me and took half-a-dozen steps towards the door.

I gave a cry of frustration when he stopped. But then Bob looked back at me and his right hand formed a fist with his thumb pointing straight up. I hadn't taught him the thumbs up sign, so he must have learned it from Nick. I made the broad pointing gesture with my arm and prayed Bob realized I wanted him to keep going. He turned and resumed walking towards the door.

I leapt into the air, pumped my fist, and shouted, "Yes!"

Fortunately, Bob wasn't watching me. God only knows how badly my actions would have confused him if he had seen them. I made a mental note to restrain myself from actions that Bob might misinterpret as additions to our tiny store of signs.

Bob stopped two more times before he finally reached the huge overhead door. I pressed my hand against the transparent wall, returned his thumbs up sign, and prayed Bob's eyesight was good enough to see my hand. It must have been, since Bob lowered his arm and stood next to the door.

I made the *come here* sign, and Bob made his slow way back to my cell. When he reached me, I immediately launched into the next part of my plan. Bob watched carefully as I swiped my hand to the right—the sign I decided meant *move*—point at my cell door and walked to it. I raised my right hand, balled it into a fist, and punched the door. The sound echoed off the walls of my cell as I did the same with my left hand. Then I punched the door, alternating hands. Right, left, right, left.

The door slid open just as my right arm shot forward. Slick dodged my fist and gave me a quick rabbit punch to the gut with the muzzle of the blaster he held. "Watch it, bub."

I staggered back two steps, rubbing my stomach. Slick was the last person on Mercury I wanted to apologize to, but I swallowed my pride and said, "Sorry, I was trying to punch the door."

"Well, quit it. Yer givin' me a headache."

Odd as it was hearing Slick speak without echoing Hammerhand, it wasn't so fascinating that I wanted him sticking around outside my cell. "I'm working out my frustrations."

"Then hit the wall."

"I like hitting the door."

"Too bad."

"Yeah, too bad for you, Slick. Because I'm going to keep punching the door." I flashed a big grin. "If you don't like it, go somewhere else."

Slick snarled something unintelligible, but I got the idea he'd just insulted my parents. Then he slapped the door control, and the cell door slid shut.

I waited a moment and then turned back to Bob. He stood there watching me. I wondered what he understood of my scene with Slick, but not for long. We still had a lot of work to do.

I went through my signs again, walked to the cell door, and began pummeling it with my fists. All I did was bruise my knuckles. But maybe Mercurians' rocky hands could handle pounding on the overhead door without hurting themselves too badly.

Not wanting to introduce any unnecessary motions to this

latest attempt at communication, I resisted rubbing my hands as I returned to Bob. Then I made the *move* sign, pointed to the door, and then mimed several punches.

Without hesitation, Bob walked to the overhead door and began punching it. The door rattled and shook with each blow. Bob kept his enormous arms pistoning at the door while he turned his head and looked at me. I gave him a thumbs up and watched him work.

The sound of Bob pounding on the door provoked a reaction from other Mercurians, the first I'd seen since I began working with Bob. Heads lifted and turned Bob's way. Some rose and ambled towards the door. One must have spoken, because I heard what sounded like someone walking through gravel.

Bob stopped hitting the door, his mouth moved, and I heard more gravel grinding. The Mercurian who spoke to Bob looked over his shoulder at the other Mercurians and spoke in a louder voice. Two dozen massive Mercurians—some of them bigger than Bob—went to the door.

Their arms pistoned.

The door shook.

Sounds boomed off the walls.

Bob spoke again, though I couldn't hear his voice over the pounding of fists on the door. The Mercurians all stopped, and I had just enough time to wonder what had gone wrong. But then Bob gave a command that sounded like two boulders smashing into each other.

And the Mercurians punched the door at the same time. They made another simultaneous punch. Then a third. And a fourth. The blows kept hammering on the door. And it slowly buckled under their combined assault.

I was so intent on watching the Mercurians that I didn't hear the cell door open. I didn't even know someone else was in the cell with me until Hammerhand growled, "Make 'em stop, Barrett."

I turned around, saw Hammerhand standing a few feet from

me, with Slick watching from the door. With a wide smile, I said, "Go to hell."

Hammerhand studied the fingernails on his left hand. "You cruisin' fer a bruisin', Barrett?"

"Tate ordered you to treat me well. Are you going to disobey him?"

"He only said I gotta do that if you do whatcha told. You gonna do what I toldja to do and make 'em stop?"

"Nope."

Hammerhand stepped forward, faked with his left, and then drove his right fist into my face. The blow knocked me back against the transparent wall. I ducked and dodged and did my best to make the ex-boxer miss. But he was too fast for me. In a matter of seconds, he had me huddling in a corner as blows rained down on me. Weirdly, Hammerhand matched the Mercurians' rhythm.

Hammerhand stopped long enough to say, "I been waitin' for a chance to smack you around some more, Barrett."

Behind Hammerhand, in the cell doorway, Slick suddenly stiffened and toppled to the floor. And, blaster in hand, Dave Hayslett stepped through the doorway.

I stared at Dave and would have rubbed my eyes in disbelief, but needed my hands for the meager defense I mounted against Hammerhand. My surprise at Dave's appearance slowed my reaction to a right cross. I ducked and blocked as best I could, but a pile-driver fist still clipped my jaw and knocked me hard into the transparent wall.

"Tell 'em to stop, Barrett," Hammerhand snarled.

Dave pointed his blaster in Hammerhand's direction and fired. A searing bolt of white-hot plasma flashed across the room and splashed against the transparent wall. Whatever the wall was made of, it was tough stuff. I thought the blaster bolt would burn right through the wall, but it only partially melted the wall where it hit.

As molten wall dripped, Dave said, "I missed on purpose, big guy. But if you hit Barrett one more time, I swear the next one will be in your ear."

Hammerhand froze with his left arm cocked for another blow. His head turned slowly and glared at Dave. But then something moved at Dave's feet, and we both looked down. Slick's hand slowly slid towards the blaster he'd dropped when Dave smacked him.

Dave saw our gazes shift down, and he glanced down, too. With a pilot's quick reflexes, Dave raised one foot and stomped hard on Slick's hand. Slick screamed, and I heard bones breaking over the Mercurians' door pounding.

Dave's eyes were off Hammerhand for only a second, but the ex-boxer had fast reflexes, too. His cocked left arm shot out, Hammerhand grabbed me by the neck, and he yanked me in front of himself. His left hand released its grip just long enough for him to slide his arm around my neck. Then he lifted me off the floor, held only by the arm pressing against my throat.

I pulled at Hammerhand's massive arm with both hands, but the man was simply too strong for me. Then I punched at him with flailing arms, but the blows lacked any real force. Already inured to physical punishment from his boxing days, Hammerhand ignored my attacks.

"Drop your blaster, bub," Hammerhand said, "or I break Barrett's neck."

"Go ahead." Dave kept his blaster leveled on Hammerhand and me. "Everyone knows I hate the bastard."

Hammerhand wasn't buying it. "Yeah? Then what're you doing here, huh? And why'd you tell me to stop hittin' him?"

"I came to get the Tate kid. I only told you to stop beating on Barrett because *I* want to beat on him."

"Nope. Don't believe you. You'd'a shot by now if you meant it, and you wouldn't worry 'bout which one of us you hit."

From the corner of my eye, I saw Hammerhand raise his right fist. He slammed it into my temple and tightened his arm around my throat at the same time. Lights flashed in my head from the blow, and darkness formed at the edge of my vision as I fought for breath.

Uncertainty shone in Dave's eyes as he raised his blaster and took careful aim.

Pain pulsed in my head.

My blood pounded.

My legs flailed.

Far away, the Mercurians kept up their assault on the wall.

Hammerhand rocked, then steadied.

Dave lowered his blaster.

Hammerhand cocked his right fist for another blow.

"Hammerhand!" Slick yelled. "Behind ya!"

The wall shattered, and a rock-skinned arm reached through the hole. Scorching air blew through the hole as a massive, craggy hand grabbed Hammerhand's right wrist. The sound of sizzling flesh reached my ears just ahead of Hammerhand's howl.

Hammerhand released his hold on my throat, and I fell at his feet as he spun to face the new threat. I drew gasping breaths, tinged with the acrid odor of burning meat. Above me, acting on instinct, Hammerhand pounded on the Mercurian's hand with his left fist. For his troubles, the flesh on Hammerhand's left fist charred and burned.

I scuttled out from under Hammerhand and tried standing. Dave appeared at my side, caught my hand, and pulled me to my feet. I swayed, only remaining upright because of Dave's support, and looked at the transparent wall.

Bob stood just beyond it, his right arm thrust through the hole he'd smashed through the wall, and Hammerhand's blackened wrist held in his firm grasp. Hammerhand leaned against the wall, softly whimpering.

I met Bob's gaze, raised my right hand and gave him a thumbs up. Bob released Hammerhand, who collapsed to the floor and curled his massive form around his ruined right hand. With his arm still stuck through the hole, Bob returned the thumbs up. Then he turned and headed back to the wall.

Slick stumbled to his feet, his horror-filled eyes locked on his partner. "Hammerhand?" The little guy ran to him and put his good hand on the big man's shoulder. "I'm here, Hammerhand. Slick ain't gonna leave ya."

Despite everything the pair had done to me, I couldn't watch their suffering. I picked up Slick's forgotten blaster and turned towards the door. "Is this when you start beating on me, Dave?"

Dave headed for the door. "I was trying to convince the guy he couldn't use you for leverage. I didn't mean it, Travis."

"Yeah, I figured that out." I followed Dave. "You know that's the first time in six years you've called me Travis without sneering or sarcasm?"

"Sounds about right."

I stopped outside the cell, and closed and locked the door. "Where to now?"

"The *Lightning's Hand* is parked about half a mile away."

"You walked here wearing a heat suit?"

"Yep."

"And now we walk back?"

"Yep. Don't worry, I brought a spare heat suit for you to wear." Dave grinned. "Trouble and Rita insisted on that."

"That's good. I burn something awful in direct sunlight."

"One thing hasn't changed in the last six years. Your jokes are still as bad as ever."

As natural as the banter felt, I put it aside and said, "Thanks for coming for me, Dave. Seriously."

Dave gave an uncomfortable shrug. "Trouble called after her brother got back. She asked me to come get you, and she wouldn't take no for an answer."

"How many times did you refuse?"

"Then there was Rita. *She* threatened to ruin my credit rating. Not that there's much left to ruin."

"How many times, Dave?"

"And don't get me started on Sam and Nick. They—"

"Answer my question, Dave. How many times did you say no?"

Dave glanced at me. Looked away. "Um... Zero."

I nodded, and we walked through empty corridors in silence. We passed an open door along the way, and it held five men, gagged and tied to chairs. I looked at Dave and raised an eyebrow. He offered a tight smile, and kept walking. At the heat lock, Dave pulled two heat suits from a locker next to the hatch, and we put them on. Just before I put my helmet on, I looked Dave in the eye. "Is your self-imposed exile over now?"

"Yeah, I guess so."

"It's good to have you back, Dave."

I sealed the helmet on my heat suit and flashed a thumbs up to Dave. He returned it, then opened the inner hatch for the heat lock. Unlike an airlock, which is almost always built small to minimize the time spent pressurizing or depressurizing the chamber, a heat lock chamber just has to have big air handlers to raise or lower the temperature. Heat locks usually double as a storage facility for tools and vehicles designed for the furnace that is Mercury's sun-side, and this one was no different.

Dave closed the inner hatch and activated the air handlers. Hot air blasted into the chamber and I watched the temperature rise rapidly on my heat suit's external thermometer. Meanwhile, I inspected the seven heat-shielded vehicles lining the wall on my right. It only took a moment to find what I was looking for.

I activated the heat suit's comm. "Hey Dave, why walk to the *Lightning's Hand* when we can ride?"

"Great idea, but only if you know how to drive that thing."

"Don't you? You bragged about your driving almost as much as you bragged about your piloting."

Dave gave a dismissive wave. "I brag about driving fast cars, which impresses fast women." He pointed at the squat vehicle I'd selected, somewhat similar to a bulldozer, and said, "*That* is neither fast nor likely to impress women."

"Fortunately for us, this thing is a lot like the rescue vehicles we carried on the *Soteria*." I opened the cab door and climbed in. "As captain, I had to understand how they worked so I could make fast decisions in life-and-death rescue operations."

"That means you can drive it?"

"That means I can drive it."

Someone had written 'Bertha' above the dashboard dials, so I asked, "Are you ready to go, Bertha?"

I pressed the ignition, and Bertha answered with a deep, rumbling roar. I carefully backed her out of her place in the line of vehicles, turned her toward the outer hatch, and we crawled forward. Dave stood by the controls, waited for the temperature equilibrium light to turn green, opened the outer hatch, and then joined me in Bertha's cab.

"How fast will this thing go, Travis?"

"About as fast as we can walk." I put Bertha in gear and drove through the open hatch. "Maybe a little faster."

He looked back at the remaining six vehicles. "None of those go any faster?"

"All of them do. But Bertha has hidden talents."

I turned left after exiting the heat lock. Dave pointed back to our right and said, "My ship is that way."

"We'll go that way in a bit." We passed the far wall of the heat locker and the outer wall of the vast research room came into view. I pointed to the battered, bulging overhead door midway along that hundred-yard wall. "But first we're going to free Bob and his buddies." I glanced at Dave. "Bob is the other friend who came to my rescue today."

Dave nodded. "I only have one question."

"Shoot."

"Why Bob? Why not 'Rocky' or something like that?"

"Too obvious." I paused for a moment, then said, "But I almost named him 'Cary,' after an actor from the dawn of spaceflight."

Dave furrowed his brow for a few seconds, then the furrows cleared. "You mean Cary Grant?"

"Close. Cary Granite." Then I laughed.

Dave groaned. "Remember when I said your jokes weren't any better than they were six years ago?"

"Yeah."

"I was wrong. They're worse. A *lot* worse."

I chuckled until we got close enough to the door to hear the Mercurians pounding over the growl of Bertha's engine. When we reached the door, I maneuvered Bertha until she was right in front of the overhead door's center. I lowered the blade adorning her front end to the ground and edged forward. The lip of the blade dug into Mercury's surface and slid under the lower edge of the door.

The pounding on the door stopped after the blade poked under it. I wished for a way to tell Bob and his people to move back, but that wasn't possible. Instead, I lifted the blade gradually and with as much care as possible. The door resisted briefly, but the Mercurians' pounding had deformed it and robbed it of much of its strength. With a metallic screech, the raising blade crumpled the door.

I edged Bertha forward, raised the blade so it caught on the inside of the door, and then backed up. With an unholy shriek, the center of the door tore free.

A lone Mercurian appeared in the hole Bertha had made in the door and looked at us. It could have been Bob, but I wouldn't swear to it. Still, I stopped Bertha, climbed out, and faced the Mercurian. I made the *come here* gesture. To my relief, the Mercurian gave me a thumbs up. Bob turned, called to the others in a gravel-toned voice, and then walked my way.

He stopped three feet from me, raised his left hand, and spread his fingers. I did the same with my right hand, prayed Norman Tate hadn't scrimped on the heat suits, and touched my hand to his. I felt Bob's prodigious heat through the thick glove, but the material didn't melt or burn.

When the contact grew too uncomfortable, I pulled my hand

back and gave Bob another thumbs up. He returned it as I said, "Take care of everybody, Bob. Okay?"

Bob didn't understand me, but I believe he caught my drift. His stony lips moved, and I heard the sound of rocks grinding against one another. Bob and I had been through a lot in a very short time, and I'd formed a strong attachment to the big guy. I wondered if we'd ever see each other again, swallowed a lump that suddenly formed in my throat, and returned to Bertha.

I climbed back into Bertha's cab and backed her away from the Mercurians still streaming through the hole I'd made in the door. Then I turned Bertha away from the Mercurians and set off for the *Lightning's Hand.*

DAVE POINTED through Bertha's front windshield. "The *Lightning's Hand* is just over that rise over there."

"We'll be there in five minutes." I glanced at Dave. "Can you check on the Mercurians? Did they all get out?"

He peered out the back window. "Crap."

"Do I need to go back? Are the Mercurians in trouble?"

"No, sorry. They're gone. Damned if I know how such big people disappeared so fast, but this is their planet. I was referring to the outer hatch for the heat lock. It's closed."

"We left it open."

"That's why I said, 'crap.' At a guess, someone sounded the alarm about your escape. Probably the big guy who was pounding on you or his scrawny buddy." Dave turned back to me. "Nick told us about Norman Tate's plan for keeping everyone quiet. That only works if you're their hostage."

I already had Bertha crawling at her top speed, but willed her to go faster. "So they'll come after us."

"That's what I'd do in their place."

"And I took the slowest vehicle in the locker." I patted the dashboard. "No offense, Bertha."

"You didn't have any choice. We couldn't leave the Mercurians where they were."

"Even if that means Tate's goons get us? They need me alive, but you're a different matter."

Dave was silent for several seconds. Then he said, "If there's one thing I learned in the six years since the *Soteria's* destruction, it's that some fates *are* worse than death."

"Hey, I just got my best friend back. I'm not ready to lose him again so soon."

Dave looked back at the facility's heat lock. "You might not have any choice. The external heat lock fans just started spinning. We've got maybe thirty seconds before they're on our tail."

"Have you kept in shape?"

"What?"

"Can you run from here to the *Hand* and still have enough breath to fly her?"

Dave eyed the rise a quarter of a mile ahead. "Why?"

"You can run faster than Bertha crawls. I can keep Hammerhand and his buddies busy long enough for you to escape."

"Let's both run for it."

I looked over my shoulder at the heat lock just as the hatch jerked into motion. "They'll catch us both if we do that. Someone has to be the diversion, and that someone can't be the pilot." I reached past Dave and opened Bertha's door. "There's no time to argue. Go!"

Dave snarled in frustration and leapt from the cab. He landed easily, cast a last glance my way, and started running for the rise. As soon as he was clear, I reversed one of Bertha's tracks and she spun to face the compound. The first pursuit vehicle edged through the widening hatch as I stopped turning and sent Bertha rumbling towards the facility. I took a quick look over my shoulder and watched a sprinting Dave angle his path, so Bertha was between him and our pursuers.

I smiled, appreciating the cleverness of his move. The longer it took Tate's men to realize only one person was inside Bertha, the better Dave's odds became. But maybe I could do even more to help him remain hidden.

I grabbed the blade control and lowered it until it scraped against the ground. Some dirt piled up in front of the blade, slowing Bertha, but the blade also kicked an expanding cloud of dust into Mercury's arid air. In seconds, the billowing dust partially obscured my vision of the path ahead. My pursuers were invisible except for the ever-present sun glinting off their vehicles. I just prayed the dust blocked their view as much as it blocked mine.

A bolt of white-hot plasma flashed through the dust cloud and splashed harmlessly against Bertha's blade. I had to assume they were shooting to disable the dozer. As I'd told Dave, they still needed me alive.

Two more blaster bolts came my way. One hit the ground just ahead of Bertha, and the other glanced off her left tread.

"Sorry for the abuse, old girl," I said. "But you're doing a great job."

The first pursuer swept past on my left, and three blaster shots flashed into the gears driving the left tread. Bertha lurched and pulled to the left, but she kept rolling. I held my breath until the same pursuer circled around Bertha and unloaded more blaster shots at her right tread.

I released my held breath and checked the clock in the heat suit's heads-up display. Dave had been on the run for almost two minutes. If he'd been running unencumbered, he'd have easily reached the *Lightning's Hand* by now. But how much would the bulky heat suit slow him down?

Two more pursuers roared by, one on each side, and poured more blaster fire into Bertha's gears. As the pursuers circled for another pass, she lurched to the left again, and this time I let her have her head. The vehicle coming up on my left ran too close, and Bertha's blade swung into its path. Bertha bucked as the vehicle smashed into her blade, then her left tread crunched over its engine.

Two heat-suited men rolled from the smaller vehicle's cab, came to their feet, and poured blaster fire into Bertha's engine. She shook, rattled, lurched forward, gave a final shudder, and her engine fell silent.

The three remaining vehicles encircled Bertha and stopped. Goons armed with blaster rifles climbed out and leveled the guns at Bertha's cab.

I gave Bertha's dashboard a last pat. "Thanks, old girl. You did great."

With a sigh, I raised my arms in surrender.

trouble on the rooftop

ONE MORE MAN emerged from the largest of the pursuit vehicles. His heat suit hung from his narrow frame like a burlap sack draped over a child. Even though reflected sunlight kept me from seeing the face behind the suit's faceplate, I recognized him.

Slick tapped his right ear, held up one finger, and then held up four fingers. I recognized the universal sign to turn my comm to channel fourteen, did so, and gave him a thumbs up.

"Hammerhand's hurt bad, Barrett," Slick said. "Real bad."

I resisted the urge to shrug, since my heat suit would render the move all but invisible. "It's not my fault."

"The hell you say!" Slick yelled. "You musta trained that… that… creature to attack him."

"Or, and try to follow my reasoning Slick, that *Mercurian* saw Hammerhand pound on me and threaten to break my neck. And *he* intervened." I took a dig at Slick and added, "That means 'to come between.'"

"I know what it means!" Slick waved his hand at the gun-wielding goons surrounding Bertha. "Somebody shoot Barrett."

In case someone obeyed Slick's command, I ducked below the dashboard. After five seconds passed without a hail of blaster fire, I poked my head up. The goons looked back and forth between each other, obviously uncertain what to do. I decided this was a good time to add to their uncertainty.

"You know Norman Tate wants me alive, right?" I asked. "If he doesn't have me as a hostage, he has no way to keep Tina and Nick from telling the solar system what he's been doing out here. So shooting me is a terrible idea."

Slick remained still for ten long seconds, then gave a dismissive wave. "Fine. Whatever. I guess me and the boys'll settle for beatin' the crap outta you when we get back inside. And when Hammerhand done healed up, he's gonna beat the crap outta you, too."

Hoping to delay the time when Tate's men noticed Dave wasn't with me, I needled Slick some more. "I'm going to be a get well present for your boyfriend? Aw, that's so sweet, Slick!"

Someone on the comm channel snickered.

"Who laughed? Huh? Who was it?" When no one responded, Slick said, "Me and Hammerhand is good buddies, is all."

I adopted a dubious tone of voice. "If you say so, Slick."

"Yeah, I say—"

I never heard Slick's next words, because the high-pitched whine of engines drowned out his words. I looked behind me, and saw a wall of dust coming towards us. The nose of the *Lightning's Hand* poked through the dust cloud's leading edge. I switched my comm back to channel nineteen, which Dave and I used before I made him take off running. "Dave?"

"Who else? What comm channel are the goons using?"

"Fourteen."

"Switching channels now."

I changed to channel fourteen, and heard Dave say, "I have my ship's guns charged and ready to fire. Back away from Barrett and the dozer, or you'll get to see what a blaster cannon bolt does to a human body."

Everyone stared at the approaching ship for a moment, then Slick said, "He's bluffing. He ain't got no guns. He'd a shot somebody if'n he did."

Dave barked a dark, menacing laugh. "Wrong, bucko. If I shoot the guns, I'll have to clean them afterwards. It's a tedious job, and I'd rather not do it. But I will unless you. Back. Off. Now."

"I'd do it, guys," I said. "Cleaning the guns takes the same time, whether he shoots one of you or all of you. Which he's likely to do if you piss him off."

No one spoke as the whine of the *Lightning's Hand's* engines drew closer. Finally, a goon said, "I don't get paid enough for this."

A man to my left turned and walked away from me. His partner glanced at Slick, then followed his friend. That was all it took, and everyone except Slick walked away. Slick stood like a sad statue as Dave brought the *Lightning's Hand* down behind Bertha. As the ship settled onto her landing struts, I climbed from Bertha's cab and walked back to the ship.

Just before I entered the *Hand's* airlock, Slick said, "This ain't over 'tween us, Barrett. Not by a long shot."

I sighed. "Yeah, Slick, it is."

When I'd cycled through the airlock, Dave spoke over the ship's intercom. "You safely onboard?"

I began peeling off the sweaty heat suit. "Yes. But don't leave yet. I want to use your ship's guns to destroy the facility's communications dish."

Dave laughed. "What ship's guns?"

"So you *were* bluffing?"

"Yep."

"Too bad. I'd really like to keep Slick and friends from reporting my escape."

In a tone of mock offense, Dave said, "Hey, remember who you're talking to. Hotshot pilots like me can do stuff like that without firing a shot."

"How?"

"Come up to the cockpit and see."

I finished pulling off the heat suit and joined Dave in the

cockpit. I buckled myself into the co-pilot's seat, glanced askance at Dave, and said, "I'm waiting."

Dave reached for the cargo compartment controls and opened its hatch. I felt the *Lightning's Hand* shudder as the open hatch interfered with her aerodynamics, but Dave compensated easily even though he only had one hand on the flight controls. He extended the winch arm and lowered the cable and hook.

I turned wide eyes on Dave. "Are you doing what I think you're doing?"

"I don't know, Travis." Despite concentrating on two sets of controls, Dave's voice was calm and controlled. "What do you think I'm doing?"

"Looping around the communications tower way too close for comfort, so you can catch the cargo hook on one of its girders, and then use the *Hand* to pull it down."

Dave grinned without looking at me. "Then yes, I am doing what you think I'm doing."

And he did it, too. Dave dragged the tower four or five miles from the facility and landed. He had me don the heat suit again and cut off the tangled end of the cable. While I removed the heat suit a second time, Dave withdrew the winch, closed the cargo hatch, and lifted off. He turned the ship's nose towards Twi-Town and flew a mere one hundred feet off the ground.

"Aren't you a little low?" I asked.

"I'm keeping her under the radar." He grinned at me. "Relax, I know what I'm doing."

As I settled into the copilot's seat again, Dave handed me the comm. "Don't you think you should check in with your girlfriend? She's been worried about you."

I tapped in Trouble's comm code. Two seconds later, she answered with a tentative, "Hello?"

"May I speak with Trouble with a capital T?"

She gasped. "Travis?"

Excited voices rose in the background.

"Your one and only," I said.

"Dave got to you? You're safe?"

"Yes, to both. It's good to hear your voice, Trouble. Are you ready to go home?"

"More than ever," she said, "but we can't."

"Why not?"

"Jacobson closed the spaceport, so no ships are coming in or out. He must have had officers follow Nick, because he has ten patrol cars outside our hotel. And Allie Winters commed to let us know that Space Patrol has orders to take us into protective custody if we leave the hotel." Trouble's voice lowered. "I believe Father ordered Jacobson to keep us trapped until a spaceship arrives to take us back to Carnegie Station." She sighed in despair. "I want to see you again more than anything, but we can't leave the hotel. Father must pay for his crimes, Travis, so you have to leave us behind."

I took a deep breath, squelched the urge to let emotion get the better of me, and spoke in the calmest, most rational tone of voice I could muster. "No, Trouble, I'm not leaving you or anyone else behind."

"You have to, Travis. The Mercurians—"

"Are free. Dave and I broke them out during our escape."

Dave leaned closer to the mic in my hand and said, "Travis freed them. I was just along for the ride."

"That's wonderful news," Trouble said. "But they won't be truly safe until the solar system knows they exist. You and Dave are the only ones who can alert Space Patrol and the Earth govs. That means you can't risk coming for us."

Dave destroyed the sun-side research facility's communications array specifically so Norman Tate and his Space Patrol lapdog, Jacobson wouldn't know I had escaped. But Tate would suspect the truth the next time he commed the facility and no one responded.

With that in mind, I asked, "What do you think will happen to you and Nick when your father realizes I escaped?"

"Nothing. Father can't risk having an investigation that involves him. He has too much to lose, especially now."

She had a good point, but it didn't go far enough. "What do you think he'll do to you two if I expose his operations on Mercury? He'll lose everything if the full weight of the Space Patrol and the Earth govs come down on him. You already said your father is vindictive. Do you believe he cares about Nick and you more than he would want revenge against the man who ruined him?"

Trouble remained silent for a moment. She had no illusions about her relationship with her father, but did she believe even Norman Tate could be so cold and calculating? In a small voice, Trouble said, "I... don't know, Travis."

"Neither do I. And that's why he can, and will, use you and Nick as hostages against my good behavior." I forced an upbeat tone into my voice. "That's why Dave and I are coming to get you."

"But how will you get through the Patrollers surrounding the hotel?"

"Why go through them when we can fly over them?"

"What?" Trouble gasped.

"*What*?" Dave shouted.

"It's a small cockpit, Dave," I said. "There's no need to shout."

"You can*not* be serious!" Dave snapped.

"Are you serious?" Trouble asked.

"Would you both please be quiet for a minute?" I asked. "I can only answer one person's questions at a time. Dave, I'll discuss this with you once I finish talking with Trouble. Okay?"

"Yeah, fine," Dave said.

"Now, are you listening, Trouble?"

"I always listen to you, Travis."

"Good. Who's in the hotel with you?"

"Nick, Laura, and Rita."

"What about Rach and Sam?"

"Rach took Sam home."

"Did Sam keep the samples of frozen Mercurian blood?"

"No, he left them with Nick. Just in case you escaped from Father's clutches."

"Good. I want you to comm Sam. He and Liz should take the kids and go to his employer's offices. Try to talk Rach and Allie Winters into joining them there. If your father gets desperate for hostages, he might find his way to them. They should be safe from him in a rival's offices."

"I'll do my best."

"You're free to move around the hotel, right? You just can't leave it?"

"That's right."

"Good. Have Nick find the way onto the roof and make sure the door is unlocked. Buy the key from the clerk, Archie, if you have to."

"You're going to pick us up from the roof?"

"That's the plan."

"Um, Travis?"

"Yeah?"

"The hotel is only five stories high. All the surrounding buildings are taller."

"What she said," Dave muttered.

"Don't worry," I said. "Dave is the best pilot in the solar system. If he can't do this, no one can."

"If you say so," Trouble said. "How long before you get here?"

I glanced at Dave. He checked the *Lightning's Hand's* location and said, "Fifty minutes."

"Then I'd better get busy," Trouble said. "I love you."

"I love you, too."

I disconnected the comm, and Dave immediately glared at me and asked, "Are you out of your mind? There's a reason they put spaceports in the middle of nowhere! The *Hand* is small for a spaceship, but she's freaking huge for city streets."

I met Dave's glare with as bland an expression as I could muster. "Do you agree we can't leave Nick and Trouble in Twi-Town?"

"From what you and Trouble said about Norman Tate? Yeah, they—"

"Since they can't leave the hotel without Space Patrol grabbing them, what other options do we have?"

Dave sighed. "I can't think of any."

"Then let's figure out how you're going to do this."

"Fine. Call up the map of Twi-Town on the nav system." Dave looked at me. "Do you think you can handle flying the *Hand* while I study the map?"

"I... guess I'll have to handle it."

"Yeah, you will. Take the controls." I caught the co-pilot's controls, did my best to ignore the ground racing by a hundred feet below us, and got a feel for the ship. Dave released his set of controls and said, "I'm going to be really pissed off if you crash my ship, Travis."

In a tight voice, I said, "Wouldn't want that."

"Damn straight, buddy."

Dave fell silent while I concentrated on flying. After I flew for five minutes without crashing, I even relaxed. A little.

After another ten minutes, Dave asked, "You know there's no way we can sneak up on the hotel, don't you?"

"Of course. Like you said, the *Lightning's Hand* is way too big for that."

"Good. I just wanted to make sure you understood that before I told you my plan."

"Which is?"

Dave took the controls from me. "I'm going to fly the *Hand* straight down Main Street to the hotel."

I stared at Dave with wide-eyed astonishment. "You're going to fly a spaceship down a city street?"

"A small spaceship," Dave replied.

"Which *you* called freaking huge for city streets."

"It is, except that Main Street is the widest street in the city. It's a good thing the hotel is on Main, or I'd have to bring the *Lightning's Hand* in from above." Dave flashed a grin at me. "Cities have all sorts of wind swirls, so *that* sure would have been tricky!"

"Trickier than flying for God knows how many miles down a city street?"

"Bringing the *Hand* down in Twi-Town was *your* idea, Barrett," Dave growled. "Don't get pissy with me just because you don't like how I'll do that."

I took a deep breath and released it. "You're right. Sorry for my overreaction."

Dave waved off my apology. "After the day you've had, you've earned the right to stress out a little. Besides, I'll only have to fly a mile or so down Main Street."

"I thought the hotel was on the edge of midtown?"

"It is. But I can bring the *Hand* down in Twi-Town Square. It has a small park with a monument to the first man on Mercury, and all the streets go around the park. Then I just have to nose her into Main Street and fly to the hotel. Easy."

"I'll just have to trust that you know what you're doing."

"It'll be just like all those asteroid field rescues we pulled off in the *Soteria*." A nostalgic smile spread across Dave's face. "We made a good team."

I shared his smile. "Still do."

Dave gave me a sideways look. "You want to make the same bet we made back then?"

"Sure," I said. "Drinks are on me if you pull this off."

"And drinks are on me if I crash and kill us both."

I reached for the comm. "I'd better tell Trouble the plan."

She listened as I described Dave's proposed flight plan, then simply said, "Then we'd better get to the rooftop."

I checked the time. "Good idea. We're about five minutes out right now. Did you get hold of Sam, Rach, and Allie?"

"Yes. Rach grumbled about your request, though I think that

is more out of habit than anything else, but they're all getting out of sight for a few days."

"Good. We'll see you in a few minutes."

"We'll be waiting."

As I disconnected, Dave said, "Twi-Town is on the horizon."

"How long before you increase your altitude?"

Dave pulled back on the controls, and the *Hand* climbed to three hundred feet. "How about now?"

I can only imagine the shocked expression on the face of the space control operator at Twi-Town's spaceport when the *Lightning's Hand* suddenly appeared on his screen. But he didn't let his surprise slow his reactions. The comm squawked, and a professionally calm voice said, "*Lightning's Hand*, this is Twi-Town control. Divert course to the spaceport and land. You are in a no-fly zone."

"You want to get that, Travis?" Dave asked. "I need to concentrate on piloting from here on out."

I grabbed the comm again, and drawled, "Twi-Town Control, this is the *Lightning's Hand*. We don't copy. Please repeat."

"You are in a no-fly zone. Come to heading two niner three and land at the spaceport. Do you copy?"

"We copy, Control."

Control waited two seconds for our course change. When it didn't come, he said, "Why haven't you altered course?"

"I said we copied, Control, not that we'd comply."

A sharp edge entered the professionally calm voice. "But you're flying into the city!"

"Huh," I said, "so we are. But don't worry. We'll be real careful not to break anything."

"*Lightning's Hand*, alter course or I swear I will ensure Space Patrol revokes your pilot's license and confiscates your ship!"

The dilapidated outskirts of Twi-Town flashed beneath us, and Dave reduced the ship's throttle. "Twenty seconds to Twi-Town Square."

Into the comm, I said, "I don't have a pilot's license, Control, and it's not my ship. I'd tell the pilot and owner, but he really needs to concentrate on flying right now."

"But—"

"Over and out, Control."

I disconnected the comm as Dave brought the *Hand* to a near-stop and descended towards Twi-Town Square. The ship's controls displayed the square, with a scale image of the *Lightning's Hand* superimposed over it. Dave hadn't been kidding when he said the monument park was small. My eyes darted back and forth between the altimeter and the display, and the square still appeared too small to hold the *Hand's* full length.

The top of an office building appeared through the ship's front viewport. We were so close to it, I could clearly read the expressions of the people working within it.

A man stared at me in open-mouthed astonishment, his hand curled around a coffee mug. As I watched, his grip loosened, and the mug fell to the floor.

Two women separated by a desk sat in an office and watched us descend, their eyes wide and their work forgotten.

Dozens of others crowded around windows, apparently heedless of the potential danger should Dave make a piloting mistake. Some shouted and pointed. Others stared with amazed expressions.

At an altitude of fifty feet, Dave gently nudged the *Lightning's Hand* to starboard. I gave a cheery wave to the office workers, and a few gave half-hearted waves in return, though one older woman smiled broadly and waved vigorously.

Main Street slid into the viewport. Dave stopped sliding sideways when he had the *Hand's* nose centered on the street. He increased the throttle, and the ship entered the man-made canyon walled by offices and stores. I glanced at the display again, saw that the ship had only ten feet of clearance on each side, and rose from my seat.

"I'm going to the cargo hold. Tell me when you're ready for me to open the hatch."

In a tight voice, Dave said, "Got it."

I felt better when I couldn't see the display or through the viewport. Sometimes, ignorance really is bliss.

The ship's intercom crackled, and Dave said, "Hotel in sight. Two blocks to go. Open the hatch."

I activated the door mechanism, and it quickly slid open. "Done."

"Trouble and the others are on the roof." A second later, he added, "Dammit. Half the Space Patrollers surrounding the hotel just ran inside."

"On their way to the roof?" I asked.

"That's my guess, but it gets worse. The remaining Patrollers have their guns trained on the *Hand*."

"Do you think they'll shoot at me when you stop?"

"This is Twi-Town," Dave said. "Count on it."

A quick glance out the cargo hatch showed it was twenty feet from the nearest building. The control display in the cockpit had only shown ten feet of clearance for the *Lightning's Hand*, so I had to find a way to get everyone across at least ten feet of open space. I glanced at the controls in the cargo hold, didn't see controls for extending a landing ramp, and didn't have time to search for them.

With a mental shrug, I ran to the controls for the cargo winch. I unrolled about fifteen feet of cable and then extended the winch arm out the cargo hatch.

"You ready, Travis?" Dave asked over the intercom.

The roof corner of the hotel slid into view through the open hatch. "As ready as I'm going to be."

A blaster bolt lanced from below and splashed off the hotel's exterior wall. Two more followed, and I heard a third bolt ping off the *Hand's* hull as Dave slid the ship closer to the hotel.

On the roof, Trouble, Nick, Laura, and Rita dashed into view. Another volley of blaster bolts drove them back from the lip of the roof.

I wrapped the cable around my left arm, got a good grip on it with my right hand, and said, "Up three feet, if you can." The *Hand* wobbled as Dave fought to keep her steady, but rose enough for my purposes. "Hold it here, Dave."

"Roger."

Blaster bolts flashed through the gap between the *Hand* and the hotel. I looked into Trouble's green eyes and the concern reflected in them, and leapt from the cargo hold. Shouts rose from below as the Patrollers spotted me. Three of them snapped off shots that sizzled the air near me, but none of them hit. Nick caught me as I swung over the hotel roof and pulled me away from the edge.

I unwound the cable from my left arm. "Half the officers are running up the hotel stairs now, so time is short." I handed the cable to Nick. "You go first so you can catch the girls and Rita when I send them over."

Nick nodded and duplicated my hold on the cable. He moved a few feet to the right so he wouldn't swing straight into a hail of blaster fire and jumped from the roof. More shouts rose from below as the officers shifted their aim, but they were too late. Nick swung into the cargo hold, landed easily, and quickly shoved the cable back to me.

I caught it and turned to Laura. "You're next."

She gave a nervous nod as I wound the cable around her left arm, then closed both hands over the slender cable in a white-knuckled grip. I guided her to the left, away from Nick's flight path across the gap.

"Don't look down," I said. "Go!"

As Laura jumped, I sped her on her way with a shove in the back. As with Nick, the blaster fire was late in adjusting to her sudden appearance. She swung safely into the cargo hold, and Nick caught her easily.

I knew we had to avoid falling into a pattern that the officers on the street below could discern. So I said to Trouble, "You go as soon as you've got the cable."

She nodded as her brother sent the cable back to us, and

didn't wait for me to catch it for her. Trouble dashed in front of me, grabbed the cable with both hands, and launched herself from the roof. The arc of her swing carried around the blaster fire from below. Nick steadied his big sister as she landed. Then she sent the cable back to me.

"It's your turn, Boss," Rita said.

I caught the cable with my left hand, wrapped my right arm around Rita, and pulled her to me. "I'm not leaving you behind, Rita."

"I'm just a Robosec, Boss." She pushed on my arm, but I didn't let go. "You're a person."

"You're a person to *me*, Rita. So shut up and let me get you to safety."

To my surprise, Rita stopped struggling. I had doubts that her thin mechanical arms—designed for clerical work, and not heavy lifting—would hold her weight. So I wrapped the cable around her middle and tied a half knot. It wouldn't hold for long, but it didn't have to.

Rita grabbed the cable with her spindly hands. "You better be right behind me, Boss."

I grabbed her torso and shoved her hard in the opposite direction Trouble went. She barely cleared the lip of the roof and swung into the gap between the hotel and the *Lightning's Hand*. She voiced a mechanical squawk as the half-knot loosened and her hands slid down the cable. Her course arced towards the cargo hold, and it appeared she would make it.

Then our luck ran out. A blaster shot sliced through the cable above Rita's hands. My heart leapt into my throat as she tumbled, and the lower section of her torso smacked into the bottom edge of the cargo hatch. Her metal hands scrabbled on the flat metal deck, but there was nothing for them to hold.

Then Nick and Trouble literally dove to her aid. Trouble grabbed Rita's arms, slowing her slide and giving Nick enough time to wrap his arms around her. Laura caught Nick's legs, leaned back, and pulled with all her might. Rita's torso popped up over the edge of the hatch. She was safe, but there wasn't enough free-swinging cable left to reach me.

Trouble hopped to her feet and ran for the winch controls. At the same time, I heard a crash behind me. I looked towards the sound and saw a door hanging limp from a broken hinge. Five Space Patrol officers charged through the door and sprinted my way.

corporate trouble

I DIVED behind an exhaust duct jutting through the roof as the lead two patrollers opened fire. Blaster bolts hotter than the sun's surface sizzled through the air behind me, splashed into the roof and gouged holes in the tiles.

"You got nowhere to go," an officer called, "and your cover won't last long."

A blaster shot slammed into the other side of the duct I hid behind, and I caught the familiar scent of melting metal. If all five officers turned their blasters on the duct, they could burn through it in seconds.

In case I hadn't gotten the message, the same officer said, "One shot and there's already a foot wide hole in the duct. I'm going to count to five, and then we're all going to shoot at it... One. Two."

The flat crack of a blaster sounded nearby, followed by two more shots. I glanced at the *Lightning's Hand* hovering tantalizingly nearby and impossibly far away. Trouble was flat on the deck with her blaster braced against the lip of the cargo hatch, taking deliberate shots at the officers.

The officer interrupted his count. "Crap!"

I heard the Patrollers scramble for cover as Trouble said, "I missed on purpose, gentlemen. I will not miss again."

"Christ, lady, are you out of your mind?" the talker yelled. "It's illegal to shoot at a Patroller carrying out his lawful orders. You're going to be in a lot of trouble if you don't stop it!"

"Who gave you those orders?" Trouble asked.

"We got them straight from Jacobson," the officer said.

"Then it's a safe bet the orders aren't lawful."

Trouble's aim shifted slightly, and she fired again. I heard a muffled curse from one officer and scrabbling as he pulled himself back under cover.

Trouble said, "Good reflexes, officer. I thought I had you. Next time you think about sneaking around on the roof, remember how close I came to hitting you."

In the *Hand's* cargo hold, Rita rose from the deck. The length of cable I'd wound around her dragged on the deck as she glided to the winch controls. The winch motor whined as she let out another ten feet of cable. That was more than enough for me to use to swing from the hotel roof to the cargo hold, except that the cable dangled midway between the two.

"Hey lady, how long do you think it's going to take Commander Jacobson to scramble a couple of Patrol interceptors?" the talker asked. "Because I guarantee that's what he's doing right now. Even the lazy ass Space Patrol pilots we have out at the spaceport can have a ship in the air in two or three minutes." He let that sink in, then said, "This might look like a standoff, but it's not. If you leave ahead of the interceptors, we get your buddy. If you stay, we get all of you. Either way, we win."

Trouble glanced at me. I nodded and waved for them to leave me. She gave me a look of grim determination and shook her head.

I glanced at Nick and Laura, who, unarmed and unable to help, huddled on the deck behind Trouble, and made the same 'get going' motion. They shook their heads in unison.

Rita didn't even wait for me to look her way before her head began swiveling back and forth atop her torso.

I couldn't see Dave in the cockpit, but he was a Space Patrol veteran and had to know Jacobson would send interceptors after us. Hell, he had the ship's sensors in front of him, and would know the second the ships lifted off.

And I could see their point of view. If the *Lightning's Hand* flew away, Norman Tate would have me to use as a hostage against Trouble's and Nick's good behavior. If the Space Patrol interceptors caught the *Lightning's Hand*, Norman Tate could release his children and hold the rest of us hostage.

Either way, Norman Tate won.

The only way Tate lost was if he held no hostages. And the only way that could happen was if I made it to the *Lightning's Hand*. Or got gunned down trying to get there.

I avoided thinking of the second outcome and waved to get Trouble's attention. When I had it, I pointed at myself and then pointed at the *Hand*. Then I mimed shooting at the Space Patrol officers. Her eyes widened when she caught my gist, but gave me a firm nod.

I held up three fingers. Then two. Then one.

I jumped up, fired two quick shots in the general direction of the officers, and then ran for the roof's edge. Trouble laid down covering fire as I ran, and I kept firing over my shoulder as I ran. I took a last shot as I stepped up onto the lip of the roof. And my foot slipped under me as I leapt for the *Lightning's Hand*.

When my foot slid beneath me, I knew my leap wouldn't carry me to the *Lightning's Hand's* cargo hold. I kicked my other foot against the lip of the roof in a desperate attempt to strengthen my leap and save myself. But I was already too far from the edge to get much force behind the kick. It helped. Just not enough.

My gaze met Trouble's across the gap, and I hated the anguish I saw reflected in her eyes. She stopped shooting and stretched her arm towards me in a desperate, futile gesture. Behind her, Laura buried her face in Nick's shoulder while he watched me, grim and helpless. My eyes flicked to Rita, but her face screen showed an image of intense concentration as she kept working the winch controls.

And I suddenly realized the winch arm was moving. Towards me. Bringing its fifteen feet of dangling cable ever closer to my hands.

I released the blaster I'd forgotten I still held and reached for Rita's lifeline. But it still dangled beyond my grasp. Trouble stuck her head through the hatch and watched as I fought panic and the urge to flail wildly for the cable. I'd only have one chance at this, and the last thing I needed was to knock the cable out of reach.

My infinitesimal forward momentum brought me closer to the cable.

Rita's work with the winch controls brought the cable closer to me.

The end of the cable entered my peripheral vision.

A fingertip brushed the cable.

I stretched.

Curled three fingers around the cable.

Pulled.

Grabbed the cable with both hands.

Felt the cable slide through my hands.

Tightened my grip.

Arrested my fall.

Swung beneath the *Hand*.

Realized the end of the cable hung before my eyes.

Shoved thoughts of how close I'd come to missing the cable from my mind.

Pulled myself up the cable.

Fought the terror of losing my grip long enough to shift my hand higher.

Brought my left hand up to join my right.

Pulled myself up again.

Wrapped my ankles around the cable.

Remembered to breathe.

And that's when I saw the building across the street from the hotel sliding past me. Dave had the *Lightning's Hand* underway again. I wondered why he'd risk moving the ship while I dangled from the cable until I noticed the blaster bolts blazing up from the street below. My ill-fated leap from the hotel made me forget the Space Patrol officers stationed down there. Only my pendulum motion at the end of the cable kept me from being an easy target.

Almost as soon as I noticed the shots flying around me, they grew even less accurate. Then less numerous. And then they stopped entirely as the *Lightning's Hand* moved out of range.

"Hold on tight, Travis!" Trouble called. "Rita is reeling you in."

Twenty long seconds later, Trouble and Nick helped pry loose my death grip on the cable. After my aerial ordeal, it felt distinctly odd having a solid deck beneath my feet.

Laura said, "We've got him, Mr. Hayslett."

The intercom crackled, and Dave replied, "Good. Time to say goodbye and good riddance to Twi-Town."

Rita activated the cargo door, and it trundled slowly closed. Trouble dragged me away from it, held my head with both hands, and asked, "Are you okay?"

I nodded. "Yeah. Thanks to Rita, you, and Dave."

Then Rita slammed into my back and wrapped her mechanical arms around me. "I thought I'd lost you, Boss!"

I turned enough to loop one arm around Rita, the other around Trouble. I squeezed Rita tightly, planted a kiss on her face screen, and said, "You saved my life, Rita."

Rita's face screen turned pink. "You're making me blush, Boss."

I arched my eyebrows in surprise. "I didn't even know you could do that."

"A girl likes having a few secrets," she said.

"I also didn't know you could work a winch."

"It's part of Rossum's basic skills software package, Boss. All

Robosecs have it." Rita pulled away from me. "Now, you need to kiss Miss Tate."

Trouble spun me to face her. "Thank you, Rita." Then she tilted her head back, melted against me, and poured all her love and fear and longing into a kiss unlike anything I'd ever felt before. I wrapped my arms around her and returned the kiss for all I was worth.

In a smug tone, Rita said, "I *told* you she was trouble, Boss."

THE *LIGHTNING'S Hand* accelerated suddenly and threw everyone but Rita onto the deck. Her repulsors kept her from falling, but the force sent her crashing into a wall. I twisted so my body cushioned Trouble, and a quiet *oof* from Nick suggested he'd done the same for Laura.

"A little warning next time, Hayslett?" Rita said.

The intercom crackled as Dave replied, "No time, sorry."

"What's happening?" Trouble asked.

"Two Space Patrol interceptors just took off from the Twi-Town Spaceport," Dave said. "Guess who they're coming for?"

I lifted Trouble off me and stood up. "I'm coming up there."

A moment later, I slid into the co-pilot's seat. Trouble stopped in the doorway, and everyone else hovered—literally, in Rita's case—behind her. The viewport showed the upper atmosphere of Mercury's dark side as the *Lightning's Hand* rocketed towards space. I glanced at the scanner display, noted the two dots on our tail, and asked, "Can you outrun them?"

Dave's eyes never left his controls as he snorted. "Did you ever see a commercial ship outrun interceptors during your career in Space Patrol?"

"No."

"You're not going to see one do it today, either."

"They're short-range ships. Can you stay ahead of them until they run low on fuel and have to turn back?"

"Maybe. I probably know a few maneuvers they don't."

The ship's radio came to life, and the most unprofessional Space Patrol voice I'd ever heard said, "You can't escape before we get you, buddy. So why don't you pull over now and save us both a lot of trouble?"

I grabbed the mic and said, "You have no reason for this pursuit. Break off and return to base."

"You flew a spaceship down a city street to pick up a bunch of fugitives. Seems like a good enough reason to me."

"That's a traffic violation, and our passengers are not fugitives."

"Then you won't mind coming back to Space Patrol HQ so we can clear this up."

While I searched for a suitable response, my chair shifted as Trouble leaned over it. "Travis, may I please have the mic?"

I rose from the co-pilot's chair and handed the mic to her. "Do you have a good reply?"

She slid into the seat. "I have a reply. We'll see how good it is in a minute."

The interceptor pilot said, "I'm tired of waiting."

Trouble keyed the mic. "I wish to speak with Commander Jacobson."

Derisive laughter came from the speaker. "Oh, no! Space Karen wants to talk to my manager!"

"I doubt you'll laugh much when you're rotting in a cell next to your commander." Trouble paused for a moment, then said, "Speak up, Jacobson. I know you're listening in."

"Why would he be listening?" Laura asked.

Trouble looked over her shoulder. "Too much is riding on this for him to leave it entirely in the hands of those two pilots. If Jacobson is even remotely like Father, he's poised to intervene at the first sign of trouble." Her lips quirked up in a brief smile. "And here I am."

"I don't know who you are, lady, but—"

"Jacobson knows who I am. He's the only one who matters."

Trouble released the mic switch. "Dave, are the interceptors in firing range?"

Dave's eyes raked over the ship's controls. "Not yet."

"How long until they are?"

"In range? A minute. Until they have a reasonable chance of hitting us? Two minutes."

Trouble looked back at Nick and Laura. "Laura, gather all the data we have on the Mercurians into a single file. Nick, record a brief statement explaining what it all means, and include the coordinates for the day-side facility where Father held you and Travis. Get it ready for broadcast as fast as possible."

"What can I do?" I asked.

Trouble caught my hand in a tight grip. "Stay with me." Then she triggered the mic. "Speak up anytime, Jacobson."

I signaled for Trouble to keep the mic active. I filled my voice with all the disgust I felt for my former commander and said, "Give it up, Tina. Jacobson's too cowardly to talk to you."

As if on cue, Jacobson snapped, "Wrong, as usual, Barrett. I will enjoy listening to you beg for your life as my interceptors blast your ship to atoms."

Trouble asked, "Are you willing to kill both Tate heirs and risk my father's wrath just to take petty revenge on Travis?"

Jacobson laughed. "Norman Tate will thank me for ridding him of his meddlesome offspring."

"He might," Trouble said, "but only in the darkest recesses of his mind. Publicly, he'll play the grieving father whose children's lives were cut short on the orders of the solar system's best-known coward."

Jacobson's voice dripped with condescension. "That is the one thing he will *not* do. Not if he has any sense of self preservation."

"Oh, Father has that in spades, which is why you'd never live long enough to face a court martial for destroying this ship." Trouble said. "Hammerhand and Slick are already on Mercury. I wonder what kind of accident they'll create for you? Heat suit failure? An ill-considered, probably drunken, trip to the Twi-Line wastes? Or maybe just something like a simple mugging gone wrong?"

Silence met Trouble's words. She took that as a good sign, and added, "The minute those interceptors shoot, we'll broadcast everything we know about the Tate Steelworks day-side research facility on all radio frequencies. Every radio receiver in the inner system will pick up that broadcast, and it will be more than enough to warrant a thorough investigation from the spacefaring Earth govs.

"The two pilots listening to this conversation and probably wondering what we're talking about might end up receiving the order to take you into custody pending investigation." Trouble's voice dropped to a purr. "If you're very lucky, you'll spend the rest of your life in prison. But I'll bet you get shipped off to a Venusian penal plantation. Either way, your remaining days will be short and unpleasant in the extreme."

Trouble stopped talking and waited for a response from Jacobson. After half-a-minute of silence, the interceptor pilot said, "The ship is in range, sir. What are our orders?"

Jacobson maintained his silence, so Trouble said, "Recall your interceptors and let us go on our way, Jacobson. We won't make any system-wide broadcasts, meaning you'll have until we reach the United Planets headquarters on Luna to disappear."

Jacobson broke his silence. "I want Barrett's word that no one on that ship will report anything until you land on Luna."

Trouble handed the mic to me, and I said, "You have my word, Jacobson."

A moment later, Dave's posture relaxed. "The interceptors are turning back." Without looking up, he said, "I suppose you want the rest of us to abide by your precious word of honor?"

"I'd appreciate it," I said.

Dave shrugged. "I'll do it as long as I can take the fastest route to Luna."

I waved my permission. "Waste as much fuel as you need. I'll cover the costs."

"Now you're talking." Dave flashed his cocky-pilot's grin. "Somebody time me, because I'm going to set a record for the fastest Mercury to Luna run ever."

He did, too.

WITHIN HOURS of our arrival on Luna, Space Patrol issued an arrest order for Jacobson. He rabbited right after Trouble's brief negotiations with him, but for once in his miserable life Jacobson's cowardice proved useful. His flight lent credence to our admittedly outlandish story, as did the disappearance of Warren, Jacobson's sycophantic assistant, and three other Space Patrol officers assigned to Twi-Town.

Three days of testimony, scientific inquiry, and negotiations followed, during which Space Patrol issued arrest orders for half-a-dozen Tate Steelworks employees in Twi-Town. Rather than trust the most corrupt Patrollers in the solar system, Space Patrol sent a special detachment to Mercury. They staged a coordinated string of raids and snatched all their suspects in Twi-Town quickly and quietly.

The group sent to the research facility fared less well. They discovered a blown up ruin, and the charred remains of twenty-eight people. Space Patrol forensics couldn't tell us much about the dead except that Hammerhand and Slick weren't among them.

Space Patrol only found six of the seven vehicles Dave and I found in the facility's heat lock, so I must assume the pair got away and are plotting revenge on the person they blame for their fall from criminal grace—me. I'm already having nightmares about them getting their hands on me or—far worse—Trouble.

After our three-day debriefing on Luna and at Trouble's

prompting, Space Patrol sent Nick and Laura back to Mercury to act as liaisons to the Mercurians. They put Trouble and me on the fastest ship available and sent us to Carnegie Station. She told those in charge that they'd never capture Norman Tate if they flooded the Tate Steelworks headquarters with officers. Trouble told them of the bolt holes her father had built into their Carnegie Station home and insisted he'd have similar bolt holes at work, too. But she suggested that subtlety might work where a frontal assault would fail.

That's why I ended up riding the same tube train I took the day Trouble burst into my life. The train's doors hissed open at the industrial district's station. The familiar smell of hot metal and humanity tickled my nose. As before, the subtle scent of exotic locales, tropical nights, and all-consuming passion blended with the industrial odors. But I didn't wonder where the fragrance came from. Because Trouble walked by my side.

As before, the surrounding crowd shrank with each foundry we passed until Trouble and I walked alone towards the blazing TATE STEELWORKS sign. Her clicking high heels echoed in the vast corridor and proclaimed doom for anyone foolish enough to stand in her way. Knowing Trouble's entrance had to be perfect, I hurried ahead and opened the office door for her.

Trouble breezed through the door and smiled at the security guard within. "Good morning, James. I'm here to see my father."

Without slowing, Trouble headed for the elevator. James smiled and touched a button hidden by his desk. As the elevator door slid open, he said, "Welcome back, Miss Tate. I hope you had a pleasant trip."

The banal greeting carried more weight than James knew. It told us that her father still played his cards close to his chest. That he even kept his security people in the dark about the Mercury project *and*, equally surprising, his daughter's role in the affair. Someone might interpret Norman Tate's actions as stupidly short-sighted. I interpreted them as unwavering confidence in himself and his position.

And a severely myopic idea of his daughter's abilities.

But we were banking on that. Or Trouble was. I was just along for moral support. But I'd also watch her back.

The elevator doors closed silently. They opened a moment later on the professionally beautiful form of Miss Aspin, Tate's secretary. She offered a dazzling smile beneath calculating eyes. "Welcome back, Miss Tate. You may go right in."

Trouble strode towards the door to her father's office. "Thank you."

I followed. "He knew we were coming?"

"From the minute we came through the front entrance," Trouble said.

"Wonderful."

I lengthened my stride, drew ahead of Trouble, and once again opened the door so she could pass through it without slowing. I closed the door behind us and we approached Norman Tate's massive desk. He sat and watched in silence as we settled into seats opposite him.

"Hello Father," Trouble said. "I'm sure you remember Mr. Barrett."

Norman Tate's snake-like eyes regarded us without blinking, but his lips spread in a fair imitation of a welcoming smile. "Indeed, I do." His gaze shifted to me. "How are you enjoying the coffee I gave to you, Mr. Barrett?"

"It's too pricey for my tastes, Mr. Tate."

Tate barked a laugh. "That's clever, Mr. Barrett! Far more clever than coming here, I might add."

"That was my idea," Trouble said.

Tate snorted. "You should have sent your brother."

Trouble returned the snort. "Nick is a terrible negotiator."

Tate smirked at his daughter. "And you're a better one?"

"Yes, though I'm not surprised you don't know that." She leveled a stare at her father. "You never gave me the opportunity to prove my worth to the business, always ignoring me in favor of Nick. He fumbled every time you gave him the ball, but you still kept sending him instead of me."

"Your brother will inherit my position someday," Tate said. "What else would you have me do?"

"Maybe you could stop living in the 1950s and recognize that a woman might be just as capable as a man. More so, with Nick and me." Trouble leaned forwards. "Do you remember his deal with Blorath, Inc?"

From Tate's grimace, he did. "What about it?"

"Blorath had massive supply issues. With a little pressure, Nick could have leveraged that into a far more favorable deal for us." Trouble sat back. "But Nick didn't do that, because Nick is a nice guy. He always will be a nice guy. I love my brother, but I wouldn't send him to negotiate for Girl Scout cookies, much less with a shark like Antonio Blorath."

Tate sat back in his chair, steepled his fingers, and said, "Interesting."

"I could have saved this company almost a million dollars on that deal." Trouble pointed a finger at her father. "And you know that figure is right because you saw the same opportunity I did."

Tate regarded Trouble for a moment, and then asked, "Tina, why haven't you reported me to Space Patrol and the Earth govs?"

"How do you know I haven't?"

Tate spread his arms wide. "Because I'm still sitting here." He shook his head. "No, you want something that only I can provide."

"I want in."

"In?"

"On the business. *I* want to sit in that chair when you step down, and that means I need the experience you keep wasting on Nick."

"Why?"

"Because I enjoy having money, Father. I like what I can buy with it, from power to..." Her eyes flicked to me. "Men."

Tate turned to me. "I thought you were Mister Incorruptible. What happened to the man who couldn't be bought?"

I let my eyes roam over Trouble's body, flashed a wolfish smile, and said nothing.

Tate's attention returned to Trouble. "You can do better than him."

"That is quite literally my affair, Father. Now, about my proposal?"

"How do I know you won't use the failed experiment on Mercury to push me out?"

"Why would I do anything to harm the company I want to run?"

Tate gave a slow nod. "What about Nick?"

Trouble gave a wintery smile. "Nick will do what I tell him to do."

"You could always make him do anything you wanted…" Tate mused. "This is a big step, Tina. I need time to think on it."

"No. You'll decide now or rot in a prison cell."

Tate tilted his head back and acted as if he was considering Trouble's proposal. That's when my comm began beeping.

"Oh darn, you took too long." I looked at Trouble. "He did take too long, didn't he?"

"Yes," she purred, "just like we planned it."

"Just like *you* planned it," I said.

"Planned what?" Tate demanded.

Trouble motioned for me to speak, but I said, "No, you go ahead. You've earned this one."

"Thank you, Travis." Trouble turned to her father. "We kept you distracted while Space Patrol slipped agents into the office, took over the networks, and locked everything down. The signal means they have everything under control and are coming for you."

Tate stared at his daughter in slack-jawed shock. He gave himself a shake and his hand darted for a drawer.

Trouble's hand slid into her purse and emerged with a blaster. "Don't even think about it, Father dear."

I drew my blaster from its shoulder holster and pointed it at Norman Tate. "Put your hands where we can see them."

Tate slowly raised his hands. "I truly underestimated you, Tina. But it's not too late for us to start over."

"It's been too late ever since Mom died, you bastard," Trouble spat. "Now shut up."

A few seconds later, four big Space Patrol officers entered the office and led Tate away.

eighteen
epilogue

I ROSE from the depths of sleep to the cusp of waking in stages. My dreams faded from memory, but the relaxation I felt told me they'd been pleasant ones. While a part of me longed to dive back into the dreamworld, something drew me towards consciousness. I came fully awake without opening my eyes and immediately identified what had pulled me from sleep.

Trouble's scent lingered in the air. It teased of exotic locales, tropical nights, and all-consuming passion.

My apartment is as far from exotic as you can get.

There's nothing tropical in the recycled air of Carnegie Station.

But those are nothing more than window dressing for the passion.

And Trouble's passion had consumed me entirely.

My lips spread into a languid smile, but it faded after I rolled over and discovered I was alone in the bed. I listened for the shower or Trouble moving around in the kitchen. Nothing sounded except the constant hum of the machinery that keeps Carnegie Station running.

I sat up, ran a hand through my hair, and spotted a hand-written note on the bedside table. Despite my certainty that

Trouble wasn't the *love 'em and leave 'em* type, my heart hammered as I reached for the note.

Dear Travis, Please forgive me for leaving the note, but you looked so peaceful that I couldn't bear to wake you. I have a couple of errands to run before we start our day. Meet me at 8:30 outside the thrift shop where we disguised ourselves before leaving for Mercury. All my love, Trouble.

My heart rate slowed after I read the note. It slowed even more after I read it a second time. The door buzzer interrupted my third reading.

I keyed the apartment's intercom. "Yes? Who's there?"

"It's me, Travis," Dave responded. "Open up."

I thumbed the door open button. "Come on in."

A few seconds later, Dave peeked into the bedroom. His eyes widened when he saw the bed. "Damn, Travis, you used to be such a stickler for neatness, but your bed is an absolute wreck." He rubbed his chin as if he was deep in thought. "Either you've become a slob in the last six years, or something... energetic... happened in your bed last night. I wonder which—"

I cut his speculation short. "Why are you here, Dave?"

"I'm here to make sure you aren't late."

"Late for what?"

"You're holding Trouble's note in your hand, yet you still asked that question?"

I glanced at the clock beside my bed. "It's already 8:15?" I jumped out of bed. "Do I have time for a shower?"

"Barely."

I grabbed some clothes, dashed into the bathroom, and emerged fully dressed five minutes later. Dave stood as I crossed the living room and fell in behind me. We entered the shopping arcade at exactly 8:30, but it took another minute to negotiate the morning foot traffic and reach the thrift shop. Trouble sat on a public bench in front of it, with Rita floating at her side.

The eyes on Rita's face screen focused on Dave. "You're late."

Dave shrugged and jerked a thumb at me. "Blame him."

Rita tutted. "The Boss—"

"Doesn't want to listen to you two squabble," I said. I bent over and kissed Trouble. "Sorry I'm late. You look gorgeous, as always."

Trouble smiled. "I bet you say that to all the girls the morning after."

Dave snorted. "Travis hasn't had enough mornings after to-*Oof.*"

Rita activated a tone of false sincerity. "I'm sorry, Hayslett. I *accidentally* rammed my elbow into your stomach."

Dave rubbed his stomach and glared at Rita. "I *could* have left you on Mercury, you know."

"Not without leaving the Boss or Miss Tate, too," Rita countered.

Trouble stood. "Stop it, both of you."

Dave straightened, almost to attention. "Yes, ma'am."

Rita swiveled her head to look at Trouble. "Whatever you say, Miss Tate."

"Rita, Trouble asked you to use her nickname," I said. "Why are you calling her Miss Tate?"

Trouble began walking across the shopping arcade. Rita followed her without answering my question. Dave shook his head, murmured, "Women, am I right?" Then he fell in behind Rita. With a mental shrug, I joined the procession.

Trouble led us to a row of offices on the far side of the arcade and headed for one with its windows covered and the door propped open. Half-a-dozen workmen were inside painting or installing wiring. I half expected them to tell us to get lost. Instead, they glanced at us, let their eyes linger on Trouble, and then all but the foreman returned to their work.

The foreman tipped his cap to Trouble. "Good morning, Miss Tate."

"Good morning, Mr. Chilson. Is it finished?"

"The door?" Chilson asked. "Yes, ma'am."

Chilson led us back outside, ripped the paper off the inside of the door, kicked away the doorstop holding it open, and let the door close. "I hope you like it."

"It's not my opinion that matters, Mr. Chilson," Trouble said. She looked at me, bit her lip in apparent nervousness, and asked, "What do you think, Travis? Do *you* like it?"

The words INVESTIGATIONS AND RETRIEVALS appeared exactly the same as they did on the door to my office in the industrial district. But *two* names arced over those words.

Our names.

TRAVIS & TROUBLE.

I stared long enough that Dave poked me on the shoulder and, in a stage whisper, said, "You're supposed to say *I love it*."

I shook myself and faced Trouble, who still bit her lip. "I love it. I *truly* do."

"But?" she asked.

"But..." I shrugged. "I thought you wanted to run Tate Steelworks. With your father's arrest, the CEO's position is yours for the asking."

"I discussed it with Nick by radio yesterday, and he's going to take the job when he gets back from Mercury. I'll offer advice, but..." Trouble offered a tentative smile. "Why would I want a life of high finance with my father's cronies when I could have a life of high adventure with the man I love?"

I smiled in return. "How could I possibly say no to that?"

Trouble grinned, and I thought she might flow into my arms for an ardent kiss. Instead, she grabbed my hand and led me into the office. "Come on! I have something else to show you."

Trouble dragged me across the outer office to a door on the far side. She turned the knob, threw open the door, and sang, "Ta da!"

The office beyond the door was bare except for two desks pushed against each other in the middle of the floor. I walked to the desks and rapped my knuckles on one. The pure knock you only get from real wood sounded.

I cocked one eyebrow. "Oak?"

Trouble nodded. "Don't they make the office pop?"

"Not as much as you do."

Then I wrapped my arms around my new partner in adventure and kissed her.

"Aw, isn't that sweet?" Rita asked.

"Sweet enough to give me sugar shock," Dave said.

I broke my lip lock with Trouble. "You can leave any time, Dave."

"Not without you, I can't," he replied. "Or did you two forget you promised Mah'Ri you'd go to Mars after you wrapped up this case?"

"No, we didn't forget." Trouble pointed to two suitcases behind the desks. "Why do you think we have those?"

Dave spun on his heel and headed for the door. "Okay. I'll go get the *Lightning's Hand* prepped for departure."

After he left, I asked, "When did you pack the suitcases?"

"I packed yours while you were sleeping. Then I stopped by Father's place and packed mine this morning. Don't worry, I brought sensible shoes." Her smile turned devilish. "Along with some more interesting items."

"I thought *I* was the one supplying the life of adventure?"

Trouble slipped from my arms, walked to the office door, and gave me a smoldering over-the-shoulder look. "There's more than one kind of adventure, Travis."

I took a moment listening to her high heels click confidently through the outer office. Then I picked up the suitcases and hurried after her.

travis & trouble
return...

...in *Trouble on Mars*. Available now.

about the author

Henry Vogel began his writing career in comic books way back in the 1980s, with the indie titles *Southern Knights* and *X-Thieves*. When the bottom dropped out of the black & white comic book market, Henry went into IT, where he worked for the next thirty-three years. Henry took up professional storytelling in 2006, and has performed all across his home state of North Carolina.

As a lifetime fan of science fiction, Henry always wanted to write science fiction novels. He began writing *Scout's Honor* in 2012, and released it to the world in 2014. He hasn't stopped writing since.

Henry makes his home in Raleigh, NC, and is hard at work on his next novel.

www.henryvogelwrites.com

also by henry vogel

Travis & Trouble

Trouble in Twi-Town

Trouble on Mars

The Fortune Chronicles

Fortune's Fool

The Scales of Sin & Sorrow

The Scout Series

Scout's Honor

Scout's Oath

Scout's Duty

Scout's Law

Scout's Training

Scout's First Mission

Hart for Adventure

The Princess Scout

Scout: The Lost Colony Adventures

Non-series books

The Lost Planet

Heart of Dorkness & Other Stories

The Connaught Family Chronicles

The Fugitive Heir

The Fugitive Pair

The Fugitive Snare

www.ingramcontent.com/pod-product-compliance
Lightning Source LLC
Chambersburg PA
CBHW020747310726
48969CB00002B/458